WRONGFULLY INFUSED

Oxford Tearoom Mysteries

BOOK 11

H.Y. HANNA

Contents

Chapter One

There is a well-known ancient proverb which says: "*The path to Heaven passes through a teapot.*" Unfortunately, the path to Hell can pass through a teapot too—as I found out all too well...

But on that beautiful spring morning, as I cycled out of Oxford and into the Cotswolds countryside, Hell was the furthest thing from my mind. I *was* thinking about teapots, though—specifically the teapots at my Little Stables Tearoom, which should have been ready and brimming with hot tea by now. *With no one to carry them out to customers*, I thought guiltily, wincing as I glanced down at my wristwatch and saw the time.

I was horribly late for work—the result of hitting the "Snooze" button on my bedside clock once too often and falling back into a deep, exhausted sleep. In fact, I would probably have still been snoring peacefully if it hadn't been for the persistence of my tabby cat, Muesli. For a creature with no opposable thumbs, she certainly managed countless ingenious ways to get me out of bed! When her mournful meowing and prodding paws had failed to rouse me, she had progressed to knocking everything off my bedside table, chewing my hair, nipping my toes, and finally sitting on my face.

And although I had erupted in a furious tangle of bed hair and blankets at the time, now I had to ruefully admit that I was grateful to my mischievous tabby cat. I glanced down at the cat carrier in the front basket of my bicycle and smiled to myself as I caught sight of Muesli's little face peering out through the bars at the side. Her big green eyes watched the landscape fly by with keen interest, and her pink nose quivered as she sniffed the scents of the countryside. Despite making this journey with me every day I went into work, she never seemed to tire of the experience.

She let out a chirrup of excitement as we crossed a bridge over a small stream and entered the quaint little village of Meadowford-on-Smythe. It was like stepping into a postcard scene of bucolic England, with thatched-roof cottages lining the sides of cobbled lanes, all winding around a picturesque village green. And at the bottom of the village high street, sandwiched between antique shops and quirky boutiques, was my traditional English tearoom. Housed in what used to be a fifteenth-century

Tudor inn, the Little Stables prided itself on offering the best in British baking, from our signature scones, served with jam and clotted cream, to traditional favourites like Chelsea buns, Victoria sponge, and delicate finger sandwiches—all accompanied by fragrant tea in beautiful bone china.

I smiled in anticipation as I pulled up in front of the Little Stables and dismounted. I was already imagining the wonderful aroma of fresh baking and the warm atmosphere of happy customers talking and laughing that would envelop me as soon as I entered the tearoom. But when I stepped through the front door, I was met by an empty dining room, with only a solitary elderly gentleman at a table in the corner.

Faltering to a stop, I looked around in surprise and dismay. *What's going on?* I glanced at the counter by the till, unconsciously seeking my best friend, Cassie, who worked at the tearoom, before recalling that Cassie had mentioned she'd be coming in late this morning. In fact, that was why I had been so concerned about being late myself, worried that no one would be around to serve the customers.

I can't believe I was worrying about that—there are barely enough people here to open the tearoom for! I thought grimly. After letting Muesli out of her carrier, I pushed through the swinging baize door behind the counter and stepped into the kitchen. There, I found my baking chef, Dora, bent over the large wooden table in the centre of the room, her arms covered in flour up to the elbows as she busily flattened a large slab of dough with a rolling pin.

"Oh hullo, Gemma," she said, glancing up distractedly. "I was beginning to wonder what had happened to you."

I gave her an apologetic smile. "Sorry! I overslept. The long hours from recent weeks must be catching up with me. Actually, I was worrying about you having to serve customers while also trying to do the baking, but when I arrived—" I glanced over my shoulder and lowered my voice. "Dora, why is the tearoom so empty?"

Dora straightened and gave a helpless shrug. "I don't know. Mr Prendergast is the only person who's come in all morning."

"The only one?" I said in horror. "But... but I don't understand... Where is everyone?"

Dora frowned. "Actually, it was like this yesterday as well... and the day before, remember? Although things did seem to pick up a bit as the day went on," she added.

I bit my lip, my stomach churning with sudden anxiety. Dora was right. Things *had* been very quiet all week, although I had been trying to ignore it, telling myself that fluctuations were the norm in the hospitality business. After all, it was one of the things I'd had to learn to deal with when I left my executive position in a large corporate firm to follow my dream of opening a traditional English tearoom. Abandoning my stable monthly salary for a fluctuating income and unpredictable expenses had been one of the hardest things to come to terms with.

But with our appealing setting, friendly service, and well-earned reputation for having the best scones in Oxfordshire, business had grown in recent months to the point where I could usually rely on a steady flow of customers daily. Not only did we have regular visits from local residents, but for many of the tourists who came to visit Oxford and the surrounding Cotswolds countryside, my tearoom had become a "must-visit" destination for those in search of the quintessential

British experience of a traditional afternoon tea. So this sudden drop in customers was both puzzling and alarming.

"Now, don't fret," said Dora briskly, seeing my expression. "It might just be coincidence, you know. Maybe a lot of people have gone away on holiday at the same time or maybe one of the tour bus companies is having a break this week."

"It still doesn't make sense," I said, furrowing my brow. "Have there been any complaints that I'm not aware of? Any customers who were really unhappy about something?"

Dora shook her head. "You'd have to ask Cassie to be sure, since she does most of the serving, but *I* haven't heard anything. I certainly haven't seen any plates returned to the kitchen."

I sighed, then reached for one of the tearoom aprons hanging from a hook on the kitchen wall. "Well, I'd better go out and check that Mr Prendergast is okay, otherwise we might lose the only customer we have!"

Back in the dining room, I found Muesli curled up in her favourite spot on the window seat overlooking the high street and Mr Prendergast leaning back in his chair, engrossed in a newspaper, while an empty teacup and plate sat on the table in front of him. A retired accountant, Mr Prendergast had been recently widowed and claimed that our scones were just like the ones his wife used to make. Thus, he came almost every day to sit at the same table and do the crossword in the daily paper, while enjoying a cup of tea and some home baking. I was glad to see that we were still part of his daily routine, and I gave him a bright smile as I went over to collect his empty plate and teacup.

"Good morning, Mr Prendergast. Everything all right with your order?" I asked casually.

"Hmm? Ooh yes, marvellous. Nothing like fresh homemade crumpets slathered with butter and honey," said Mr Prendergast, making a lip-smacking noise. "I say, you wouldn't happen to have any idea what this clue could mean, would you?"

He held up his newspaper and I bent over to read the crossword clue: *Nosiness victim, visual sweep (3, 4).*

I gave a helpless laugh. "I have no idea! I'm not very good at crosswords— I never have the patience for them."

"My dear, I'm no great shakes either but I do like giving them a shot." Mr Prendergast tapped the side of his temple and smiled. "Keeps the brain nimble, you know."

"Hmm…" I read the clue again. "Well, I presume 'nosiness victim' means 'a victim of nosiness'… what's another word for nosiness?"

"Inquisitiveness? Prying?" said Mr

Prendergast.

"Or 'curiosity'?" I suggested.

"Hmm… yes, curiosity," Mr Prendergast mused. "A 'victim of curiosity'…"

"*Meorrw!*" came a little voice by our feet.

I looked down to see that Muesli had left the window seat and come over to join us. She rubbed herself against Mr Prendergast's chair and looked up at us with her big green eyes.

"Cat!" cried Mr Prendergast, staring at Muesli.

I looked at him, startled. "Er… yes, we've got a resident feline at the Little Stables. This is my cat Muesli; you've met her before, remember—"

"No, no, the crossword!" said Mr Prendergast, pointing at his newspaper. "The answer is 'cat'—as in 'curiosity killed the cat'."

"Oh yes, of course!" I cried, feeling foolish that I hadn't made the connection.

"Hmm... so the first word is 'cat' and the second word... four letters... something that goes with 'cat'..."

"Catcall? Catsuit?" I guessed. "Catfish? Catwalk?"

"None of those really fit the clue for the second word," said Mr Prendergast. "Also, they're really one word, aren't they? This answer requires two separate words, the first of which is 'cat'."

I shook my head. "It's beyond me."

"Ah well... I suppose I'll just have to keep thinking about it," said Mr Prendergast. He folded his newspaper and glanced around the dining room, then observed, "A bit quiet here this morning, isn't it?"

I flushed slightly. "Yes, I suppose it is a bit."

"Must be that new place that everyone's gone off to," he said.

I stared at him. "New place?"

"Yes, you know—down by the Cotswolds Manor Hotel, on the other side of the village. Haven't you seen it?"

I shook my head. I had been so busy at work that I'd barely had any free time, and when I did, I usually went straight home. I certainly hadn't made much effort to wander around the village or the surrounding area lately.

"Don't fancy the look of it myself," continued Mr Prendergast, "but young people like these fancy new places, don't they? Calls itself a 'tea bar' and menu's full of odd things... and tea cocktails! Bah! What's a 'tea cocktail', I ask you?" he said, his moustache bristling. He looked down at his empty cup and gave an emphatic nod. "A good cup of tea is brewed dark and strong, with milk and sugar—or a slice of lemon perhaps—but nothing else!" He raised his head and smiled at me. "And there's no better cup of tea than what one can get here at the Little Stables."

"Oh, thank you," I said, flushing again but this time with pleasure. "That's really kind of you to say."

"It's no more than the truth," he said gruffly. Tucking his newspaper under his arm, he stood up and added, "Well, I'd best be off. If you could let me have the bill, my dear...?"

A few minutes later I stood at the tearoom doorway and watched Mr Prendergast's erect figure walk, with almost military bearing, down the high street. My eyes followed him, but my mind was busy going over what he had told me. A new 'tea bar' on the other side of the village? Could that be the reason business had slumped so much lately?

My musings were interrupted by the arrival of Cassie, looking even prettier than usual with her windswept dark hair curling wildly about her head and her eyes sparkling from the exertion of her cycle into the village. Like many talented artists who unfortunately found that their art didn't quite pay for their living, Cassie had always had to work additional jobs to make ends meet, and she had been delighted when I returned to England, after several years working overseas, to open my tearoom. Not only did she get her childhood best friend back, but she also found the perfect job to fit around her painting—and her many years of waitressing experience had been invaluable in the early days when the tearoom had first opened.

Cassie was feisty and spontaneous, and, like many artists, had a healthy disrespect for convention. She had been brought up in a warm, riotous family who championed creative self-expression above all else. It was the complete opposite of me with my repressed upper-middle-class upbringing and my constant worry about meeting social expectations. You wouldn't have thought that such different personalities could become best friends, but we'd been inseparable since meeting each other in primary school and, when I'd returned to Oxford, our friendship had picked up exactly where it had left off.

Now I gave her a warm smile as she came clattering up the steps, all fired up and breathlessly indignant.

"Bloody hell, Gemma, I thought I was never going to get here! There was a car accident in Jericho—some plonker didn't bother to look before reversing out onto the street—and the police blocked all the roads off. But they made a right mess of things; total bottleneck and no one could get anywhere! And it was the morning rush hour too, when everyone's desperate to get to work on time. I practically had to cycle through several

back gardens just to get out of Oxford—
" She broke off and looked at me quizzically. "What are you doing, standing there on the doorstep? Shouldn't you be inside looking after the customers?"

"I would be, if we had customers to look after," I said with a sigh, turning and leading the way back into the tearoom.

"Bloody hell!" Cassie burst out again as she stopped short just inside the door and surveyed the empty dining room in dismay. "Where is everybody?" she cried.

"I wish I knew," I said gloomily. "By the way, have you heard about some new 'tea bar' that's opened on the other side of the village? Somewhere near the Cotswolds Manor Hotel?"

"A 'tea bar'? What's that?" asked Cassie, wrinkling her nose. "Sounds like a poncy London invention." She paused.

"Hmm… but I *have* heard that the corporation which owns the Cotswolds Manor Hotel has recently expanded and developed the site, and there are several new restaurants and bars there now, in addition to the hotel itself. Your 'tea bar' is probably one of them."

"Well, Mr Prendergast says it's doing booming business," I said, grimacing. "Everyone is going there. That's probably why we have no customers today."

Cassie pulled her phone out of her pocket and began doing a search, whilst I peered over her shoulder. A few minutes later, we both stared down at the glossy image filling the screen, announcing the grand opening of the new Yin-Yang Tea Bar earlier this week. It was an impressive website, filled with beautiful, professional photography showing a variety of food and drink in vivid, mouth-watering colour, all accompanied by sleek cast-iron teapots and dainty china cups that lent everything an Oriental air.

Cassie whistled as she ran her eyes down the page. "My God, they're offering 'bottomless tea and coffee' with any food order… and a free glass of bubbly with every afternoon tea package… and look at these prices! It's no wonder everyone is going there! How can they be charging so little? They can't be making any profit with prices like that!"

"It says it's an opening-month special," I said, pointing to the little label on the page. I shifted uncomfortably as I continued looking down at the sleek design and glamorous images on the screen. The Little Stables's plain website, with its few amateur photos and the simple list of menu items, looked completely archaic and unsophisticated in comparison. "Cripes, it makes our website look pretty bad, doesn't it?" I asked.

Cassie bristled. "There's nothing wrong with our website. Besides, at the end of the day, it's the food and the ambience of the place that matter. We know we're the tearoom with the best scones in Oxfordshire and we provide an authentic British afternoon tea experience."

"Yes, but not everyone knows that. I mean, tourists and visitors make up half our business and they don't know our reputation. They can only go by what they've seen or heard online..." I indicated the glossy website in front of us. "And that looks amazing."

"People aren't going to be taken in by some fancy pictures online," insisted Cassie. "Don't worry, Gemma. I'll bet this is just an opening-week thing. It'll all die down next week and people will be back here when they realise that it's genuine quality that matters, not all this PR nonsense."

Chapter Two

Unfortunately, though, as the week wore on, Cassie's predictions didn't come true. Instead of things returning to normal, they only seemed to get worse. Most mornings only saw Mr Prendergast at his customary table, and we were lucky if we got a few village regulars in the afternoons. By the start of the following week, I was feeling seriously alarmed and panicking about what to do. At this rate, my tearoom would be lucky to get to the end of the month without closing permanently!

I sighed as I turned away from the window, where I had been standing, looking out onto the village high street and hoping to catch a glimpse of customers approaching. The large oak table beside the window was empty and I felt a pang as I thought of the four little old ladies who usually sat there. Known affectionately as "the Old Biddies", Mabel Cooke, Glenda Bailey, Florence Doyle, and Ethel Webb were four senior residents of the village who combined a penchant for prying into other people's business with a ghoulish appetite for mystery and murder. Their attempts at amateur sleuthing had landed me in trouble more than once, but I had to admit that, despite my exasperation with their meddling ways, I'd become very fond of them. Even if they were nosy and interfering, it was hard not to admire their dogged persistence, not to mention their amazing network of community intel (otherwise known as local gossip!).

The Old Biddies had come to treat my

tearoom—and this table by the window in particular—as their own personal HQ, and normally came almost every day to hold court here and gossip with other village residents or pounce on any hapless tourist who'd caught their interest. But their spot had remained empty all last week, and I sighed again now as I looked down at the unoccupied chairs.

But it's not because they've abandoned me, I reminded myself. I knew that the Old Biddies had gone away on holiday to visit some friends on the Norfolk coast. *They were meant to have been back yesterday though*, I thought with a frown. I would have expected them to be in here first thing this morning, brimming with news of their adventures in the Fens. *Maybe I've got the date wrong and they aren't back yet?* I wondered.

The tinkle of bells—the usual herald of new customers—interrupted my thoughts, and I looked eagerly towards the tearoom door. My heart lifted as I saw the group who had just entered. They looked to be an Indian family: a mother and father, a young man and a teenage girl who were obviously their children, and an elderly lady with long, braided grey hair, dressed in a beautiful silk sari, who I guessed to be the grandmother. As I led them to their table, I gathered that the son was a student at Oxford University, and that the family had come to visit him from overseas.

"Sanjit told us that this tearoom was featured in the university student handbook as one of the top places to go for tea." The mother beamed at me as she took the menu I handed her.

"Oh, thank you." I felt my face glow with delight, although my smile slipped a bit as I heard the teenage sister mutter:

"Don't know why. This place is a hole.

We should have gone to that tea bar on the other side of the village. That looked way cooler."

The mother shushed the girl. "Priya! That is not a nice thing to say. This is a lovely establishment. That tea bar place looked very modern."

"What's wrong with that?" demanded the teenage girl. She cast a disparaging look around. "This place is like sitting in a museum. A really *old*, boring museum."

The mother gave me an apologetic smile and leaned towards me, murmuring in an undertone, "I'm sorry... I think it is her age. Nothing seems to please her these days."

"Stop saying that!" cried the girl indignantly. "You're always going on about my age and... and my hormones! You're always making fun of me! You won't listen to me, even when I'm right—"

"That's enough, Priya," said the father sharply.

The girl subsided with a scowl, and an awkward silence fell over the table. The mother looked at me again, an embarrassed expression on her face. "I'm so sorry—"

"That's okay," I said quickly, keeping my smile in place, although my cheeks were beginning to feel stiff from the effort. "Um… I suppose we do have a… *er*… more traditional style of décor here," I said, glancing at the dark, exposed timber framing around the whitewashed walls, the flagstone floors, and the original inglenook fireplace. I had always loved interiors with this type of quaint, period charm, but I supposed that not everyone shared my tastes— especially teenagers obsessed with being "cool and trendy".

"Well, I like it," the father declared. "I wanted a traditional English tea, and this is exactly the kind of place I imagined having it in."

His words made me feel better and, as I returned to the kitchen with their order, I thought feverishly that I had to make sure they left the Little Stables having had the most wonderful, satisfying experience.

In the kitchen, I found Cassie lounging in a chair and chatting to Dora, who was busily mixing some kind of batter in a bowl. They looked up as I entered, brandishing the order pad, and Cassie said hopefully:

"Customers?"

I nodded, smiling. "And they've put in a big order too. In fact, they chose us over that new tea bar, so we'd better make a bloody good impression!"

"Give them some of the new batch of scones that's just come out, then," said Cassie, indicating the counter where rows of golden-brown scones studded with raisins were cooling on a rack.

"Nothing like freshly baked scones, still warm from the oven."

"Ooh, that was good timing," I said, picking up a plate.

But as I turned towards the counter, I tripped and stumbled, nearly losing my balance. Glancing down, I found a little grey-and-white tabby cat weaving between my legs, looking cheekily up at me.

"*Meorrw?*"

"Oh, Muesli—what are you doing in here?" I asked in exasperation. "You know you're not allowed in the kitchen."

"Which is exactly why she keeps trying to sneak in," said Cassie with a grin.

She bent to pick up the cat, but Muesli nimbly evaded her hands. The little tabby darted sideways and leapt up onto the counter, then trotted over to the rack of scones and bent to sniff one.

"*Meorrw?*" she said, throwing me another cheeky look. Then she reached out a paw.

"No! Muesli, don't touch that!" I cried, lunging towards her.

It was too late. With a deft swipe of her paws, Muesli sent the scone flying off the rack to smash on the floor. Then she did it again to the next scone, except that this time, her paw knocked the entire rack sideways. It teetered on one edge, then flipped over, causing all the scones to tumble to the floor.

"*Muesli!*" I cried, furious and disbelieving.

Instead of looking repentant, Muesli jumped off the counter and trotted away with an impish look over her shoulder.

"Just you wait... I'm going to wring your little neck," I muttered as I crouched down to clean up the mess.

"It's all right, Gemma—I can make up a fresh batch of scones," said Dora, reaching for a fresh packet of flour. "They only take twenty minutes to bake so they'll be ready in a jiffy."

"Take them some of our other cakes and buns in the meantime," suggested Cassie. "Compliments of the house."

"Hmm, great idea." I hurried to load up a tray with a selection of fresh baking.

Thankfully, the Indian family seemed perfectly happy to wait for a fresh batch of scones and delighted to tuck into the alternatives I'd provided first. In fact, the grandmother beamed at me after tasting a slice of our Victoria sponge and addressed me eagerly in rapid Hindi.

"Nani is saying that your cake is the most delicious she's ever tasted," the mother translated, smiling. "In fact, the softer sponge and cream is much easier for her teeth than scones, so thank you!"

By the time the family had finished the complimentary treats and were on their second pot of tea, the freshly baked scones were just coming out of the oven. I brought them, still warm, to the table and hovered surreptitiously as I waited for them to be sampled. I knew they were a great batch: golden and crusty on the outside, soft and buttery on the inside, and it was wonderful to hear the exclamations of delight and pleasure as the family tucked in. Even the teenage daughter grudgingly admitted that the scones were "not bad".

"That's high praise, coming from Priya," said the father with a wink at me.

When they finally departed, he left a generous tip along with the payment for the bill; but more than the welcome earnings, it was their obvious enjoyment that really soothed my soul. Still, the elation was short-lived. After they left, no other customers arrived, and the tearoom remained morosely empty all afternoon.

At half past four, Cassie made an impatient sound and said, "That's it, Gemma. We're not going to just sit around here, moping, any longer. It's obvious no one else is going to turn up today. Let's shut early, so we can get there before they close."

I looked at her in surprise. "Get where? Where are we going?"

"To check out the competition," said Cassie grimly. "If everyone's over at that new tea bar, then we've got to go and see what it's like. You can't fight a battle unless you know your enemy."

"That's a bit melodramatic, isn't it?" I protested.

But my best friend was right: sitting here, desperately waiting for customers to show up, wasn't going to fix our problems. I looked around the empty tearoom once more, then sighed and nodded. "All right. Let's go."

Chapter Three

Cassie and I stared at the modern façade in front of us, with its gleaming metal accents and large expanses of glass and concrete. There were floor-to-ceiling, steel-framed windows leading out to a wrap-around terrace, and through the open front entrance, we could see a large oval-shaped cocktail bar in black marble, dominating the dining room like a sleek alien spaceship. It was surrounded by ebony tables and chairs, which harmonised with the darkly exotic palette of the interior décor.

Even if we hadn't seen the large sign proclaiming "Yin-Yang Tea Bar", we would have known we were in the right place from the loud hubbub of talk and laughter that could be heard as we approached. Now, we stared disbelievingly at the queue of people snaking out of the front entrance and the crowds spilling out onto the terrace. When we'd finally shuffled to the front of the queue, an attractive young woman in a slinky dress, that looked more like a cocktail outfit than a waitress's uniform, came up to us with a tablet.

"Do you have a booking?"

"No," said Cassie evenly. "Do we need one?"

The woman pursed her lips, then tapped importantly on the tablet with a well-manicured finger. "We could squeeze you in on an extra table at the back, if you don't mind things being a bit tight."

"We'll take it," said Cassie before I could reply.

A few minutes later, we were seated at a small, cramped table next to a corridor that obviously led to the kitchen at the rear of the building. It had been a feat even getting to our table—the place was packed to the seams, and there was hardly space to squeeze past chairs seating other customers. This didn't seem to deter the waitstaff, though, who came jauntily out of the corridor every few moments, carrying trays laden with food and drink, and manoeuvring with expert ease between the crowded tables.

"Wow... what's that?" I said, turning in my seat as my eyes followed a waiter who sailed past us, bearing what looked like a towering column of food.

"Looks like their 'Grand Opening Afternoon Tea Special'," said Cassie, bending over the menu. "Come on, let's order it and see what it's like."

A short while later, we leaned forwards to survey the structure that had been placed on our table. It was a three-tiered cake stand, although it looked very different to the traditional style usually found in tearooms and posh hotels. Instead of round plates joined by a central column, it featured square plates set inside a tall rectangular frame of brushed, black metal. The delicacies on the plates were not the traditional teatime treats of finger sandwiches, scones, and sponge cakes either. Instead, there were wasabi-cream-cheese wonton tarts and miniature BBQ-pork buns, tropical-fruit rice puddings and wakame-seaweed sandwiches. Even the cakes were presented in strange geometric shapes, decorated with minimalist chocolate cut-outs and covered with bright technicolour frosting.

"Bloody hell…" muttered Cassie, eyeing the food with trepidation. She pointed to a squat little square coated with a lurid green jelly and a blob of foam on top. "What the hell is that?"

I checked the menu. "Um… I think that's the lime-and-kale delice with wheatgerm curd, matcha sponge, and pea-shoot foam."

Cassie made a face. "Is it edible? Sounds like something you'd plant in the garden."

I laughed. "Well, I guess there's only one way to find out."

There was silence as we both began cautiously sampling the range of treats.

"Hmm…" said Cassie, chewing on a bite. "Well, I have to say, this looks a lot better than it tastes."

Swallowing a mouthful of my own, I had to agree. Everything looked fancy and expensive, but once in the mouth, each dish tasted surprisingly bland and similar, with no particular flavour or texture standing out. Still, we worked our way diligently through the various tiers until we reached the square "scones" at the bottom.

"Ugh…" said Cassie, putting hers down after one bite. "I don't know what that is but it's not a scone."

"Maybe the teas are better," I said, reaching over to pick up one of the distinctive Oriental-style cast-iron teapots that had been brought with our tea set. I glanced at the menu again, then said, "This is an organic infusion of green tea, lemon myrtle, and eucalyptus." I indicated the other teapot on our table. "Or you can have the other, which is 'smoky black tisane with ginseng and stone-fruit aroma'."

Cassie groaned. "Isn't there anything that's just plain, normal tea?"

Still, she took the cup I offered her and obediently took a sip. Then she wrinkled her nose. "This doesn't taste of anything. You might as well have given me a cup of hot water." She put the cup down and leaned back with an expression of disgust. "Honestly, Gemma, this is all just a load of pretentious crap—that's all it is! Style over substance."

I glanced around the packed dining room. "Well, it seems to be working." I sighed. "Maybe we're behind the times, Cass. Maybe this is what people want now, and simple home baking and traditional teas just aren't good enough anymore."

"Bollocks!" said Cassie, scowling. "I don't believe that." She stood up. "Come on, I've had enough of this place."

We paid our bill, then sucked our stomachs in as we tried to squeeze our way past tables to get out. Just as we were nearing the entrance, however, Cassie let out a cry of indignation and pointed to a table by the wall.

"I can't believe it!"

I followed the direction she was pointing in and saw four little old ladies with white helmet hair, sensible orthotic shoes, and lavender handbags huddled around a table. *The Old Biddies!* A sense of betrayal washed over me. So they *had* returned to Meadowford—they just hadn't come back to my tearoom! Feeling terribly hurt, I would have slunk away, but Cassie grabbed my arm and dragged me over to their table.

The four old ladies looked up as we approached and gave a guilty start.

"Gemma!" cried Mabel Cooke, her booming voice almost drowned out by the noise of the crowd around us. As the bossiest and most opinionated member of the Old Biddies, Mabel was renowned for her thick-skinned sangfroid in the face of any awkward predicament. For once, though, she looked uncomfortable and slightly at a loss for words. "Er... fancy seeing you here, dear."

"What are *you* doing here?"

demanded Cassie.

"Cass!" I remonstrated. Turning back to the old ladies, I forced a smile and said in a neutral voice, "I thought you were still away on holiday."

The Old Biddies exchanged slightly shamefaced looks, then Mabel said:

"We came back yesterday, and we *did* mean to come to your tearoom this morning, dear, but then Glenda found the flyer in her letterbox and we thought we'd just pop in here first."

"What flyer?" Cassie asked.

"I've still got it here somewhere... I'll show you..." Glenda rummaged in her cavernous handbag, fishing out various cosmetic compacts, tissues, hair accessories, and several tubes of pink lipstick. Despite being in her early eighties, Glenda still had the soul of a teenage girl, complete with the make-up obsessions, romantic fantasies, and flirtatious manner towards any handsome male. She pulled a printed leaflet triumphantly out of her handbag at last and thrust it towards us.

I looked down, my eyes scanning over the bold printed words. I don't think I'd ever seen so many exclamation marks squashed into one small space:

YIN-YANG TEA BAR - GRAND OPENING SPECIAL!!!!!

Delight your senses with a unique twist on the traditional high tea!

Ditch the stuffy old tearooms and come enjoy yourself in sophisticated, contemporary surroundings!!

Mouth-watering sweets and savoury delights with bottomless tea and/or coffee and a free glass of bubbly for every customer!!!

~ limited number of Afternoon Tea packages! ~

This special offer could end at any time!!

GET IN QUICK BEFORE YOU MISS OUT!!!!!!

"Aha… so they're using 'scarcity'!" hissed Cassie in my ear. "Oldest trick in the book: *'limited number'*… *'could end at any time'*… *'get in quick before you miss out'*… *That's* how they're packing them in! Nothing galvanises people like the thought of missing out on a great bargain. Even if they were planning to go somewhere else, this would motivate people to come here first, before the special offer ends. Very clever." She looked back at the Old Biddies. "Did you each get a flyer in your letterboxes?

The four old ladies nodded.

"And everyone in our bingo group too," said Glenda. "In fact, the ladies were thinking that they might come here for our get-together tomorrow evening instead of the Little Sta—" She broke off suddenly, looking embarrassed, then cleared her throat and added hastily, "Just this week, of course. You know, because of the promotion."

"We still think you're the best, Gemma," said Ethel loyally. The quietest of the Old Biddies, Ethel was gentle and sweet, with a kindly manner that had endeared her to everyone when she used to work in the village library.

"Oh yes, your tearoom is ever so much nicer. We just thought it would be fun to try somewhere new—just to see what the fuss was all about," said Glenda in an apologetic tone.

I gave them a smile. "It's all right, you don't need to apologise. I mean, you're not obliged to come to the Little Stables all the time. Of course you'd want to check out the new place, especially when they're offering such a good deal."

"Well, I have to say, I'm not very

impressed, now that I've tasted the food," commented Florence, her plump face puckering in disappointment. If there was one person who loved her food, it was Florence, and she was always worrying that I wasn't eating as much as I should. She frowned now as she looked around the dining room. "It *is* a nice setting, I suppose. But it's no use having a fancy place to sit in if the tea and scones aren't any good."

The other Old Biddies nodded.

"Yes, the food is very disappointing," agreed Glenda. Then she gave an impish giggle. "The lad who brought it over to us was very handsome though! Ahh, if only I was sixty years younger…" She glanced at me. "Maybe that's what you need, dear: a few sexy chaps to help serve the scones at your tearoom—"

"That's it!" cried Cassie. She turned eagerly to me. "Maybe that's what we need to do: get sexier!"

I gaped at her. "Huh?"

Cassie grabbed the menu from the Old Biddies' table and started reading out some items. "Listen to this: 'fluffy buttermilk scones with silky cream and pure fruit compote'—huh!" She cast a contemptuous look at the crumbling remains on one of the Old Biddies' plates. "Talk about making a silk purse out of a sow's ear! Their scones are stodgy and tasteless, whereas ours are genuinely fluffy and delicious—but they're much better at making their stuff sound appealing. Think of our menu: it doesn't sound as good when we just list them as plain 'scones with jam and clotted cream', does it?"

"I suppose not," I said doubtfully. "But—"

I broke off suddenly as I realised that a woman had come up to the table and was standing beside us, listening. She looked to be Chinese, or of similar East Asian descent, with long, silky black hair that was caught up in a high ponytail and a striking face: high cheekbones and slanted, almond-shaped eyes, which had been enhanced by black eyeliner. She was not conventionally beautiful—there was something hard in her face and her thin, tight-lipped mouth—but she was the kind of woman who commanded attention when she walked into a room. Now, she regarded us with a speculative look, although her expression and voice were coolly polite as she said:

"Hello ladies, is there a problem?"

"Oh no, we just happened to see our friends here and stopped to say hello," said Cassie, indicating the Old Biddies.

"How nice." The woman's smile didn't reach her eyes. "Would you like me to have the waiters bring some extra chairs—"

"Oh no, that's okay. We were just leaving, actually," I said.

"Well, I hope you enjoyed yourselves.

Ah… I see that you ordered the Grand Opening special," she said, eyeing the square cake stand on the Old Biddies' table. "I'm so glad. It highlights the best of our menu and is the most delectable selection of teatime treats!" She turned to me with a smug smile. "Don't you think our scones are the *best* you've ever tasted?"

"Er… well…" I stammered, torn between the characteristic British compulsion to "always be polite" and the reluctance to give false praise for something that had tasted so horrible.

Before I could decide how to answer, Mabel cut in with her characteristic forthrightness.

"No, they were not. In fact, the scones were very stodgy and dry."

The woman looked taken aback. She raised an eyebrow. "Really?"

"Yes," said Mabel, jutting her chin out. She continued, her voice rising above the din of the room: "And if you really want to see what good scones taste like, you should go to Gemma's tearoom." She nodded in my direction. "Now, *those* are what I call proper scones, and they really *are* the best you've ever tasted!"

Several customers at nearby tables turned our way, their attention caught by Mabel's booming voice. I groaned silently and hunched my shoulders, not knowing where to look. I felt both touched by Mabel's championing of me and embarrassed by the attention.

The Chinese woman glanced at the customers around us, who had obviously heard Mabel's comments and were eyeing me with interest, and her face hardened. Turning back to me, she narrowed her eyes. "You own a tearoom?"

I cleared my throat. "Yes, on the other side of Meadowford-on-Smythe. It's called the Little Stables."

"Oh... that old place," she said, her lips curling.

I felt a flash of resentment, my embarrassment fading. My tearoom might not have been slick, modern, and sophisticated, but I was proud of it and I loved my little business. Cassie bristled next to me and opened her mouth, but I laid a hasty hand on her arm before she could say anything. I didn't want to cause a scene but I wasn't going to allow myself to be put down either. I raised my chin and looked the other woman straight in the eye.

"Yes, in fact, we're known for having the best scones in Oxfordshire," I said evenly.

"Really?" she said in a disdainful tone. "Well, I suppose I ought to visit and check it out."

The last thing I wanted was this cold, supercilious woman in my tearoom, but I dredged up a polite smile and said: "Of course, you're welcome any time." I glanced at Cassie, whose face was still flushed with indignation, then added, "Um… anyway, we'd better go. Thanks again for… um…"—my tongue tripped over the words "a lovely tea" and instead, I amended it to—"… er… an interesting experience."

I bid the Old Biddies a hasty goodbye, then hustled Cassie out of the tea bar as fast as I could. As we stepped out of the entrance and walked away, however, I could still feel the woman's eyes on me, boring into my back, and I couldn't help an uncomfortable sense that somehow I had made an enemy.

Chapter Four

I felt emotionally drained after the outing to the tea bar and just wanted to head straight home to flop on the sofa with a hot drink and some mindless TV. But as I strapped Muesli's carrier into the front basket and wheeled my bicycle out of the tearoom's stable courtyard, I remembered with an inward groan that my mother was expecting me for dinner that evening. In fact—I glanced anxiously at my watch—I was in danger of being late. In my mother's book, it was punctuality and not cleanliness that was next to godliness, and I'd never hear the end of it if I wasn't sitting at the table by the time she was ready to serve the starter.

There was no chance of going home for a change of clothes or to drop off Muesli first. I would have to head straight to my parents' house and take my little cat to dinner with me, I decided, as I hopped onto my bike and began pedalling furiously. *Not that she'll mind*, I thought with a wry smile. Muesli loved going over to my parents' as she was spoiled rotten there. For a couple who had never professed to like animals and who had always fussed over the smallest stain on their upholstery or dirt on their cream carpets, Muesli had somehow managed to win my parents over to the point where my mother kept a bowl perpetually filled with cat treats and my father insisted on leaving her favourite armchair empty—just in case she visited.

Muesli sat up in her carrier and gave a chirrup of delight as we pulled up in front of my parents' elegant Victorian townhouse in North Oxford. I could see from her smug expression that she recognised where she was and was already looking forward to an evening of chin rubs on demand. I parked my bike, heaved the cat carrier out of the front basket, then raced up the front steps, hoping that I might still slide into my seat at the table before my mother noticed the time.

As I burst through the front door, however, my headlong rush was stopped by the sight of my father in the front hallway, bending over and carefully arranging pairs of fluffy slippers in a row alongside the wall.

"Dad?" I blurted.

"Ahh… hello, darling." My father, Professor Philip Rose, straightened and gave me his customary absent-minded smile.

A semi-retired Oxford don, my father

was a gentle, mild-mannered man who lived a happily henpecked life, spending most of his time either deep in his academic textbooks or following the progress of the latest cricket match on TV. I had expected to find him sitting in his usual place at the head of the dining table by now, obediently waiting to be served his bowl of soup, and I stared at him in bewilderment.

"What on earth are you doing?" I asked, starting across the threshold. But I'd barely taken a step before my father sprang forwards, barring my way.

"Oh, no, no, darling," he said, looking flustered. "You must remove your shoes before coming into the house."

"Remove my shoes? Why?" I glanced down at my feet. "I haven't stepped in mud or anything—"

"Your mother has decided that everyone must remove their shoes when they enter the house and put on these slippers instead," my father explained.

"What?"

"Darling!" cried an indignant voice above us. "Haven't I taught you any manners? Don't say 'what'—it is so uncouth. Always say 'I beg your pardon?' when you are unsure of what you have heard and would like something repeated."

I looked up to see my mother, Evelyn Rose, descending the staircase that led into the main hallway. She was dressed in a navy wool ensemble, with a pearl brooch at her throat and her hair gleaming in an elegant coiffure, with not a strand out of place. As usual, she instantly made me aware of my own dishevelled appearance in comparison— clad in a pair of corduroy trousers and faded sweater that had seen better days, with my hair windblown and my cheeks flushed from my recent hectic cycle into town.

"Mother, my shoes aren't dirty," I said impatiently.

"All shoes are dirty, darling," said my mother, coming to join us. "They track all manner of unseen grime and bacteria into the home. The outdoors is an extremely unclean space, you know! Besides, it's not merely a matter of hygiene but a sign of respect to remove one's shoes when entering someone's home."

"Huh? 'A sign of respect'?" I looked at my mother, perplexed. I wondered where she was getting these ideas from. "But surely it would be more respectful not to walk around barefoot?" I argued.

"Ah, that's why slippers are provided," said my mother with a complacent smile. "'One must change into appropriate footwear before entering the corresponding spaces.' Mrs Chu explained it all to me."

"Who's Mrs Chu?" I asked, feeling

lost.

"Oh, she's a lovely Taiwanese lady I met through OISS—you know, the Oxford Immigrant Support Society," my mother explained. "I've been volunteering in their outreach programme, where established residents help new arrivals in Oxford settle in. Mrs Chu arrived in England only a few months ago and it's all been a bit of a culture shock for her, poor thing— especially as her English isn't very good. She is finding things quite difficult."

"What made her decide to move, then?"

"Well, she has three grown-up daughters living in the UK. They were sent here for boarding school and then they all got into Oxford. The two older girls have graduated now but the youngest is still a student. When Mrs Chu was widowed last year, her eldest daughter felt that she should come and live here, where she would be closer to them. She is *such* a sweet lady!" my mother gushed. "So gracious and charming. I've been showing her around town and sharing some of our English customs, and in return, she has been telling me all about the Chinese traditions they observe at home."

"Wait, I thought you said she's Taiwanese?" I said, puzzled.

"Mrs Chu is *ethnically* Chinese but she's from Taiwan," my mother explained. "Mrs Chu told me that a long time ago, her ancestors used to be pig farmers in South China—fancy that! And like a lot of other farmers and fishermen, they found their way to Taiwan and settled there."

"Taiwan is an island, isn't it?" I asked, trying to remember my geography.

My mother nodded. "A little island off the south-west coast of China. Mrs Chu says it's beautiful, with mountains and forests and rivers and beaches... oh, and lots of earthquakes every year, apparently, because it sits right on the Pacific Rim."

"It's the politics that's complicated, my dear," my father told me, adjusting his spectacles and assuming the voice he used for university lectures. "Taiwan has had a colourful history: its original inhabitants were aboriginal tribes, but due to its fertility and strategic position, the island has always been highly coveted. It has been, at various times, a Dutch colony and a Japanese colony, then in the 1940s, when the Communist government took over China, the losing party retreated to Taiwan and set up a separate government there. They imposed harsh martial laws for many years; I imagine it was quite a shock to the community who had been living peacefully in Taiwan until then—people like Mrs Chu's ancestors who had settled on the island much earlier—but thankfully, things have improved greatly and the country is now considered a liberal, modern democracy. Of course, there is still the thorny question of its status as an independent nation. China claims that it is a renegade territory, whereas Taiwan considers itself a separate country."

"Oh yes, Mrs Chu told me that Taiwan is quite different to China in many ways," my mother chimed in. "But they do still follow many of the old traditions of Chinese culture. And I've decided that since Mrs Chu is trying to embrace our English customs, it's only fair that I should try to do the same in return!" She beamed.

"Certainly, the best way of understanding another culture is to walk in their shoes," my father agreed. "Or—" He gave a dry laugh. "—to remove your shoes, in this case."

"Mrs Chu has even helped me source some authentic 'Made in Taiwan' slippers!" My mother gestured proudly to the row of plush pink slippers, each somehow made to resemble the head of a white cartoon cat with a big red bow on one ear. "Aren't they delightful? Apparently, they're all the rage there."

"Delightful" wasn't quite the word I would have used. "Nauseatingly cute" would have been more accurate—the kind of thing you'd expect five-year-old girls to adore. And to add to the kitsch factor, each slipper was embroidered with pastel hearts and emblazoned with the words "Hello Kitty" in swirly pink letters.

I balked slightly as my mother reached for a pair and thrust them at me. "So… um… are we all going to be wearing slippers in the house from now on?"

"Not just slippers, darling," trilled my mother. "We're going to follow many of the traditions of a Taiwanese household… starting with dinner tonight!" She turned and sailed grandly out of the hallway into the dining room, with my father at her heels.

Wondering what on earth that meant, I stuffed my feet into the slippers and started to follow my parents, then paused as I heard the doorbell sound.

"Oh, darling—will you get that? And make sure they take off their shoes and put on the slippers!" my mother's voice drifted out.

I turned back to the door with a sigh, wondering which of my mother's "pearls and twinset" brigade would be joining us for dinner. But when I saw the man standing on the front steps, I broke into a smile of delighted surprise. With his dark, brooding good looks and air of cool authority, Devlin O'Connor was the walking cliché of "tall, dark, and handsome". He had been my first love—and was still the only man who could make my heart race, even though we'd known each other for over a decade now. True, we hadn't spent most of that time together: after a whirlwind romance as college sweethearts at Oxford, we'd broken up when Devlin had asked me to marry him, and I'd said no—not because I hadn't loved him, but because I knew my mother and family social circle didn't approve of Devlin, with his working-class roots and his lack of wealth and status. They'd insisted that I could never be happy with someone from such a different background and, young and uncertain as I was, I had bowed to the pressure.

Devlin had been hurt and furious, we'd parted bitterly, and I'd spent the next eight years overseas trying to ignore my broken heart and the feeling that I'd made the worst mistake of my life. Imagine my shock when I returned to Oxford last year to find that Devlin had not only become a top CID detective but was also independently wealthy, with a luxury car and a beautiful property in the Cotswolds—whilst I had been reduced to living with my parents again whilst struggling to get my tearoom business off the ground. Perhaps it had been a form of karma.

Although karma's also been kind enough to let us find our way back into each other's arms again, so I suppose I can't really complain, I thought with an inward smile. And the experience had certainly made me older and wiser, plus helped me cut the apron strings and step out from my mother's shadow at last!

There were still times, though, when I couldn't quite believe that Devlin and I were back together. I felt my heart give a familiar little flip now as his vivid blue eyes met mine, and his expression softened.

"Devlin!" I threw my arms around his neck. "This is a nice surprise."

He gave me a playful kiss on the tip of my nose, and I leaned back in his arms, laughing. Then my smile faded as I noticed that he was still in the three-piece suit that he normally wore for work and realised that he must have come straight from the police station.

"Is something wrong?" I asked, disengaging myself and stepping back.

"No… at least, I'm not sure," said Devlin, giving me a slightly quizzical smile. "I received a message from your mother saying that she needed my help and wanted me to come over straight after work. I thought perhaps her car had been vandalised or something…?" He turned and quickly scanned the street with a policeman's characteristic alertness, but the tree-lined avenue looked quiet and innocuous.

"She hasn't mentioned anything to me. It was probably just a ploy to get you to come to dinner," I said with a dry laugh as I turned to lead him into the house. Then I stopped short just inside the door. "Oh, I nearly forgot—you have to take your shoes off and put on a pair of these."

Devlin stared incredulously at the fluffy pink slippers I had handed him. "You're winding me up."

I stifled a laugh at the horrified expression on his face. "No, I'm serious. New house rules." I gave him a coaxing smile. "It's just for tonight. And it would mean a lot to my mother."

Devlin swallowed, then manfully nodded, and attempted to shove his size-eleven feet into the plush pink footwear. He managed to wriggle half his foot into one and squash most of the other into its twin, then shuffled his way down the hall. I followed, trying not to chuckle at the sight of my six-foot-tall boyfriend stumbling in fluffy *Hello Kitty* slippers.

Five minutes later, we were all sitting in the dining room, staring in puzzlement at the table in front of us. Instead of the usual soup starter, we had each been given an empty plate and a pair of chopsticks.

"Um… aren't we having soup, Mother?" I asked.

"Oh, no," said my mother. "Mrs Chu says Taiwanese families have soup at the *end* of a meal, not at the beginning, because otherwise, it would just fill you up before you've even reached the main course. It *does* make so much more sense, when you think about it—don't you agree? They usually have little cold dishes as appetisers instead."

"Oh… well, I suppose that's a bit like us having prawn cocktail or egg mayonnaise," I said.

"And that's exactly what I've prepared!" said my mother, trotting off to the kitchen.

When she returned, however, instead of setting little individual servings in front of us, like I'd expected, she placed an enormous bowl of cooked, peeled prawns drizzled with bright pink sauce in the centre of the table.

"You may all help yourselves," she said grandly, gesturing to the bowl. "One is really supposed to have a pair of communal chopsticks for serving, of course, but since we're all family…"

I gaped at her. My mother had an almost fanatical devotion to dining etiquette, and even simple family meals often involved full place settings with a barrage of fish knives, pastry forks, and dessert spoons. For someone who considered it practically blasphemy to use the "wrong" knife to butter the bread, I couldn't believe that she was now encouraging us to all dive into the same bowl with our own cutlery.

"Er… don't we usually each have our own?" I asked.

"Oh no, Mrs Chu says in a family, food should really be shared from communal dishes," my mother said earnestly.

"Sharing food is very important. It's a sign of trust, and of community and togetherness."

I looked doubtfully down at the pair of slender, tapered bamboo sticks next to my plate. "Um... can I use a fork instead?"

"Certainly not, darling!" said my mother, frowning. "Mrs Chu says knives and forks are never used at the table because they have sharp edges and are a sign of disharmony."

"Well, Mrs Chu hasn't seen the signs of disharmony from me trying to use chopsticks," I muttered under my breath.

Glancing over at my father and Devlin, I could see both men eyeing my mother with wary disbelief. Then, clutching their chopsticks with clumsy fingers, they bravely attempted to snag a prawn from the bowl at the centre of the table. I held my breath, watching as

Devlin's chopsticks slipped and a prawn dangled precariously from one tip. Cocktail sauce dripped slowly down, one lurid coral-red droplet quivering ominously over my mother's snowy white tablecloth, like a slow-motion scene from a horror movie, before Devlin—his face white with concentration—regained his grip and managed to transfer the prawn to his own plate. He sagged back in his chair, looking more stressed than if he'd been overseeing a hostage shootout, and I stifled the urge to laugh.

Then my amusement vanished as I remembered that I still had my own turn. Taking a deep breath, I picked up my own chopsticks and waded into the fray.

Chapter Five

For several minutes, there was an agonised silence at the table as we each attempted to chase slippery pink crustaceans around our plates with our chopsticks. Finally, my father swallowed his hard-earned mouthful and sat back, wiping his forehead.

"Oh, surely you're not going to just have one, Philip?" said my mother.

"I… er… I'm saving space for the main course, darling," said my father. Then he turned hastily to Devlin before my mother could reply and said: "So… er… how is your work going, Devlin?"

"Very well, sir," said Devlin, looking relieved to have an excuse to put down his chopsticks as well. "In fact, I might be in line for a promotion soon."

I looked at him excitedly. "Ooh, Devlin—you never told me! Is this for Chief Inspector?"

He nodded, smiling. "Yes. Nothing's official, but the Super—that's my immediate boss, the Detective Superintendent," he explained to my parents, "—the Super's dropped a few hints about having a word with the DCC—the Deputy Chief Constable. I think I stand a good chance. He's been keeping an eye on my performance, and I think he's been impressed—"

"He bloody well should be," I said.

"Gemma!" My mother gave a small scream and clutched her throat. "A lady never uses coarse language."

"Sorry, Mother," I muttered, then I turned back to Devlin. "You've solved more cases than any other detective at Oxfordshire CID! Probably because you work more hours than any other detective," I added, trying to keep the note of resentment out of my voice.

Devlin heard it and looked as if he wanted to say something, then he glanced at my parents and changed his mind.

"Well, I think that's marvellous news, Devlin!" said my mother, smiling at him. "How very exciting. We're all so proud of you."

I hid a smile. I never thought I'd see the day my mother would be telling Devlin O'Connor that she was proud of him. There had been a time when she couldn't even stomach the thought of him joining us at a family meal, and it had been a long struggle to convince her that he was good enough for her only child. But to her credit, once my mother had finally decided to accept Devlin as my boyfriend, she had embraced him whole-heartedly as her blue-eyed boy (literally, in his case!).

Devlin gave an embarrassed cough. "Well, I wouldn't get too excited yet. Nothing's been confirmed and I'm sure it all still depends on how I handle my next few cases."

"Oh, I'm sure that's just a formality," said my mother airily as she rose to return to the kitchen to fetch the main course.

A few minutes later, she came back into the dining room bearing a large platter. She set this down in the centre of the table and we all breathed silent sighs of relief to see that it contained nothing more exotic than roast chicken, albeit a completely deboned and shredded version—presumably to make the meat easier to pick up with chopsticks. There was also an accompanying bowl of peas and a side plate of roast potatoes, thankfully both with serving spoons... although this wasn't much help once the food was on our plates!

My mother served us each some peas and potatoes, then she sat back down and said: "When it's official, Devlin, we must have a party at Gemma's tearoom to celebrate—"

"If it's still running," I muttered darkly.

My mother stopped and looked at me. "What do you mean?"

I sighed, then took a deep breath and told them all about the demoralising time I'd been having at work, starting with the lack of customers and ending with the intimidating visit to the swanky new tea bar.

"...there were queues going out the door and the place was packed to bursting and they're offering bottomless tea and coffee, and even free sparkling wine with their afternoon teas!" I said gloomily, slumping down in my chair.

"It's hopeless. I'm never going to be able to compete."

"Nonsense, darling!" said my mother briskly. "You said yourself that the Little Stables serves *much* better food and drink. You just need to make sure that everyone knows that."

"How?" I asked despairingly. "I can't start offering crazy discount packages like this tea bar is doing to bring people in. There's no margin for profit at all and—"

"You don't need to offer deals like that," said my mother, waving a dismissive hand. "A couple of small promotions, perhaps, but in actual fact, I think you could simply repackage what you offer and that would already make a big difference."

"People don't seem to want the traditional favourites anymore," I said morosely. "This tea bar was serving all sorts of exotic things, like wonton tarts and seaweed sandwiches; even their scones were square!" I sighed. "Does this mean I have to switch to weird fusion food to compete?"

"Of course not. People come to your tearoom for the traditional British experience. But maybe what you should do is put more things into set menus."

"What do you mean?" I asked, frowning. "I thought people would prefer having more choice and being able to mix and match from the menu, instead of being forced to eat a set list of items."

"Oh no, darling. People like things presented in packages. It takes all the effort out of choosing. And a set menu always feels like a better deal, even if the savings are minimal. You could offer a 'Classic English Afternoon Tea' set menu with all the traditional favourites or a 'Tea for Two' package, perhaps..."

"Yes, I agree with your mother," my father chimed in. He gave me an encouraging smile. "It would be far better than trying to copy the other place. You'd just be an imitation, a poor second, otherwise. It's always best to be yourself, darling."

"Being myself hasn't helped me much so far…" I muttered, slumping even lower in my chair.

My mother frowned at me. "Honestly, darling, you're not going to get more customers just moping and feeling sorry for yourself—"

"I'm not feeling sorry for myself," I cried, sitting up indignantly.

My mother ignored me and turned to Devlin, saying in the kind of indulgent tone normally reserved for grouchy toddler: "Gemma gets dreadfully sulky if she's told that she's acting silly."

"*Mother!*" I cried furiously, ignoring the fact that I was sounding exactly like the petulant child she was describing.

I glanced at Devlin, waiting for him to

tell my mother what a shining example of mature adulthood I was. Instead, he shrank in his seat, studiously avoiding both our eyes, and looked desperately across the table. My father, however, was engrossed in wrestling with a roast potato using chopsticks, and was no help at all.

Finally, Devlin turned back to me and said in a neutral voice: "Uh… you know, Gemma, your mother might have a point. Not about you feeling sorry for yourself," he added hastily, seeing my expression. "But perhaps it's not as bad as you think. You just need to adjust things a bit and relaunch your menu." He gave me an encouraging smile. "I'm sure once you do a bit of promotion, business at the tearoom will be booming again. After all, it's true that you have the best scones in the county."

"Speaking of scones," said my mother, oblivious to my scowling face. "Can you make an extra batch to bring along tomorrow night, darling?"

"Tomorrow night? What's tomorrow night?" I asked irritably, still not quite ready to forgive her.

"Oh, didn't I tell you? The OISS committee has arranged a cross-cultural evening for new arrivals to get to know each other and the resident volunteers. And since food is a great bridge between cultures, they've decided to have a potty luck dinner!"

"I think you mean *pot*luck, Mother," I said, starting to grin in spite of myself. "Everyone has to bring a dish to share—is that right?"

"Yes, each person should bring a dish from their own country, so we can all exchange and share, and taste and learn!" My mother beamed. "Mrs Chu is going to bring Taiwanese dumplings, Mr Odongo says he'll show us his famous *mandazi* recipe, and Mrs Singh says she'll bring some Indian dessert to match that; Mrs Kim is bringing home-made *kimchi* and Miss Petrović says she's going to try and get hold of some Istrian ham... so I thought: what could be more English than scones with jam and clotted cream?"

Before I could answer, she continued blithely, "And you must come too, Devlin! That's what I wanted to speak to you about tonight, actually. We think you'd be marvellous in our community outreach programme."

Devlin had had his head down, swearing under his breath as he tried to pick up peas with his chopsticks, but now he glanced up and said distractedly, "Me?"

"Yes, we'd love you to speak at our event tomorrow evening. Some of the new residents come from countries where there isn't much trust in the authorities, so this would be a wonderful way to help them build up trust in the British police."

"Er… well, actually, community policing isn't really part of the work of the CID…" Devlin demurred. "It's not an area that I have much experience in—"

"Oh, you don't need to do anything special. Just a simple presentation, really, about what the police do and how they protect the community. I think the members just want to meet a friendly face and ask a few questions."

"Yeah, I'm sure the ladies will enjoy meeting *your* friendly face," I teased, chuckling as I glanced at my handsome boyfriend. "You'll be inundated with invitations to go and sample their home cooking!"

Devlin reddened and rubbed the back of his neck in an embarrassed gesture. "I still think perhaps it might be better if I asked one of my colleagues in Uniform or maybe even one of our PCSOs—er, that's Police Community Support Officers—to come and—"

"Oh no, you must come," insisted my mother. "I've been telling the committee all about you and everyone's dying to meet you!"

There was no arguing with my mother when she was in this mood, and before he realised what he was doing, Devlin found himself obediently promising to present himself the next evening.

"Er... where and what time is it going to be?" he asked.

"It'll start at eight p.m. and as for place... well, actually, we're not sure yet," said my mother with a slight frown. "It was supposed to be held at the Oxford Town Hall but there's been a last-minute mix-up and our room's been given away, so now the committee is scrambling to find a substitute venue. They're having a meeting about it tonight, actually. I'll let you know as soon as I find out tomorrow."

The rest of the dinner passed in

relative peace, bar the occasional missiles of peas evading our chopsticks and shooting off our plates. Muesli decided it was a great new game and stationed herself under the table, watching and waiting to catch the wayward peas with her paws. When my mother finally brought out the ice cream for dessert, we were all hugely relieved to discover that she didn't expect us to eat *that* with chopsticks.

After we'd bade my parents goodnight, Devlin and I stepped out of the house together and paused on the front steps.

"Hey... maybe after you've done your talk tomorrow night and I've done my duty with my mother's friends, we could go out for a drink?" I suggested. "We should be able to get away by ten at the latest."

Devlin gave me an apologetic look. "Sorry, Gemma. I've got a really early start the next day and I actually have some paperwork that I'm supposed to be doing tomorrow night, which I'll have to deal with after I get home."

"Oh." I swallowed my disappointment.

It felt like Devlin and I had hardly seen each other lately. He had always worked long hours—a detective's job certainly didn't have predictable routines—but recently, it seemed like he barely stopped, except to eat and sleep (usually alone!). I bit my lip, reminding myself that I'd always known that Devlin was dedicated and driven, often going above and beyond the call of duty in his quest for justice. Still, it was hard to stifle the flicker of hurt and resentment.

He could at least sound a bit more sorry that we can't spend time together, I thought peevishly. I knew Devlin was not the type to offer flowery declarations of love, and normally I told myself that I was glad. I didn't want a man who just spouted the usual cheesy clichés. Still, there were times when I wished he could be a bit more expressive. Sometimes even the most independent, modern-minded girl wants a bit of good old-fashioned passion and romance. It would have been nice to be told occasionally that he had been thinking of me and missed me.

Devlin glanced at my silent profile and touched my hand in a gesture of apology. "I'm sorry, Gemma. I know it's been tough lately with me cancelling dates at the last minute and not even having time to give you a call. It's just been a really bad spell at work, you know? Plus, ever since I knew my name had been put forward for the DCI promotion, I've really wanted to make sure that I'm giving a hundred percent—d'you know what I mean?"

I sighed. "Yes, of course, Devlin. It's okay. I understand."

"Thank you." He smiled at me. "Now, do you want me to drop you off home?"

"No, I'll be fine. It'll be a pain trying to fit my bike in the boot of your Jaguar and you haven't got a bike rack on the back. It's only a short cycle through the centre of town to my place anyway," I said, trying to inject a cheerful note into my voice.

"Okay, well… I'll see you tomorrow night then." Devlin hesitated, then bent and gave me a quick kiss before striding to his car.

I stood beside my bike, though, lost in my thoughts, long after his tail lights had faded into the distance.

Chapter Six

Wistful longing for romance was the last thing on my mind the next morning, though, as I sat down with Cassie to discuss a plan of action for my ailing tearoom. Much as I hated to admit it, my mother's words at dinner the night before had been spot on. I had been wallowing in self-pity like a maudlin pig in a mud bath and it was time I stopped, picked myself up, and "got back in the ring". In fact, I had arrived for work feeling more upbeat than I had in days, and even the sight of the empty tables in the dining room hadn't dampened my spirits.

"You know, I think with just a bit of extra promotion, we could really turn things around," said Cassie, catching on to my optimistic mood. "I was thinking of that flyer that the Old Biddies received through their letterboxes. Well, we could do something similar! I could easily rustle up a couple of designs and we could get a few hundred printed and distributed in the local villages... maybe even Oxford—"

"Yes... Oxford... the coach tours!" I cried. "We're already pretty friendly with several of the operators. They're used to bringing their groups here. Why don't we ask them if they'd be happy to hand out some of our flyers to their customers when they board the coaches?"

"No, no, even better than that—sampler boxes," said Cassie. "We can ask Dora if she can make up some mini-scones so we give them out as free samples. You know, like they do with cosmetics and things in department stores… I mean, we know our baking speaks for itself."

"That's a great idea, Cass!" I agreed. "If I'm going to take a loss on these promotions, I'd rather it was for people to sample our baking than just giving crazy discounts…"

"You won't need to offer crazy discounts after most people have tasted our scones," Cassie declared. She reached for an order pad and flipped it over so that she could scribble on the blank rear side of the pages. "We need to think up some good text to put on the flyers. You know, the kind of slick marketing copy that sounds really impressive—I know!" she sat up. "I'll look up some of our online reviews. Genuine customer comments are always a great place to start…" She trailed off as she grabbed her phone and started searching and scrolling.

"I hate to admit it, but my mother's comments about packages and set menus were pretty astute," I said, adding with a wry grin: "Who would have thought a Fifties Housewife devotee could come up with such cool marketing strategies? And I was thinking—"

"BLOODY HELL!" Cassie shot up out of her chair, her face red.

"What? What?" I asked, startled.

"We've had a whole load of one-star reviews online!"

I leaned over her phone, my eyes widening in horror at the score of negative reviews underneath my tearoom's listing. "I don't understand… who are all these people?" I asked miserably. "I don't remember anyone complaining recently, do you? We always try to make it up to customers if they're unhappy about anything."

"It's all bollocks! Look—" Cassie jabbed her finger at her phone screen. "What's this about us serving stale eclairs with rancid cream? We don't even have eclairs on the menu! And we don't open for dinner either, so this bit about the poor service and undercooked fish pie is either about a totally different place or it's completely made up!"

Her eyes narrowed as she scrolled up and down the screen again. "You know what? I bet these are fake reviews, posted by one person."

"What?"

"Yes, look... all the one-stars were posted either yesterday or today. There's no way that that many people could have had a bad experience here in that time. For one thing, we've barely had three customers! And that Indian family definitely left here very happy."

I stared at her. "Are you suggesting that someone is posting fake reviews just to sabotage us?"

"Why not? And I'll bet I know who it is," added Cassie grimly. "That cow who owns the Yin-Yang Tea Bar—you know, the woman who came up to us when we were talking to the Old Biddies."

I thought back to the coldly glamorous woman we had met and couldn't help remembering the lingering unease I'd felt as she'd watched us leave her tea bar. Still, it was hard to believe that anyone could do something so purposefully malicious.

"But why would she do something like this?" I asked.

"Duh… to get rid of the competition, of course!" said Cassie impatiently. "She's obviously done some research and realised that we'd be a serious threat to her business. And with her shoddy food, the only thing she's got to offer is her crazy discounts—but even that won't be enough to get people to return if the food isn't that great. So she obviously decided to tip the balance in her favour, by putting people off our place. It's absolutely despicable! I'd like to go over right now and give her a piece of my mind!"

I caught Cassie's arm. "Wait, Cass... we have no proof that she's responsible for those reviews."

"I don't need proof! I mean, come *on*, Gemma! Don't you think it's suspicious that we met her last night and she learned that you own a local tearoom with a fantastic reputation—and by the way, I could see that she was seriously narked when the Old Biddies were talking up your scones and all the customers around us were listening—and now, all of a sudden, there's a flood of one-star reviews about us?"

"Well, it does seem to be a bit of a coincidence," I agreed doubtfully.

"A *bit*?" Cassie said, her voice shrill with sarcasm. "Besides, you know how easy it is to hide behind these fake user names when you're posting anything online. She could have even paid one of those dodgy services which posts reviews for you."

"What dodgy services?"

"I read an article in *The Guardian* about businesses paying for fake five-star reviews online. There was even a man in Italy who was found out for selling fake Tripadvisor reviews to hotels and restaurants—he ended up jailed for months. Well, if people can buy fake positive reviews to boost their own profile, why not fake negative ones to damage competitors?"

I stared at my friend. The thought of someone maligning us in such a low, vindictive way made me feel slightly sick. It was one thing to face an attacker head-on, to be able to meet and defend yourself against an assault, but this kind of sly, stab-in-the-back ambush left you feeling helpless and violated.

"But we can't just accuse her, Cassie," I said worriedly. "Especially given her success. It'll just look like sour grapes."

"I don't care what it looks like," Cassie fumed. "She's got to be confronted with it, otherwise she'll just keep attacking us. We've got to show her that we're no pushovers."

I hesitated, then said: "Look, I'm seeing Devlin tonight. I'll ask him what we can do, if it *is* her—"

"It is!" Cassie insisted.

"—but we don't want to make things worse. The important thing now is getting our own business back up again. Getting sucked into some kind of nasty PR slanging match or defamation suit isn't going to help."

"Fine," said Cassie grudgingly. "Speak to Devlin and see what he says—"

She broke off as the bell attached to the tearoom door tinkled merrily and we looked up to see a young couple entering the dining room. Delighted at the prospect of customers at last, I got up to greet them, shoving the whole unpleasant subject from my mind. For the rest of the day, I tried hard not to let my thoughts stray to the topic, telling myself that there was no point seething about it until I'd had the chance to speak to Devlin. In fact, after the constant worries and stress about the tearoom, I was almost looking forward to my mother's "potty luck" dinner—it would be nice to be forced to think about something else for a few hours.

However, the reprieve was short-lived. I'd agreed for my mother to give me a lift to the event, as it would be easier to transport the big platter of scones that I was bringing in her car, rather than on my bicycle, and I paid little attention to the route during the drive. But as my mother turned into the car park of a large set of buildings, I sat bolt upright in my seat. We were in the sprawling estate of the Cotswolds Manor Hotel group, heading towards the cluster of restaurants and cafés that made up the new extension.

"The potluck dinner is being held here?" I asked in dismay as my mother slid the car into a parking space in front of a familiar gleaming façade of glass and concrete, surrounded by a wrap-around terrace and boasting a huge black-marble cocktail bar that was visible through the front entrance.

"Yes, the committee were almost in despair at finding a suitable alternative venue, but luckily Mrs Chu's eldest daughter, Azalea, came to the rescue," said my mother. "Azalea's a very successful businesswoman; she's just opened a new bar, and she's been fabulously generous! She said OISS could hire the place for nothing this eve—" My mother broke off suddenly. "Oh my goodness, darling, is this the place you were telling us about yesterday? The committee just said it was a 'bar' when they sent the details through this morning; I didn't realise it was a *tea* bar!"

I sighed. *So much for avoiding the subject of my tearoom dramas*, I thought sourly as I got out of the car and unloaded the food I had brought from the back seat. I was not looking forward to meeting Azalea Chu again. Especially now that I had suspicions about her ruthless, underhanded methods of tackling business competition, it was going to be difficult maintaining a civil and pleasant demeanour!

My mother had spotted a friend and hurried to join the other lady, and the two of them were already heading into the tea bar, their heads together, talking animatedly. I followed a bit more slowly, carefully balancing my platter of scones and containers of jam and clotted cream, as I mounted the steps to the tea bar entrance. I was glad now that Dora had spent extra time making a fresh batch of scones for me to bring. A wonderful buttery aroma rose from the platter, and I glanced down with pride at the rustic little rounds, soft and lightly flaky, with a beautiful golden crust across the top of each. If I had to face Azalea Chu tonight, at least I would have the satisfaction of knowing that I was presenting the best of my tearoom's baking!

I was pulled from my thoughts by the sound of an angry exclamation, and I looked up to see a man hovering just outside the tea bar entrance. He was dressed in the standard chef's uniform of white double-breasted jacket, black-and-white checked trousers, and apron, although his head was bare of the traditionally accompanying *toque blanche*. Still, there was no doubt that he was a professional member of the staff. I was just wondering if he had strayed from the tea bar kitchen when he shocked me by reaching up and grabbing one corner of a promotional poster which had been stuck to one of the windows.

As I watched, open-mouthed, he tore it down, then crumpled the poster in his hands before throwing it on the floor and stamping viciously on it, cursing all the while in a voice that shook with fury. Then he whirled around and stopped short as he saw me. I hesitated, embarrassed to be caught staring and not sure how to react. He scowled at me and seemed about to say something, then he turned and stalked off without a word. He walked around the outside of the building rather than going into the tea bar as I'd expected. I found myself unconsciously drifting after him to keep him in sight and I watched as he walked down the length of the wrap-around terrace.

I realised that the terrace didn't just surround the tea bar but continued along the entire cluster of buildings, tapering off by the edifice of the main hotel complex. The man had reached the end now and disappeared through a door which led into the hotel. I stared thoughtfully after him. Was he a chef who worked in one of the hotel restaurants? What had he been doing here?

I shivered suddenly as I recalled his face when he'd whirled around after destroying the poster. There had been such a naked expression of bitterness and hatred, I had almost reeled back from the force of it. I'd often heard the phrase "if looks could kill..." bandied around, but I'd never fully appreciated it until now. If the look in his eyes had been anything to go by, that man had been willing to commit murder.

Chapter Seven

When I finally entered the tea bar, I found that the interior had been rearranged so that most of the tables had been pushed to the sides and an empty space had been created in the centre of the room. A large crowd of people, of a wide mix of nationalities, were milling about, talking and laughing as they sipped drinks and munched food from the buffet laid out on the black-marble bar.

I made my own way across to the bar and carefully slid my platter of scones into an empty space at the end.

"My goodness, those look delicious."

Glancing up, I found a statuesque woman standing next to me. She looked to be somewhere in her fifties, with grey-streaked blonde hair swept back from her face in a glamorous style reminiscent of Catherine Deneuve and an elegant wool dress accessorised by an Italian silk scarf. I was startled when she extended a hand and introduced herself as Professor Gillian Bennett, the Tutor for English at Pendlebury College, one of the constituent colleges of Oxford University. She looked more like an "Old Hollywood" movie star than the usual stereotype of the stuffy Oxford don!

"And you must be Evelyn Rose's daughter, Gemma," she said with a smile.

I blinked in surprise. "How did you know?"

Her smile widened and she indicated the platter of scones. "We've all heard so much about you and your wonderful scones. Evelyn says they're known as the best in Oxfordshire."

I felt my cheeks reddening. Although I was warmed by my mother's pride in me, it was still embarrassing to be faced with your parents' bragging.

"Er... I hope they live up to the hype," I said with a self-conscious laugh. Hastily, I changed the subject. Pointing to the plate of flattened meatballs she was holding, I asked: "Are those yours?"

"Oh, heavens no," said Gillian Bennett with a laugh. "I just offered to help Mrs Akbas bring her *koftas* over to the buffet. I can barely boil an egg! But luckily I don't have to cook my own meals, as I live in college and one of the perks is being able to eat at High Table every night."

"Yes, I do miss that sometimes. Not the High Table, of course, but being able to eat in Hall," I said with a reminiscing smile, thinking back to my own student days. "There's something really nice about just having to turn up and knowing that dinner would be ready, without worrying about planning or cooking a meal. Even if it meant that you had to change and wear a gown to be allowed at the table," I added with a grin, referring to the quaint Oxford tradition of requiring their students to don black academic gowns for many university occasions, including dinners in their own college.

"Ah yes, of course, your mother mentioned that you were at Oxford. Did your college not have Informal Hall as well?" she asked, referring to the earlier, more casual sitting.

"Oh, it did, and a lot of my friends did prefer that, especially if it meant that they didn't have to worry about having to return to their rooms to change and wear their gowns. But I usually found it too much of a rush to eat so early, so I preferred Formal Hall. Anyway, it's not too bad being a girl; I mean, you don't actually have to wear a dress—you can get away with wearing trousers and a nice top, as long as you have your gown over everything. Besides, I think a lot of women actually like having an excuse to 'dress for dinner'," I added, chuckling. "It's much harder for the boys, though, because they have to wear a jacket and tie, in addition to their gowns."

"Yes, well, that's something the members of Pendlebury haven't had to worry about until recently," said Professor Bennett dryly. "It's all changed now, of course. Pendlebury College lost its 'ladies-only' status this year and we now admit men as well as women."

"Do you mind the change?" I asked, curious at her tone of voice.

"Well... I support greater diversity in the student body, of course," she said mechanically. "But I do think our unique nurturing atmosphere and environment at the college will be irrevocably damaged once men are on the scene." She scowled. "Girls are better able to focus on themselves, and their own personal growth and empowerment, when they are not being distracted by the opposite sex. Instead, with males around, they often waste a lot of time and energy on angst and romance, which does nothing other than drain their self-esteem!"

"But… surely falling in love is part of the experience of being a woman?" I asked, startled by her vehemence.

Professor Bennett sniffed. "Perhaps. But it's certainly not vital nor the most important part of the experience—and yet we all act like it is. There is still a strong expectation to be a 'good girl', to marry and have children and become a devoted wife and mother… otherwise you're somehow seen as a failure as a woman. That is certainly *not* true, as I can assure you from personal experience."

"I think things have changed nowadays," I protested.

"You mean all that talk about career women and gender equality?" she said scornfully. "That's just political lip service! In any case, if there *is* any change, it's limited to liberal circles in Western society. In many of the more traditional communities, especially non-Anglo-Saxon ones, there is still intense pressure on girls to conform. You won't believe how much they suffer under the weight of parental and cultural expectations."

I was slightly taken aback by her blunt opinions, and it must have shown on my face because she gave a sheepish laugh and said, "I'm afraid you've stumbled on my personal crusade. I feel very strongly about this because in my position, I see so many promising young women, with so much potential, throw away their dreams and squander their talents just because of social and cultural pressure to conform."

I thought suddenly of my own struggle to find my identity when I'd left university and the disapproval I'd faced when I finally decided to give up my high-flying career to open a tearoom... and I felt a surge of liking for Gillian Bennett. Perhaps if I'd had someone like her in my life when I was younger, I wouldn't have felt so dominated by my mother's "traditional" opinions and the expectations of the conservative, middle-class society that I'd grown up in.

"I think the girls are lucky to have you support them and champion their personal aspirations," I said, smiling at her.

She sighed. "Well, I try my best. It was one reason why I was keen to get involved with OISS, actually. So many daughters in immigrant families deal with this cIash between the expectations of their culture and their own dreams. I thought if I could get to know some of the parents and chat with them on a more friendly, casual basis, I might be better able to persuade them to see my point of view."

She nodded suddenly across the room, and I turned to see who she was indicating: a petite, middle-aged lady with almond-shaped eyes and a gentle face, who was chatting with my mother.

"Take Mrs Chu, for instance," said Professor Bennett. "She has three daughters who all graduated from Oxford or are enrolled at present, and who are all expected to bring honour to the family name. The eldest, Azalea, has become a top entrepreneur with a successful hospitality business.

"The second daughter, Magnolia, has done the next best thing to becoming a doctor herself: she's married one," continued Professor Bennett dryly. "And produced two beautiful children. Which leaves the youngest daughter, Freesia, who is currently in her second year at Pendlebury and is probably my most promising student," she added. "Well, Freesia is under immense pressure to walk in the footsteps of her sisters—but she is nothing like them! She's a wonderfully creative, sensitive dreamer who wants to be a writer, and that's definitely something that's *not* approved of! So I've been trying my best to befriend Mrs Chu and convince her to support Freesia's dream and ambitions."

"If her elder sister has built a successful career for herself, wouldn't she be a good ally to help you challenge the traditional mindset?" I asked.

Professor Bennett's mouth tightened. "Azalea Chu? She's the biggest part of the problem. Mrs Chu is actually a very sweet lady and I think all she really wants is for her children to be happy. But from what I've seen, she seems to defer to her eldest daughter in everything—in fact, the whole family seems to be dominated by Azalea. And Azalea has very fixed ideas about how her youngest sister should live her life. She's contemptuous of anything to do with the creative arts; she even tried to stop Freesia reading English at Oxford—can you believe it?"

"What did she want her to do?"

Professor Bennett's mouth twisted. "Oh, Engineering or PPE or one of the sciences, probably. Something more acceptable and 'useful' than an airy-fairy subject like English. Well, it's high time someone told her that her little sister's life is none of her business!" She sighed. "But that's one of the challenges with Chinese culture: there is so much respect for elders that even when it comes to siblings, the oldest is often regarded like a parent and has so much more influence over the younger siblings than you'd normally find in the West."

I was just thinking of a reply when I

heard my mother's voice calling me from across the room. Making my excuses to Gillian Bennett, I responded to the summons—only to find myself facing the very lady that we had been discussing.

"Darling, I must introduce you to Mrs Chu!" my mother said, indicating the dainty woman next to her.

"Is nice to meet you," said Mrs Chu in soft, accented English, her black eyes regarding me with interest as she inclined her head in a slight bow.

"Yes, it's lovely to meet you too," I said, hesitating as I stretched out a hand, then changing my mind and doing an imitation of her half bow instead.

She beamed at me, obviously appreciating my gesture. "Your mother talk about you very much. She is very proud of you. Very good daughter. Very beautiful, very clever."

"Er... thank you," I said, flushing with embarrassment.

"You must be very proud of your daughters too, Mrs Chu. They are all so talented and have done so well for themselves," my mother said.

I forced a smile as I nodded and said to the Taiwanese lady: "Yes, I believe your eldest, Azalea, has just opened this place and it's been doing very well."

The woman's face lit up with pride, but she said modestly, "Oh, no, no... is just lucky. Good business luck." Her eyes brightened suddenly as she looked over my shoulder and she said eagerly, "Ah! Azalea come now. I introduce you. Is good you make friends!"

My heart sank and I turned reluctantly to see the coldly glamorous woman I'd met yesterday coming towards us.

Chapter Eight

Azalea Chu's silky black hair was once again pulled back in a sleek ponytail, and her make-up seemed to be even more dramatic than yesterday, with thick black liner giving her fierce cat's eyes and dark red lipstick emphasising her thin lips. She was talking rapidly on her phone and, as she approached, I heard her voice, sharp and sneering:

"...don't threaten me, Kai, or you'll be sorry. I will destroy you. Don't think I won't... So? I don't care, that's your problem... well, you should have thought of that before you decided to call in the divorce lawyers, shouldn't you?"

She pressed a button on the phone with flourish, abruptly ending the call, then turned to face us.

"Azalea! Look, this Mrs Rose daughter, Jem-Ma," said Mrs Chu. "She also have business like your one. Very good, can make a new friend, no?"

Azalea shot her mother a brief, impatient glance, then she said: "My tea bar is very different from Gemma's... uh... vintage tearoom." The corners of her lips curled in a superior smile.

I stiffened, resenting her deliberate attempt to make the Little Stables sound like some sad old relic. But—glancing at Mrs Chu's eager, smiling face and my mother's expectant expression—I bit back the retort that sprang to my lips and instead pinned a polite smile to my face.

"I actually already met your daughter yesterday when my friend and I came over to her tea bar," I said to Mrs Chu. "But it's nice to be officially introduced," I added, turning back to Azalea and offering my hand. "Congratulations on the grand opening. It looks like everything is going great."

She gave me a coy look and said with a laugh: "I hope you weren't here yesterday trying to steal ideas?"

I stifled a gasp of anger. *The nerve of the woman!* Making a determined effort to keep my voice neutral, I said: "Well, as you mentioned, our styles are very different, so I doubt there's much overlap."

Before Azalea could respond, a young man entered the tea bar and sauntered over to join us. He had a thin, clever face with shrewd eyes and a fixed smile on his lips, which somehow reminded me of a shark's toothy smirk. He was dressed in black drainpipe jeans and a black, tight-fitting jacket, with a professional-looking camera slung over one shoulder.

I wondered if he was Azalea's husband or partner as I watched him pause beside her and give her a peck on the cheek. Somehow, he wasn't the type I'd pictured in my mind.

"Sorry I'm late. The train from London was a nightmare! Tell me, have I missed anything? Any scandals, bust-ups, murders?" he twittered, casting a speculative look over the rest of us.

Azalea turned to her mother and said: "Ma, this is Mark Scott. He's the journalist I told you about, remember? He's a good friend of mine—I asked him to come tonight so you can get some PR for your event."

Her mother furrowed her brow. "P-R?" she said hesitantly.

"Publicity," said her daughter impatiently. "You want to be in the news; you want people to talk about you. Mark has lots of readers and followers on social media."

"I certainly do," said Scott with a complacent smile at my mother and Mrs Chu. "I have a lot of power, ladies. I can make or break a business."

"But... we're not really a business," said my mother, looking puzzled. "OISS is a voluntary organisation providing a community service and outreach programme."

"You can never have too much publicity," said Azalea firmly. "Mark will make sure that people find out about the great work you do. And not just the individual volunteers but the businesses who help OISS, like my tea bar," she added brightly. "We all deserve recognition for our donation of time and resources to charitable causes." Leaning towards Scott, she added in an undertone, "Make sure you get one of our menus in the frame when you're taking your shots. I've put a pile of them by the buffet. And don't forget an exterior shot with the name of the tea bar."

I turned away, disgusted. So that was why Azalea had so "generously" offered the use of her tea bar: as a way to gain free publicity and engineer a façade of community goodwill for her business. *It was clever and resourceful*, I admitted grudgingly. The woman knew how to make the most of an opportunity, and I couldn't blame her for aggressively promoting her business. It was the kind of thing *I* should have been doing myself, the kind of thing one ought to be doing in the competitive field of hospitality. And yet... I couldn't shake off the feeling of distaste at the mercenary feel of the whole thing.

Mrs Chu suddenly piped up, beaming: "Ah! Very good idea. Your friend can write about Jem-Ma business also. She is also helping OISS."

Azalea stiffened. "What?"

"Oh no, that's..." I cut in quickly,

trying not to squirm under Azalea's sharp gaze. "That's sweet of you to suggest it, Mrs Chu, but it's really not—"

"Don't be shy." Mrs Chu patted my arm, smiling. "Your mother say you make best English scone! Most famous in Oxford! She say you bring some tonight for everybody to eat?"

"Er… yes, I've brought some scones. I've put them with the other food on the bar counter," I said, giving her a weak smile. Hastily trying to change the subject, I added, "The buffet looks great, by the way. So many different choices. And everything looks so delicious! I can't believe it's all home-made."

"Well, it's not *all* home-made," said Azalea. She gestured to the bar counter. "My tea bar has donated a significant number of items from our best-selling afternoon tea packages, so people can at least enjoy some things created by a professional chef with the highest level of expertise and a sophisticated approach to culinary presentation."

I glanced over at the counter and noticed for the first time—tucked amongst the lopsided home-made cakes and homely bowls of thick stews and chunky salads—several large trays of delicate finger food. There were chicken tofu tacos and fried-shrimp parfaits, ginger miso cheesecakes and coconut rice puddings, plus an assortment of cakes decorated with geometric chocolate cut-outs and bright, technicolour frosting. They looked so incongruous amongst the worn pots and chipped bowls filled with home cooking— it was like finding exotically coloured poison dart frogs in the middle of an English country pond.

I had to admit, though, that they did look much more impressive than the home-made efforts or even my scones, which—despite being professionally made—were deliberately baked to achieve a rustic look. Suddenly, I found myself wishing that I had brought a selection of things from my tearoom and not just the plain, simple scones. Then I berated myself. *Don't be silly. Don't get into a bragging match with Azalea Chu,* I told myself irritably. *You have nothing to prove to anyone.*

Still, I watched anxiously from the corner of my eye as a large crowd approached the buffet and began helping themselves to the food, and I was inordinately pleased when I saw many people reach eagerly for one of my scones. Soon, the entire platter was empty, and I found myself surrounded by several members of the OISS committee, all plying me with compliments. My mother beamed with delight, nodding graciously as if opening a tearoom had been *her* idea all along, as people gushed:

"Oh, those are the most delicious

scones I've ever tasted!"

"Yes, so light and fluffy—and yet still so rich and buttery in flavour."

"And they look like they've come straight out of your own kitchen, not some pretentious café. I like that," a man declared.

"I never think I like English cakes, you know," another lady confided in me. "Always so sweet, so much cream! But your scone is very delicious. Very light. I enjoy very much."

"Thank you... thanks a lot," I said, flushing with pleasure, although I was also uncomfortably aware of Azalea Chu watching the scene with narrowed eyes, her lips pressed into a thin line. I was relieved when there was a commotion at the entrance which distracted everyone's attention.

My mother looked over and exclaimed with delight: "Ah! Marvellous, they've arrived at last!"

Curious, I turned and was surprised to see Devlin entering the tea bar, followed stealthily by four little old ladies. *The Old Biddies! What are they doing here?* Hastily, I followed my mother as she sailed across the room to intercept them.

"I was worried we'd be late, Evelyn, but luckily we saw Inspector O'Connor arriving just as we did," said Mabel in her customary booming tones. "It was a bit tricky finding all the necessary props at first, but then Glenda recalled a certain gentleman she goes dancing with, who had a very tall sister. Sadly, Paula is no longer with us, but I'm sure she'll be delighted to know that her wardrobe is going to a good cause."

"Ooh yes, Percy talks about his sister all the time and how much Paula loved dancing," said Glenda. "She even used to enter competitions, you know, and had entire wardrobes of costumes."

"So when we couldn't find any

stockings in the right size, Glenda immediately thought of Percy and decided to ask him," Florence chimed in.

"How lucky for us that he should have kept his sister's things and that he should be happy for us to borrow them!" Glenda gave a girlish giggle. "Percy did say I owed him a private dance in return—such a naughty man! And so sexy for seventy-five." She sighed dreamily. "He's always asking me out for elevenses, you know, and if I hadn't sworn off boy toys, I would seriously consider accepting."

"I'm still not sure the things will fit properly, though," said Ethel, turning to eye Devlin doubtfully. "Inspector O'Connor is so much taller than we thought."

"Oh, not to worry," said my mother brightly. "Once the wig is on, nobody will notice the little details."

Devlin, who had been listening to this

exchange with an increasingly uneasy expression, now cleared his throat and said, trying to sound as business-like as possible, "Er… so where would you like me to set up? I've brought a portable projector and a PowerPoint presentation that our PCSOs use when they're giving talks in the community—"

"Oh no, no, Devlin, we've had a change of plan," my mother said blithely. She indicated the Old Biddies. "When I was telling Mabel and the others about our outreach programme, they thought it would be much less intimidating if you were to do the talk in a casual manner, in the vein of 'fun entertainment' rather than as a professional presentation. And then Mabel had an absolutely marvellous idea: why not do your talk as a lady in a lovely dress, with matching hair and make-up?"

Devlin gaped at her. "You want me to dress up as a woman?"

Chapter Nine

"Yes, isn't it a fantastic suggestion?" beamed my mother. "What could be more reassuring than seeing one of our top CID officers in lipstick and fishnet stockings?"

Devlin looked lost for words.

"That's... that's the most ridiculous idea I've ever heard!" I spluttered.

Mabel bristled. "And why do you say that, young lady? It is a most efficient suggestion. After all, not only will Inspector O'Connor be informing everyone about British policing, but he will also be introducing them to one of the key aspects of British culture at the same time."

"What?" I said. Then seeing my mother's frown, I said hastily, "I beg your pardon? I don't understand... what on earth are you talking about?"

"The great British tradition of cross-dressing, of course," said Mabel proudly. "It would be good for those new to this country to learn how much our chaps love dressing up as women."

"Yes, I so agree," said my mother. "After all, it's a time-honoured tradition that goes back to Shakespeare's days when all the female parts in Elizabethan theatre had to be played by men."

"Not to mention all the great comedy acts in British film and television," said Mabel, nodding emphatically. "*Monty Python, Carry On, The Two Ronnies—*"

"And don't forget pantomimes!" Ethel piped up. "The hero is always played by a girl, and the witch or ugly stepsisters or other old ladies are played by a man."

"Oh, I do so love a pantomime dame," said Florence with a happy sigh.

Glenda burst suddenly into song: "*Ohh... there is nothing like a dame... nothing like a dame...!*" she warbled, waving her arms.

The other Old Biddies joined in, leaning their heads together and swaying in unison as they sang at the top of their voices:. "*...THERE IS NOTHING LIKE A DAME!*"

Oh God. I didn't know whether to cringe or cry. I glanced at Devlin, who was eyeing the distance to the tea bar entrance and looking as if he might make a run for it. Before he could decide, however, Mabel had clamped a hand on his arm and was hauling him towards the rear of the restaurant.

"Come along, Inspector, we've got to get you ready!"

I watched in disbelief as my tall,

muscular boyfriend was frogmarched away by four little old ladies. I was just wondering whether to follow when I felt a hand on my arm.

"Hey, Gemma... fancy meeting you here!"

I swung around to find myself facing a slim, pretty girl in her late twenties. With her silky black hair, delicate features, and the smooth porcelain skin that all East Asian women seemed to possess, she looked like a fragile china doll, but I knew better. Jo Ling—or Dr Josephine Ling, to give her her proper title—was a highly skilled forensic pathologist working with Oxfordshire CID.

I had to admit, I'd once been terribly jealous of Jo and her easy intimacy with Devlin, and there was still a tiny part of me that felt a prickle of envy whenever I met her. After all, what woman wouldn't feel insecure when confronted with so much charm and confidence, all wrapped up in such a beautiful package too! But since getting to know Jo Ling, I'd also developed a genuine liking and respect for her, and now I greeted her warmly.

"Jo, how nice to see you! I didn't realise... are you involved with OISS?"

"My parents are," she explained. "They've been living in the UK for years now, of course, but they like to help the new arrivals, especially anyone that's come from Asia and the Far East. They went through the same culture shock themselves, you know, when they first moved here from Taiwan, so they can really relate."

"I didn't realise you're from Taiwan," I said, looking at her with new interest.

"Well, I've grown up here so I'm really a Brit," she said, grinning. "But yeah, my parents are both from Taiwan, and they love it whenever they meet anyone who comes from there."

"Like Mrs Chu?" I asked quickly.

Jo gave a rueful laugh. "Oh yeah, my mum's been getting really friendly with her. In fact, all she's talked about the last few weeks is Mrs Chu and her daughters." She rolled her eyes. "Honestly, I probably know more about Azalea, Magnolia, and Freesia now than about my own friends from school! And she's been desperate for me to meet them. It's actually why I'm here tonight—you know, family duty to please your parents and all that. It's a Chinese thing."

"Oh, I know exactly what you mean," I said with a wry smile. "It can be an English thing too. Why d'you think *I'm* here?"

Jo laughed. "Sorry, yes, you're right. Well, my mum's been trying to get me together with Mrs Chu's daughters for ages—especially the eldest daughter, Azalea. She thinks we'd be great friends just because we're both a similar age and both come from Taiwanese families." She sighed in exasperation, then glanced around and lowered her voice. "To be honest with you, after some of the stuff my mum's told me, I'm not sure I want to go anywhere near Azalea Chu."

I looked at her in surprise. "What do you mean?"

"She sounds like a poisonous shrew," said Jo bluntly. "All these stories about the nasty way she treats people—"

"Surely her own mother didn't tell your mum that?"

"No, no, of course not. But the immigrant Taiwanese community isn't that big, and people talk. I mean, I know you can't believe everything you hear, but still, there's no smoke without fire, I always say. Like... everyone's been talking about the messy divorce that Azalea's currently going through, and if even *half* the things I've heard are true…"

"Like what?" I asked, feeling guilty for gossiping but unable to help myself.

"Oh, crazy stuff that you'd think only happens in TV soap operas! Like apparently *she* was the one who cheated on him, but she made *him* move out of their townhouse in North Oxford. Then she filed a report with the police claiming that her husband 'threatened' her, and the devious cow put his *new* address as her place of residence. So the poor bugger ended up with a restraining order against him, preventing him from entering his own flat! This has gone on for a few weeks now and he's had to live in a hotel room, without access to his clothes or any of his things, and still having to pay the rent on his empty flat." Jo shook her head. "Have you ever heard of anyone so vindictive?"

"That's pretty ruthless," I agreed.

"Apparently she's like that in business

too," Jo continued. "My mother told me this dreadful story about how she forced a competitor into bankruptcy by planning a campaign of slander against him. It was a restaurant down the street from her first tea bar in London. There are even rumours that she paid an online service to flood the internet with hundreds of fake negative reviews about his restaurant—"

"*What?*" I gasped. The sudden, unexplained flood of negative reviews about the Little Stables sprang to my mind. *Was Cassie right about the perpetrator after all?* "So what did this other owner do?" I asked urgently.

Jo shrugged. "What could he do? He tried to defend himself and also have the reviews taken down, but it was really his word against hers. In fact, she went on social media saying that *he* was targeting her, just because of 'sour grapes'."

"Oh God..." I said, my heart sinking as

I thought of my own predicament. "You said Azalea forced him out of business in the end?"

"That's what my mum said. She really turned the public against him. People started boycotting this guy's restaurant. In the end, he had to shut down."

I shook my head, partly in horrified disbelief, partly in desperate denial. If Azalea could do this once, she could do it again. I felt a sudden rush of fear for my little tearoom.

"Gemma? Are you okay?"

I glanced up and realised that Jo was looking at me in concern. I gave her a wan smile. "Yeah. I'm all right. I just... I've got a situation at my tearoom that's worrying me."

"Anything I can do to help?" Jo asked.

I shot her a grateful look. "No, I don't think so. But thanks for offering. In fact..." I glanced towards the back of the tea bar. "Devlin's the person who might be able to help me. Excuse me, I need to go and speak to him—"

"Dev's here?" said Jo in delight. "I didn't realise. Did he come with you to offer moral support?"

"Sort of. He's actually been roped in to help with the OISS outreach programme—you know, give a talk about British policing."

"Ahh... my mother asked me to give a talk too," said Jo, grinning. "But I told her, the less the public knows about the details of my job, the better!"

I'll say, I thought as I gave her a parting smile and went off in search of Devlin. It always struck me as ironically amusing that Jo Ling, who looked like she must have a career in fashion or modelling, actually spent her days cheerfully elbow-deep in body cavities!

Chapter Ten

When I stepped into the staff room at the back of the tea bar, I had to fight the urge to burst out laughing as I saw Devlin sitting dejectedly on a bench alongside the wall—dressed in a sequinned pink top, black frou-frou skirt, and fishnet stockings. He was trying not to squirm as Glenda hovered in front of his face.

"…you have such lovely long eyelashes, Inspector O'Connor!" Glenda was saying as she peered at Devlin's face, causing him to lean back nervously. "I don't think you'll even need much mascara. But *definitely* some rouge. Oh, where has Mabel gone with the make-up bag? Excuse me a moment while I go and find it."

As she trotted past me out of the room, I saw suddenly that my boyfriend was not alone. Sitting on the bench next to him, looking almost as miserable and embarrassed as Devlin, was another young man I knew well.

"Lincoln!" I exclaimed. "What are you doing here?"

Lincoln Green was the son of my mother's best friend, Helen Green, and for years it had been their dearest dream to see us get together. With his similar social class and background, not to mention his position as an eminent doctor, Lincoln was ideal son-in-law material, and I'd had to fend off several embarrassing matchmaking attempts when I first returned to Oxford.

Thankfully, my mother seemed to

have finally accepted Devlin as my choice. Nevertheless, I could see that she still had a soft spot for Lincoln. To be honest, so did I. In fact, I'd be the first to admit that if Devlin hadn't been on the scene, I could have seen myself falling for Lincoln. He was charming, amiable, and good-looking to boot, with gentle brown eyes, and that calm, reassuring doctor's manner that instantly put you at your ease.

Right now, however, he looked like he was in desperate need of reassurance himself as he sat, hunched over, plucking uncomfortably at the strange pair of trousers he was wearing. They were a bright paintbox red and each leg was covered in multiple tiers of gold ruffles from hip to ankle, so that he looked like a cross between a wedding cake and a flamenco dancer.

He glanced up and looked slightly abashed as he saw me taking in his outfit. "Uh... hullo, Gemma. I... um... got roped in to help with tonight's entertainment." Then he glanced sideways at Devlin and added with a wry laugh, "Although I thought my lot was bad until I saw Devlin and heard what *he* had to do."

Devlin grinned and clapped Lincoln on the shoulder. "I don't know, mate—dressing up as a sexy female is a bloody sight better than being a lion's bum!"

The two men laughed uproariously and I looked at them, half in surprise, half in delight. Things had always been awkward between Devlin and Lincoln, with Devlin on the defensive because he knew that Lincoln had been my mother's first choice and was considered "superior", with his similar background and his "public-school" (a singular British term which paradoxically meant expensive private school!) education. Lincoln, for his part, had always been stiff and embarrassed whenever they met, and while the men had never been outrightly hostile with each other, there had always been a certain wariness between them. But tonight, for the first time, they seemed relaxed, joking and laughing as they teased each other about their respective costumes. It warmed my heart to see them bonding like this.

"Lion's bum?" I asked, chuckling. "I'm almost afraid to ask."

"One of the ladies on the OISS committee has two sons enrolled at a martial arts school in Oxford and they've been busy practising a traditional lion dance. So she thought it would be great to have them perform it tonight, as a way to share Chinese culture," Lincoln explained. "Except that the younger son, who was the rear end of the lion, has fallen ill with the flu and they needed someone to replace him at the last moment. Jo rang me up at work today and told me about their predicament and asked me to be their knight in shining armour… or in red ruffled trousers, rather!"

I noted the mention of Jo Ling with interest. I'd been wondering for a while if Lincoln and Jo were officially dating, although I was too embarrassed to ask outright. Lincoln had always made it clear that—despite his embarrassment with our mothers' heavy-handed matchmaking—he himself would have liked to see me as more than "just a friend". I'd felt very bad when I'd had to reject him. It would have been nice to know that he was now happy with someone else.

Pulling my wandering thoughts back to the present, I asked: "Have you done a lion dance before?"

Lincoln shook his head, saying with a rueful laugh, "I have absolutely no idea what I'm supposed be doing. I was just going to grab the waist of the chap who's the front half and hang on for dear life!"

Next to us, Devlin stood up from the bench and tried to walk in his borrowed high-heeled shoes. He tripped and nearly fell over. I caught his arm and steadied him, trying hard not to laugh as he pulled himself back upright, his face red.

"I swear, if anyone in CID finds out about this, I'm never going to live it down..." he muttered.

I giggled as I watched him valiantly trying to hobble across the room. And a sudden rush of love and gratitude swept through me. I was ashamed for being annoyed with Devlin the previous night. Yes, it was true that he hadn't had much time to spend with me recently, but suddenly I realised that love—*real* love—wasn't just about champagne and roses; it wasn't the cheesy declarations you read in romance novels or constant sweet nothings whispered in your ear. No, real love was the sacrifices you made, the inconveniences you put up with, to make the person you loved happy. It was Devlin giving up his evening, swallowing his manly pride and dressing up in sequins and fishnet stockings, just to please my mother—because he knew that was important to me. And that was worth more than a thousand flowery "I love you"s.

When the Old Biddies returned, armed with bright pink blusher, eyelash curlers, and red lipstick, I backed out of the room and left the two terrified men to their fate. As I returned to the main dining room, I was waylaid by Mark Scott, Azalea Chu's reporter friend.

"I say, are you the person who brought those smashing scones?" he asked without preamble. "They're absolutely delicious!"

I felt myself thawing towards him. "Thank you."

He gestured around the tea bar. "So you run a place like this as well?"

"Well, not exactly like this," I said, glancing at the gleaming chrome and modern fittings around us. "I have a traditional English tearoom which is housed in a fifteenth-century Tudor inn. It's on the other side of the village."

"And… if I were to turn up, would there be a chance of afternoon tea on the house?" He smirked at me. "I'd be sure to mention your tearoom in my regular column, of course."

I stiffened. So the man was after a free meal in exchange for a review! It certainly wasn't the first time that I'd been made such an offer—after all, the practice was fairly standard in the hospitality industry—but still, something about Mark Scott's smooth manner made my hackles stand on end. Then I thought of Azalea Chu and reminded myself that I needed to be more open to opportunities to promote my business.

Taking a deep breath, I gave him a polite smile and said, "You're welcome any time, Mr Scott. We're always happy to showcase our delicious baking, and if you're able to share your experience with the public, that would be great."

"You got a card or anything?" he asked.

I groped for my pockets, then realised with annoyance that I didn't have any pockets since I'd caved to my mother's urging to "wear a nice dress for once".

"Sorry, I don't have any on me. But I might have a couple of spare menus in the car," I told him. "I'll just pop out and have a look."

It was cold outside—although it was officially spring, the evenings were still chilly—and I shivered as I hurried towards the car, wishing that I'd put on my jacket before coming out. I was pleased to find a couple of Little Stables menus on the back seat and grabbed one quickly, keen to get back to the warmth of the tea bar.

As I approached the front entrance, however, I saw two figures standing on the terrace outside. They were partially obscured by the pillars around the edge of the terrace and standing in the shadows, but I recognised one of them as Azalea Chu. The other was a young girl with long black hair and a passing resemblance to Azalea. I guessed that this was the youngest sister, Freesia. Her slight figure was huddled in an oversized blue knitted jumper paired with tight jeans shoved into Doc Marten boots and she was slouched against one of the pillars, one hand holding a cigarette which she drew on with quick, nervous motions.

Azalea Chu's voice, sharp and accusing, drifted across to me and, almost without realising it, I moved closer so that I could hear what they were saying:

"...can't believe you're sneaking out here to have a cigarette! Smoking is the most filthy, disgusting habit. I thought I told you to give it up?"

"I'm twenty years old. I can smoke if I want to," said the girl defiantly. "It's none of your bloody business."

"Of course it's my business! What you do matters because it affects everyone in the family, especially Ma who has to look after you—"

"I don't need her to look after me!" Freesia snapped. "I'm perfectly capable of looking after myself."

"Oh yeah? So who's been doing the laundry that you take back to Ma every week? And who's been giving you pocket money to spend?" Azalea jeered. "Who pays for your living expenses—have you thought of that? No, of course not. Because you never think of anyone except yourself."

"That's not true!" Freesia cried. "I've been doing part-time work to earn some money and I've been helping out around the house when I can. And I even applied for the Oxford Emerging Writers scholarship, which would give me a grant towards living expenses—"

"What? A *writer's* scholarship?" Azalea laughed contemptuously. "Where did you get that stupid idea from?"

"It's not a stupid idea! Professor Bennett agrees with me. She… she says I could be a writer… a *real* writer, like a best-selling author, and—"

"Best-selling author? Do me a favour! Everyone knows that most authors hardly earn a penny. It's a notoriously unstable career, with no regular income and everything dependent on whether you get your next book deal. And if your first book doesn't sell, your publishers drop you like a hot stone. Besides, book advances these days are a pittance. How do you expect to make a living on that?"

"There *are* successful authors who make a very good living. Like… like

James Patterson... and Dan Brown... and Nora Roberts—"

"Those are the outliers! For every Nora Roberts out there, there are a dozen authors starving in the gutters," said Azalea. "What makes you think you even have a chance of becoming one of the exceptions?"

The girl's chin jerked up. "Professor Bennett thinks I've got great talent. I showed her my novel and she thought it was really good."

"*You*'re writing a novel?" Azalea gave a scathing laugh. "So where's this masterpiece?"

"I've been working on my novel since I was sixteen! I've rewritten it three times now and... and revised it and edited it and everything... I've got the printed draft in my bag, inside. I can show you, if you like—"

Azalea made a rude noise through her nose. "Spare me."

The younger girl flinched, then she straightened her shoulders and said, "I'm going to try and get it published and... and I don't care if I don't earn lots of money. Being super rich isn't everything, you know! I don't need to have designer handbags and go on luxury holidays like you. I don't think the only goal in life is getting on the Sunday Times Rich List—"

"Oh, so you think being poor is more romantic?" Azalea sneered. "You won't be thinking that when you're sitting in your ivory tower and wondering where your next meal is going to come from."

"Well, I won't be coming to *you* for help, so you needn't worry about that!"

"Don't be a bloody idiot!" snapped Azalea. "Freesia, you have to live in the real world. You'll have an Oxford education. You can get a prestigious job, a real career where you'll earn a good, stable income and be able to buy a house and invest for your retirement.

Why throw your life away on some silly fantasy when you could be so much more?" She stepped closer to the younger girl, her voice rising. "You think it's fun being poor and hungry? You think it's cool making grand gestures? It's easy to say big words, but wait until you're actually homeless and starving and all you've got to show for your troubles are a hundred rejection letters from publishers. And guess who'll be picking up the pieces then? Me, that's who!"

"I'll never take anything from you, even if I'm starving to death!" cried Freesia, her voice trembling with emotion. "You think you know everything but you're not the boss of me, so just SOD OFF!"

"I *am* the boss of you when I'm paying your college fees," said Azalea coldly. "And I can tell you from now, little sister, that if you even *think* of applying for this scholarship or trying to get this pathetic novel of yours published, I will withdraw all financial support. You won't be able to finish your precious English degree, you'll have to drop out of Oxford, you won't have your devoted professor buttering you up anymore... I'm sure you won't want that."

"I... you..." Freesia looked almost too angry to speak. Her chest was heaving and her eyes burned with loathing. "Who the hell do you think you are? We're not all slaves for you to order around, you know! You think you're so clever, so superior, but you can't just keep treating people like this without it coming back to bite you one day. And by the time you regret it, it'll be too late!"

Flinging her cigarette to the ground, she stamped on it, then pushed past Azalea and stormed back into the tea bar.

Chapter Eleven

I jerked back and plastered myself against the side of a pillar, keeping to the shadows as Freesia Chu rushed past me. Her face was red and blotchy, and I could see the shimmer of tears in her eyes. My heart went out to the girl. Although I could see the practical reasoning behind Azalea's attitude, her words had seemed unnecessarily harsh and cruel.

The sound of a click made me turn and peer around the other side of the pillar, back towards where Azalea was still standing. She had taken a slim gold lighter out of her pocket and was now lighting a cigarette herself. Smoke curled upwards into the night sky. *What a hypocrite!* I thought indignantly. I was glad when she turned and began strolling towards the other end of the terrace, away from me. Taking advantage of her turned back, I darted from my hiding place and hurried up the front steps back into the tea bar.

Once inside the welcome warmth, I paused to scan the room for Freesia, then began moving through the crowd, searching for her. The girl's tearful face had stirred something in me. Perhaps it was the memory of my own recent struggle when I'd decided to give up my prestigious corporate job and sink all my savings into opening a tearoom. I knew what it was like to have an unconventional dream and I could sympathise with the challenges of going against family and social expectations. I wanted instinctively to offer Freesia some support and encouragement.

But the girl was nowhere to be seen and, finally, I gave up. *She probably wouldn't have appreciated a stranger offering sympathy anyway. She might even be embarrassed!* I thought. *The Chu family tensions are none of my business and I really shouldn't get involved.*

As if to underline the sentiment, I saw Azalea come back into the tea bar and her eyes narrow as her gaze fell on me. I was still fuming from what Jo Ling had told me earlier and I was itching to confront Azalea. But I also didn't want to upset my mother, Mrs Chu, and the others by causing a scene, so it would have been a strain if I'd had to make polite small talk with the ruthless tea bar owner. Thankfully, she strode right past me and I watched from the corner of my eye as she made a beeline for the rear of the restaurant.

Trying to put her from my mind, I

joined a group of people by the buffet and noticed that most of the food was gone. It looked like the "cross-cultural potluck dinner" had been a roaring success. Several members of the OISS committee were clearing things from the marble counter, no doubt tidying up and clearing the area for the night's "entertainment". I hurried to collect my own food containers and found the empty platter which had been holding my scones easily enough. But I then spent several minutes hunting unsuccessfully for the ramekins I'd used to bring the jam and clotted cream. Overhearing a committee member instructing another to take items into the kitchen, I realised that my things had probably been mistakenly included with the tea bar's own crockery and returned to the kitchen.

Reluctantly, I started towards the rear of the restaurant once more, hoping that I wouldn't bump into Azalea. I glanced absently into the staff room as I passed, wondering if Devlin and Lincoln might still be in there with the Old Biddies, but it was empty. I made my way slowly down the rest of the corridor, which ended in large double swing doors that led into the kitchen. They were heavy and I had to make an effort to push them open. Inside was a vast industrial kitchen, filled with gleaming stainless steel and huge professional appliances surrounding a large central island.

Stepping through the doors, I scanned the large space, wondering where my ramekins might be. I spotted a couple of industrial sinks in the far corner and guessed that that was where the OISS members might have taken used crockery and utensils from the buffet. I started towards them, skirting around the large central island and looking admiringly around me as I went. The whole place was impressively neat and clean, with all the stainless-steel surfaces shining and spotless. There were sauces, condiments, and spices arranged in meticulously labelled containers, and bags of supplies organised with almost military precision on the shelves.

On the large central island, I could see a variety of large pots and bowls, some containing meat and vegetables, others eggs and tofu, all soaking in different sauces and marinades which gave off a delicious aroma of herbs and spices. It was obviously the main preparation space, but even here, there were none of the sauce stains or food spills that I'd expected to see in a big working kitchen. Azalea Chu obviously ran a very tight ship!

She's probably the type to keep her staff late without overtime until they've cleaned and scoured every corner to her satisfaction! I thought sardonically.

I heard a clatter and glanced up to see movement through kitchen windows along the far wall, which backed onto an alley at the rear of the building—probably where vans with food deliveries could park and bring items in through the service door. The glow of the streetlights caught the flash of blue knit and the shimmer of sleek black hair as a figure darted past the window, then disappeared into the darkness.

Distracted, I didn't look where I was going, and as I rounded the side of the central island, I nearly stepped into a large puddle of red wine. *Oops! Looks like Azalea's minions missed a spot here...*

Then I froze, my foot hovering in mid-air. *Wait... that's not red wine...*

I jerked back, stumbling and nearly falling over in my haste to retreat. I stared at the puddle in horror.

It was blood.

Slowly, almost unwillingly, my eyes followed the pool of red to where it disappeared around the corner of the central island. My heart pounding, I took a step to the side, giving the blood a wide berth, and walked around the corner of the island. Then I stopped, the breath catching in my throat.

Azalea Chu lay sprawled on her side, her legs and arms splayed out where she had fallen. Her head was turned to one side, her eyes staring lifelessly ahead, and her silky black hair was tossed around her face, half covering the gaping wound in her temple where someone had smashed in her head.

I should probably have screamed in reaction or yelled for help or something. Instead, I stood frozen for several seconds, staring at Azalea's lifeless body. Then I turned and walked slowly out of the kitchen. I felt as if I were moving in a dream, and when I tottered back into the main dining room a few minutes later, everyone seemed to be very far away, their voices muffled and distant.

"Gemma?"

I blinked and focused. My mother stood in front of me, holding a cup of tea, a smile on her face:

"I was just having a chat with some of the new ladies about the right way to eat scones—you know, whether it should be jam first and then clotted cream, or the other way around—and I thought it would be nice if you—" She broke off and peered at me. "Is everything all right, darling?"

"I… I need to find Devlin," I said in a faint voice. "Do you know where he is?"

"Devlin? I'm not sure. I think I saw him with Lincoln." My mother waved vaguely towards the other side of the tea bar, then she peered at me again. "Are you *sure* you're all right, darling? You look awfully pale."

"I'm… I'm fine… just… don't let anybody go in the kitchen, Mother—

especially not Mrs Chu. It's really important, do you understand? Don't let her go in there, whatever you do!"

Leaving my mother staring after me in bemusement, I turned and pushed my way through the crowd. Craning my neck, I searched for Devlin whilst a voice in my head repeated feverishly: *Where is he? He needs to secure the kitchen… it's a crime scene… I need to find Devlin… it's a crime scene…*

Then I spotted him, standing with Lincoln in the far corner of the room by the end of the black-marbler bar. They were dressed in their respective costumes, with lurid make-up on their faces, but unlike earlier, they were looking incredibly jolly as they swigged beers and talked with gusto. The smiles faded from their faces, though, when I stumbled up to them.

"Gemma!" Devlin caught my arm in concern. "What's wrong?"

"Devlin... in the kitchen..." I gasped, feeling the room suddenly reeling around me.

"Sit down," said Lincoln swiftly, his voice firm. It was his doctor's voice. He pulled up a chair from a nearby table and pushed me into it, then gently bent me over so that my head was between my knees. "You look like you're going to faint. You need to raise your blood pressure and get blood back into your brain."

Lincoln crouched down next to me and took my wrist, feeling for my pulse, whilst Devlin crouched on my other side, watching worriedly. I took a few slow, deep breaths, feeling my head clear, then jerked upright again.

"Steady on..." said Lincoln, putting a hand on my shoulder. "You mustn't get up too quickly."

"What happened, Gemma?" asked Devlin, his anxious gaze roving over me, checking for injuries. "Have you been hurt?"

"No, no… I'm okay," I said breathlessly. "It's not me… it's Azalea Chu. She…" I took a shuddering breath. "She's dead."

"Dead?" both men chorused, looking stunned.

I nodded. "In the kitchen—"

"Was there an accident?" asked Lincoln, rising quickly. "She might still be alive. I'll go and see if I can—"

"No, wait… you don't understand," I cried, grabbing Lincoln's hand to stop him. Turning back to Devlin, I swallowed painfully, then looked up into his puzzled blue eyes. "She's been murdered."

Chapter Twelve

By the time the ambulance and police arrived, I had recovered some of my composure—helped by the strong cup of sweet black tea which Mabel Cooke had forcibly made me drink. And although I normally found her bossy tendencies exasperating, now I was grateful for Mabel's brisk, no-nonsense manner and commanding voice. Together with the other Old Biddies, she helped to bring some calm and order to the mayhem that ensued after news of Azalea's death spread through the tea bar.

I was grateful, too, that my mother

immediately took Mrs Chu under her wing and kept the Taiwanese lady preoccupied, so that she didn't observe the grim little party of police officers, forensics team, and other emergency personnel that arrived at the tea bar and made their way to the rear of the premises. Devlin had disappeared into the kitchen with them, together with Jo Ling, and as I thought of them, a voice suddenly said in my head: *If you ever wanted to get murdered, you couldn't do it at a better place than at a party where a CID detective and a forensic pathologist are present!*

I pulled myself up, horrified at my own thoughts. How could I be seeing any kind of levity in this situation? *It must be a reaction*, I told myself. Gallows humour was a well-known strategy for coping with shock and horror, and I was willing to clutch at anything that would help me deal with the memory of my grisly discovery. A vision of Azalea's crumpled body rose in my mind's eye again and I hastily rose from my seat, pushing the mental image away.

I looked restlessly around. Lincoln had told me to sit and rest whilst he went to attend to some of the other guests, but I couldn't bear to stay still any longer. Almost without realising what I was doing, I found myself making my way to the rear of the tea bar once more. I needed to know what was going on. Somehow, being "involved" in some way made me feel better than just sitting there helplessly.

I found that the kitchen was already roped off with crime-scene tape and, through the propped-open swing doors, I could see some members of the forensics team making their meticulous way through the entire room, taking samples, examining surfaces. Beyond them, I could see Jo Ling crouched next to the area where I'd found Azalea, although thankfully the view of the actual body was blocked by the central island.

"Miss Rose? You seen the inspector anywhere?"

I turned to find a young man with a trendy jacket and meticulously gelled hair standing behind me. It was Devlin's sergeant.

"I've just arrived. CID are short-staffed at the moment and they called me away from a case in Cowley," he explained. "Can't seem to find the guv'nor anywhere."

"I'm not sure where Devlin is," I said apologetically. "He doesn't seem to be in the kitchen with the SOCO team and—"

I broke off as Devlin himself appeared suddenly in the corridor. He was still dressed in his costume, although he had kicked off the high-heeled shoes and now strode towards us in fishnet-stockinged feet. The detective sergeant swung around, his eyes bulging as he saw his superior officer.

"Not a word, Sergeant," Devlin said through gritted teeth as he came up to us.

The younger man ignored him. "S-sir... are you in *drag*?" he asked, an incredulous grin spreading across his face.

Devlin gave a curt nod. "And I'll have your hide if you breathe a word of this to anyone in CID."

"Y-yes, sir!" said the sergeant, his voice wobbling. "Um... one of your eyelashes is falling down, guv'."

Devlin reached up and yanked the false lashes off his eyelid. Trying to look as dignified as possible, he said: "I was asked to help with the Oxford Immigrant Assistance Society community outreach programme. They thought it would be more entertaining and approachable for me to give the talk in costume."

"As... as a woman?" guffawed the

sergeant. Then, seeing Devlin's glower, he hastily rearranged his face into a serious expression. "Ah, right... sir."

"My appearance isn't important. What's important is starting to question everyone," said Devlin. He jerked his head towards the doorway of the staff room further down the corridor. "We can use that as an interview room. I'll get started while you go back out there and find everyone who has had any interaction with Azalea Chu this evening. Leave her mother alone for the time being, though." His voice softened as he turned to me and added: "If you feel up to it, Gemma, I need to ask you what happened when you found the body."

I nodded and followed him into the empty staff room. He shut the door behind us and gestured to the bench that he and Lincoln had sat on earlier. I couldn't help a sad inner smile as I remembered their cheery banter. How much things had changed in the space of a couple of hours!

"Now, I want you to tell me everything you remember, starting from—" Devlin broke off as the door to the staff room suddenly swung open and a middle-aged man in a shiny suit walked in. I stiffened as I recognised him: Inspector Roberts, one of the other CID detectives in Devlin's unit.

I had never like Roberts, a self-important man with a huge chip on his shoulder, who blamed Devlin for his own stagnating career instead of considering that it might have been his own laziness and ineptitude that was the cause. He had also made no secret of resenting my involvement in past investigations and never missed an opportunity to put me down whenever I'd encountered him at the police station in the past.

"You're off duty, O'Connor. This is my case," he said without preamble.

"I was here on the scene when the

murder occurred," said Devlin evenly. "I have first-hand experience of the situation. That gives me a unique perspective and an advantage as lead investigator on the case."

Roberts gave Devlin a contemptuous look, taking in the sequins and black lace, the fishnet stockings and lurid make-up. "Yeah, I can see that you've been having a *unique* experience," he sneered. "But some of us don't have Oxford degrees like you and we don't need fancy methods for detective work. We just use good old-fashioned policing. Besides—" His gaze swept to me. "—I heard that your girlfriend found the body? Well, there's a conflict of interest, then. You can't be working a case where you're personally involved with a suspect."

Devlin made an impatient noise. "Gemma isn't a suspect! She just happened to be the first on the scene—"

"I'll be the judge of that," Roberts cut

in. "Until I question her and establish her alibi, she's the top suspect in my book."

"That's ridiculous!" Devlin exploded. "You have no basis for—"

"I have *every* basis. *You're* the one who's on slippery ground, O'Connor." He jabbed a finger at Devlin's chest. "Don't think just because I didn't go to Oxford, I don't know the meaning of the word 'nepotism'."

"What?" said Devlin angrily. "What the hell are you on about?"

"I'm talking about you giving your girlfriend preferential treatment and access to CID information," said Roberts. "You think I don't know about all those times when you let her and those nosy old friends of hers meddle in our investigations?"

"The Super knew about their involvement in those situations and he was grateful for their input. Without their help, we wouldn't have solved half of those cases," said Devlin. "He's acknowledged that Gemma isn't a 'normal' member of the public and that the usual rules don't apply."

"He doesn't know the half of it!" Roberts growled. "You've been giving him the sanitised version. But I've been keeping tabs on you, O'Connor. I know about all those times you broke protocol and shared confidential information with your girlfriend or let her get away with serious offences, like… like impersonating a CID officer and questioning suspects without permission. Did you tell the Super about that? Huh?"

I winced. Everything Roberts said was true and I knew that Devlin had often covered up for me. Suddenly, I felt terribly guilty. I'd always been so caught up in finding the murderer and helping those who had been wrongly accused, that I'd never really thought about Devlin's side of things. I knew that he had frequently been exasperated by my sleuthing attempts and by the Old Biddies' snooping, but I never really considered how our actions might affect his position in the CID.

Roberts took another step towards Devlin, thrusting his face aggressively close. "You think you're better than the rest of us, don't you, O'Connor? You think you don't have to abide by the same rules, just because you're the Super's 'golden boy'. Well, I'm not putting up with it! I haven't spent thirty years working my arse off, to be side-lined for a promotion just because some cocky young—"

"I'm not responsible for your inadequacies, Roberts," Devlin snapped. "If you're looking for someone to blame for not being promoted, you should be looking in the mirror."

The other man flushed. "You… you…!" he spluttered. "I don't care what you say—you're not winning this time! You think you're untouchable, but I'm not afraid to go higher up the ranks. The Super might let you pull the wool over his eyes, but the DCC and others on the committee won't be so complaisant. Let's see if you can make Chief Inspector when you've been hauled up for disciplinary action!"

I sprang up and caught Devlin's arm before he could answer. I could feel his body rigid with anger. "It's all right… I'm happy for Inspector Roberts to question me," I said quickly, trying to inject some calm into the tense atmosphere.

Devlin said nothing for a moment, then finally he gave a curt nod. "Fine. I'll go and find Sergeant—"

"No, O'Connor, you're going home now!" insisted Roberts. "This is my case!"

I caught Devlin's eye and gave him a slight shake of my head. He hesitated, then finally said: "I'll be speaking to the

Super first thing in the morning." Giving my hand a quick squeeze, he turned and reluctantly left the room.

I looked at Roberts, who was standing with a smug look on his face. He gestured me to sit down again, then said brusquely:

"Now, Miss Rose, I want you to give me an exact account of your movements this evening, starting from when you arrived."

Chapter Thirteen

I was no stranger to being questioned by the police, especially following a murder, but I'd never had to endure as tough a grilling as what Inspector Roberts put me through. He was merciless, attacking me like a terrier worrying a bone, making me go over and over the same details, and constantly trying to trip me up so that I would look like I was lying. After forty minutes of this, I had a pounding headache and an overwhelming desire to thump him on the head. But I contained my temper with an effort and tried my best to keep my voice cool and neutral.

"...so you're saying that after you spoke to that reporter chap, you went out to the car park and then, on the way back, you decided to spy on Azalea Chu talking to her sister—"

"I didn't *decide* to spy on them," I said, irritated despite my resolve not to react to his baiting. "I just happened to be walking past on my way back and saw them on the terrace. I couldn't help overhearing some of their conversation."

"You mean you deliberately eavesdropped," said Roberts. "Come on, admit it, Miss Rose. You were up to your old tricks again, snooping and spying on people."

"I wasn't spying on anyone!" I said, trying to ignore the flicker of guilt as I remembered that I *had* deliberately gone closer and concealed myself in the shadows, so that I could hear what the sisters were saying. "I didn't—"

"So did either of them see you?" he cut in.

"No."

"Did you speak to anyone when you came back into the tea bar?"

"No, not really."

"So what were you doing?"

"I was looking for Freesia Chu, actually."

"Why?"

I hesitated. I knew that if I mentioned Freesia's distress and the hostile interchange between the two sisters, I would be exposing the girl to Inspector Roberts's suspicion. I felt suddenly reluctant to incriminate the youngest Chu daughter in any way.

"Oh, no particular reason. I… I just hadn't had a chance to chat with her yet."

"And did you find her? Did you speak to her?"

"N-no. I didn't see her in the main dining room so I gave up."

"And then?"

"I've told you twice already," I said impatiently. "I went to collect my empty things from the buffet—"

"Is there anyone who can vouch for that? Anyone you spoke to?"

"No, I didn't happen to speak to anyone by the buffet. I searched for my things and when I couldn't find some of the containers, I realised that they must have been taken into the kitchen by mistake, along with the tea bar's own stuff. So I went into the kitchen to collect them and that's when I found the body."

Inspector Roberts leaned back and regarded me coldly. "There's a long gap between the time the reporter spoke to you and the time you reported the discovery of the body. There's no way of verifying what you were really doing or where you really were during the time between those two points."

I eyed him warily. "What do you mean?"

"Well, I only have your word that you were out in the car park and then returned and went to the buffet and all the rest of that. There's no one to corroborate your movements, since the two Chu sisters didn't see you outside and you didn't interact with anyone when you came back in—until the moment you reported finding the body." Roberts gave me a challenging look. "Instead of going out to the car park, you could have easily sneaked into the kitchen and lain in wait for Azalea, killed her when she came in, and then used the back alley to circle around the building and come in the front entrance. Then all you had to do was make up an excuse to go to the kitchen and pretend to 'discover' Azalea's body."

"*What?*" I stared at him. "That's... that's the craziest thing I've ever heard!"

"I'm simply stating the facts," he said loftily. "Unlike your boyfriend, Miss Rose, I don't try to bend the truth to cover up for personal favourites."

"No, you just bend the truth to fit a ridiculous, convoluted theory so that you can pin the crime on me!" I snapped, all efforts to maintain a cool façade forgotten. "This is just your way of getting back at Devlin, isn't it? If you actually do your job properly and take the time to interview a few other people here tonight, I'm sure you'll get lots of witness statements confirming that they saw me after I returned to the tea bar. Even if I didn't speak to them, it wasn't as if I was invisible!"

Roberts had flushed a dark, angry red at my comment about "doing your job properly" and now started to retort, but I rushed on:

"And besides, it's absolutely ludicrous to suggest that I might have murdered Azalea Chu! Why on earth would I have wanted to kill her? I barely knew the woman! Whereas if you ask around, you'll quickly see that she had a lot of enemies, some of whom might have even been here tonight—"

"Oh yeah? Who?" sneered Roberts. "Next you'll be telling me that you saw a furtive figure running away from the crime scene."

"I—" I broke off as I recalled the movement I had seen outside the kitchen windows just before discovering the pool of blood and Azalea's body.

"Well?" demanded Roberts. "Did you see anyone?"

I hesitated, trying to remember exactly what I'd seen. There had been a flash of shiny black hair caught in the glow of the streetlights—I remembered that clearly. Had it been a man? A woman? The figure had been slim, so probably the latter, although it could also have been a slightly built man... And had I seen a glimpse of blue knitted fabric? Suddenly, I remembered someone who had been wearing an oversized blue sweater: the youngest Chu daughter, Freesia.

"Miss Rose?"

I jumped and came back to the present. As Roberts's sharp gaze bored into me, I wondered frantically what to do. If I didn't mention what I'd seen, I'd be withholding potentially important information in a murder investigation. It could be considered "lying by omission" if Roberts ever found out. But on the other hand, if I mentioned the figure I'd seen and the possible resemblance to Freesia, I'd be directing police suspicions onto her.

I thought back to the girl's distraught face and the shimmer of tears in her eyes as she had stormed past me. Then I thought of Mrs Chu's bright, happy smile earlier that evening, and then the sight of her broken figure standing next to my mother when Devlin broke the news. My heart went out to the family. They were already having to deal with a shocking, brutal death—did I really want to add to their troubles by foisting someone like Roberts onto them? *Besides*, I argued to myself, *Freesia couldn't possibly be the murderer!* So by not mentioning her, I would actually be "helping" the investigation, in a way, because I'd be preventing them from wasting time on a false lead.

Taking a deep breath, I looked up and met Roberts's eyes. "No, I didn't see anything suspicious," I said, deliberately choosing my words so that I wasn't exactly lying. It was true—I hadn't seen anything suspicious. At least, nothing that I *thought* was suspicious.

Roberts stared at me for a long moment, as if trying to decide whether to believe me, then finally he said: "So where are all these 'enemies' that could have been here tonight, then?"

"Well, there was a man outside the tea bar much earlier in the evening," I said, pleased to change the direction of the interview. "I saw him as I arrived. He tore down one of the promotional posters announcing the grand opening and crumpled it up, then threw it on the floor and stamped on it. He looked really angry, like he wanted to do someone an injury—"

"And you think that makes him a deadly enemy?" said Roberts with a derisive laugh. "He could have been anybody! Maybe he was a local resident annoyed at this development disturbing the peace of the countryside and wanted to vent his frustration on the new businesses opening up; maybe he was a nutter who just likes to go around tearing down posters."

"No, it wasn't like that," I insisted. "I saw his face. It was personal. There was some kind of history between him and Azalea Chu—I'm sure of it. Besides, he wasn't a random member of the public. He was wearing a chef's uniform. He probably works in the main hotel—that's where I saw him heading to afterwards. Come on, you'll be going through the CCTV footage, won't you? Surely you can try to identify him and at least question him about his actions?"

"I don't need you to tell me how to do my job." Roberts scowled.

"And it's not just him," I rushed on. "There's also Azalea's husband—or rather, soon-to-be ex-husband."

"What's that?"

I recounted the gossip about Azalea's messy divorce proceedings that Jo Ling had told me. "It's well known that murders are often committed by those known to the victim," I said as I concluded. "And here, you've got an ex-partner with a lot of reason to hate Azalea and want revenge, after the ruthless way she's treated him."

"I'm not going to waste police time on petty slander," said Roberts with a dismissive wave of his hand. "If you had any experience of *real* detective work, you'd realise that we conduct our investigations based on serious evidence and reliable information gleaned from police interviews, not from women's gossip."

"What's the difference between that and interviews?" I asked in frustration. "When you question people, you're relying on what they tell you, which could include gossip they'd heard."

"It's completely different, but I wouldn't expect an amateur like you to understand," said Roberts pompously.

He folded his arms and gave me a hard look. "I know what you're doing, Miss Rose. You're attempting to distract police attention from your own motives and actions. Well, you might be able to bamboozle your boyfriend, but your tricks won't work with me." He narrowed his eyes. "I'm going to make sure you're thoroughly investigated, just the same as any other suspect. You won't get any special treatment from me. And if I find even a sniff of a possibility that you might be involved in this murder, I won't hesitate to arrest you and lock you up."

Chapter Fourteen

It felt strange the next morning to set off for work on my bicycle, almost as if nothing had happened. In fact, as I left the hustle and bustle of Oxford's busy streets and pedalled along the country lanes leading to the little village of Meadowford-on-Smythe, I could almost convince myself that I had somehow imagined the nightmarish events of the night before. But then, as I freewheeled around a curve, reality came rushing back as I caught a glimpse of a car over my shoulder. It was unmarked and cruising nonchalantly at a consistent distance behind me, but I knew instantly that it was the police. Inspector Roberts had assigned someone to tail me.

I felt a surge of indignation mingled with annoyance. Not only did I resent the surveillance, but it also seemed a stupid waste of resources when the police should have been concentrating their manpower on other aspects of the investigation. Still, there was nothing I could do about it, so I took a deep breath and faced the front again, determined to act as if I hadn't noticed.

Luckily, once the Little Stables opened, I didn't have time to dwell much on the subject. It seemed that, with Azalea's tea bar closed as a crime scene, several of the would-be customers had decided to come over to my tearoom instead. Business wasn't quite at the old level of our peak but it was a lot better than it had been recently. I was kept busy enough that I only paid cursory attention when a young man, who was obviously a detective constable despite his attempts to blend in, came into the tearoom and skulked over to a table in the corner. I didn't recognise him from my occasional visits to see Devlin at the police station, and I guessed that he must have been one of the latest new recruits to Oxfordshire CID. I almost felt sorry for him as I watched him look around in dismay. Sitting in a quaint Cotswolds tearoom, drinking endless cups of English Breakfast, probably didn't fit the image of high danger and excitement that had motivated him to join the CID!

Then the Old Biddies caught sight of him and I winced in real sympathy. The nosy foursome had been busy gossiping since arriving at their usual table by the window an hour earlier, but now, having exhausted the topics of the postman's hernia, the butcher's new wife, Mrs Harrison's missing toilet brush, and the Lord Mayor of Oxford's strange moustache, they were casting around for new diversions. I saw their eyes light up as they noticed the young detective constable at the nearby table and they pounced on him with glee.

"Hello, young man," Mabel Cooke boomed. "You look a bit lonely sitting there by yourself. Are you having morning tea alone?"

"Perhaps you're waiting for your girlfriend to join you?" asked Ethel.

"No… uh… I'm workin—I mean, I don't have a young lady," amended the young DC hastily, throwing a wary glance in my direction.

"You don't have a young lady?" said Glenda, appalled. "But why ever not? A handsome young chap like you…"

"Well, you're never going to impress a lady if you order like that," said Florence, looking doubtfully at the solitary cup of tea on the table in front of him. "Girls like a man who is generous when taking them out. Being stingy is so unattractive."

"I hope you're not one of those young people who follow that dreadful modern practice of 'going Danish'," said Mabel, glowering at him. "Splitting the bill in half—whoever heard of such a thing? A gentleman always pays for the meal."

"It's Dutch, Mabel, not Danish," remonstrated Ethel.

"What—the Dutch men do it too?" said Mabel, scandalised.

"I once went out with a Dutch gentleman," said Glenda with a dreamy sigh. "He had a wonderful moustache. And such sensitive hands. He didn't pay for the meal, though."

Florence turned to the bewildered DC. "You're not Dutch *or* Danish, are you?"

The young man shook his head nervously.

"What about your hands? Are they sensitive?" Ethel persisted.

"Never mind his hands," said Mabel impatiently. "How are your bowels?" she asked the young constable.

He gulped. "M-my bowels?"

"Yes, I hope you go regularly, young man. Healthy digestion is very important to male virility. You'll never get a girl if you don't eat enough fibre. Men who have problems with their bowels have higher rates of erectile dysfunction, you know."

"Mabel! Don't scare the poor boy," chided Glenda. "I'm sure at his age, he has no problems getting his willy up."

The DC sprang to his feet, nearly knocking his chair over. "I… uh… I have to go!"

Throwing some money on the table, he bolted for the door. I watched him leave, torn between pity and laughter. Well, that was one way to get rid of police surveillance! Going over to the Old Biddies' table, I gave them a mock frown and said laughingly:

"That's no way to treat an officer of the law."

Four pairs of beady old eyes regarded me with surprise. "What do you mean, dear?"

"That was a DC from Oxfordshire CID, didn't you know?" I told them.

"A detective constable!" cried Mabel, looking deeply chagrined. "If only we had known! We could have pumped him for information about Azalea Chu's murder."

"But how did *you* know who he was?" Florence asked me.

"I think he tailed me from Oxford. There was a car following me when I cycled in this morning." I made a face. "You know Inspector Roberts has this crazy idea that I'm a prime suspect. I think he's got me under surveillance."

"That's ridiculous, dear," cried Ethel.

"Everyone knows that her husband did it."

I looked at her, startled. "How can you be so sure about that?"

"It's what always happens in books," Ethel told me blithely. "When I was a librarian, I read practically all the murder mysteries we had on the shelves, and it always seemed to be the husband or wife who was guilty."

"Yes, but this isn't a nov—" I started to say.

"Oh, but it's true in real life too," said Florence earnestly. "I read in the papers the other day that nearly half of all murdered women are killed by their romantic partners."

"And Azalea's husband would have had a very good motive," added Glenda. "We all heard about the terrible things she did to punish him for trying to divorce her. She forced him to move out of their home, then she manipulated things so that he couldn't even live in his new flat—"

"Yes, I heard about that," I said, recalling what Jo Ling had told me. "Azalea made a false report of assault or something and got a restraining order put on her husband, which prevented him from entering his own place and he ended up having to stay in a hotel, while paying for both places."

"That's not all she did," said Mabel. "She also purposefully left all the lights on in his new flat and set the heater on the highest setting, while leaving all the windows open, so that his bills would be astronomical. She even left the tap running at full flow in his kitchen sink!"

"Wow…" I said, unable to believe that anyone could be so vindictive.

"Any man who was treated like that would be very bitter and angry," declared Mabel. "You wouldn't be surprised if he wanted revenge. In fact, some of the other OISS members, who had known Azalea awhile, even said that they thought she had it coming to her."

Wow, it looks like Jo and I weren't the only ones indulging in a good gossip last night, I thought dryly. *And there certainly doesn't seem to be a lot of sympathy for Azalea!*

"I did mention all this to Inspector Roberts," I said. "But he just dismissed it as malicious gossip and slander. And to be fair, Azalea's husband wasn't there last night."

"How do you know?" demanded Mabel.

"Well, I didn't see him. I'm sure someone would have pointed him out if he had been there. Besides, I heard Azalea talking to him on the phone when she first arrived," I added.

"He could have been speaking to her from somewhere nearby," Mabel pointed out. "For instance, he could have been sitting in a car, outside in the car park. Or in the lobby of the main hotel."

"Yes, and then he crept into the kitchen from the alley at the rear of the building and smashed Azalea's head when she wasn't looking!" said Ethel with relish.

I eyed her askance. It never ceased to amaze me how sweet old ladies could have such bloodthirsty imaginations.

"Well, the police can check his alibi easily enough—if they would just take him seriously as a suspect," I said, sighing with exasperation. "I kept trying to tell Inspector Roberts about him but he just wasn't interested."

"You'll never achieve anything if you wait for the police, my dear," said Mabel. "If you want anything done properly, you have to do it on your own. We just need to find Azalea's husband and question him ourselves."

"Or perhaps his neighbours?"

suggested Ethel. "Neighbours always know what you're doing."

"Yes, Margery told me that her neighbours knew her granddaughter was pregnant before anyone in the family realised," said Glenda. "They even knew the sex of the baby!"

"What about his hairdresser?" suggested Florence. "People always tell their hairdressers everything."

"Or his dentist!" said Ethel excitedly. "People will reveal anything under pain and torture—"

"Whoa—stop! Stop!" I said, putting my hands up, palms out. "You can't go around questioning random people about Azalea's husband! Aside from anything else, you promised Devlin—as part of your New Year's resolutions—not to meddle in any more investigations, remember?"

"That was back in January," said Mabel with a dismissive wave of her hand. "Besides, we promised not to meddle in *his* investigations. Since Inspector O'Connor is not the lead investigator on this case, it doesn't apply."

"But you can't—" I broke off as my phone rang and I turned away to answer. It was Devlin. He sounded angry and frustrated as he recounted his meeting with the Detective Superintendent that morning.

"...was sympathetic but he wouldn't give me the case. Says that Roberts has a point about the conflict of interest because you're involved."

"But I've been involved in other cases before," I protested. "Your boss never had a problem with you working on them."

"I know," said Devlin with an irritated sigh. "To be honest with you, Gemma, I think he's getting pressure from above. He wouldn't come out and say it, but I think the DCC's had a word with him. It's been on the grapevine for a while that Roberts's brother plays golf with the DCC—they used to know each other at uni or something—and so Roberts has been using his brother as a way to get a private word in the DCC's ear."

"What? I can't believe Roberts was making all that fuss about nepotism when he's happy to use it himself!"

"That's pretty much Roberts to a T," said Devlin with wry cynicism. "Anyway, don't worry. The Super might have approved Roberts to lead the investigation but he's not going to swallow his idiotic theory about you being a top suspect, so there's no danger of you being—"

"Oh, I'm not worried about *me*," I said impatiently. "It's the *case* that's going to suffer if Roberts wastes time following false leads. He should be investigating Azalea's enemies, not wasting resources trying to prove that I'm guilty!"

"Gemma, I think this is one of those situations where you're going to have to let it go. It winds me up as well, but unfortunately there's not much we can do—"

"But there *is*!" I said, thinking suddenly of what the Old Biddies had been saying before Devlin rang. "*You* might be officially off the case but that doesn't mean that I can't do some sleuthing on my own. Mabel and the others were just discussing some ideas—"

"No, Gemma," said Devlin firmly. "Whatever those nosy old coots are dreaming up, you can't let them meddle in this investigation and you have to stay out of it as well."

I made an indignant noise. "Surely you're not going to let yourself be scared off just because Roberts has a chip on his shoulder—"

"It's not about being scared off—it's

about playing politics," said Devlin with a sigh. "Roberts has long nursed a grudge against me and now he's got the perfect opportunity to stick it to me. He'll be looking for any way to discredit me. He's already accused me of unprofessional behaviour and nepotism; he's even saying that my relationship with you could be a threat to police security—"

"What? That's ridiculous!" I cried angrily.

"It might be, but it's also something the DCC and others higher up are very sensitive about. You know the Super has always looked on you with a kindly eye and he's been pretty lenient about your involvement with CID investigations— well beyond any normal civilian. But the DCC is not so insouciant about things, and right now I can't afford to antagonise him. Not when he's the one who could swing the decision for the next DCI position," said Devlin grimly.

"So I'm telling you, Gemma, there's no room for you or the Old Biddies to play Miss Marple on this case—do you understand? My promotion to Chief Inspector could be on the line."

Chapter Fifteen

I hung up from the call feeling torn. On the one hand, I seethed at the unfairness of Roberts's behaviour and the stipulations levelled at my own head, but on the other hand, I didn't want to do anything to jeopardise Devlin's chances of promotion either. A movement next to me pulled me out of my thoughts, and I looked up to see an excited flurry of activity as the Old Biddies collected their things and left their table.

"Where—?" I asked in surprise.

"No time to chat, Gemma," said Mabel briskly as she walked past me. "We're off to Azalea Chu's house to see if we can question her neighbours."

"Wait... no, you can't... Devlin said—WAIT!" I shouted at their retreating backs.

But it was too late. The tearoom door swung shut behind them with a merry tinkle of bells and I found myself standing in the middle of the dining room, surrounded by customers at other tables, all staring at me curiously.

I flushed and looked around with an embarrassed smile. "Er... I was worried they might have forgotten a handbag."

For the rest of the day, I alternated between fretting over what the Old Biddies might be getting up to and fuming over Roberts's lousy management of the investigation. There wasn't much time for brooding, though, as the tearoom only got busier as the day went on. After the lull in the past week, Cassie and I were unused to suddenly having to field orders from multiple tables, and we found ourselves run off our feet. Dora was swamped as well, for she had reduced the amount she prepared each morning so that we wouldn't have as much food wastage following the lack of customers. Now, she had to rush to bake extra batches of scones, and other buns and pastries, for the unexpected influx of customers at the tearoom.

It seemed that much of the business that Azalea Chu had stolen from us was returning, with many customers sheepishly confessing that they had been lured away by the big discounts on offer, but that, in fact, they had missed the homely ambience and genuine quality of baking at the Little Stables. The victory was bittersweet, however— in fact, I felt slightly guilty that the reason was because my competitor had been murdered!

"I wouldn't feel guilty," said Cassie crisply when I voiced my feelings. "If the tables had been turned, Azalea wouldn't have wasted a second, feeling sorry for you."

Still, my troubled conscience meant that when my mother rang later that evening and insisted that I accompany her to Mrs Chu's house to offer our condolences, I didn't put up much resistance. Maybe by going to offer my sympathies to Mrs Chu, I might feel better about profiting from Azalea's misfortune…

"*Meorrw?*" said Muesli, looking hopefully at me as I examined my reflection in my bedroom mirror. She knew the signs of me planning to go out for the evening and was not happy about being left out.

"Sorry, Muesli, you can't come with me," I said distractedly, eyeing my clothes and wondering if I should change.

I had only got home from the tearoom half an hour earlier and was still in the basic top and jeans that I normally wore for work. Aside from the fact that my mother would probably be horrified by my casual attire for the sombre occasion, I didn't want to inadvertently come across as disrespectful. Deciding to play it safe, I changed quickly into a pair of dark wool trousers paired with a black silk blouse, then ran a hurried comb through my hair.

Glancing at the oversized tote bag I normally carried for work, which I'd slung carelessly onto my bed when I'd got home, I pondered whether to swap handbags. My tote bag was worn and faded, and had been chosen more for its cavernous depths (perfect for carrying all the various things I needed to lug back and forth to the tearoom each day) than for its stylish appearance. I knew my mother would complain—as far as she was concerned, no lady was "properly dressed" until one had suitably matching accessories!—but I decided that I really couldn't be bothered to transfer things into a smaller, more elegant bag.

I'll put on some make-up instead, as a concession, I thought, grabbing a tube of coral-pink lipstick and leaning forwards to apply it in the mirror. Then, pausing only to extract my laptop to lessen the load, I swung the bag over my shoulder and turned to leave the room. I grimaced as I switched off the lights and started downstairs. My tote bag still seemed to weigh a tonne! *I really need to sit down and go through all the rubbish I've got in here*, I thought as I descended the stairs. *I'm probably lugging around all sorts of unnecessary junk!*

Downstairs, I went into the kitchen and poured out some extra cat food into Muesli's bowl, as a sop for having to leave her alone that evening. I heard the faint tinkle of her bell but she didn't come trotting into the kitchen when I called. *Little minx. She's probably sulking and deliberately snubbing me. Oh well, I'll make it up to her later with an extra chin rub when I get back*, I thought as I left the cottage.

I'd expected my mother to drive us over to the Chu residence and was surprised when I arrived at my parents' place to find that we were going on foot instead.

"Oh no, we're walking, darling. Azalea Chu's house is just around the corner from us," my mother said as we set off down the street. "When Mrs Chu came from Taiwan to live, she moved in with Azalea, and when the OISS committee found that she was so close, they thought I'd be the perfect volunteer to be paired with her."

"Have you seen her since last night?" I asked, heaving my tote bag more securely over my shoulder. It seemed to be getting heavier with every step I took.

"No, although I did ring earlier today to see if she was okay. She seems terribly shell-shocked, poor thing, and no wonder. What a dreadful thing to happen..." My mother shook her head.

"Do you know if the police have questioned her?"

"I'm not sure, darling. They spoke to her last night, of course, but they hadn't been to see her again by the time I rang."

What is *Roberts doing?* I wondered irritably. Surely interviewing the family of the murder victim was one of the most important first steps in an investigation?

Within minutes, we found ourselves standing on the front steps of Azalea Chu's home: a spacious, renovated Victorian townhouse that resembled many of the other elegant residences in this area of North Oxford, except for the fact that someone had stuck a square piece of white paper, painted with a single black Chinese character, onto the gleaming black front door. I noticed, too, that the front door was slightly ajar and that all the windows facing the street seemed to be open.

We rang the bell and were greeted a few moments later by a slim young woman dressed in black, with her long black hair worn loose and a face bare of make-up. For a moment, I thought it was Freesia—then I realised that this woman was older. The resemblance to both Azalea and Freesia was still strong, though, and I guessed that this was the middle sister, Magnolia. She seemed like a softer, paler version of her older sibling, with shadows of fatigue under her eyes and faint lines of discontent marring the porcelain smoothness of her face. She looked at us blankly for a moment, then she gave a perfunctory smile as my mother explained who we were.

"Of course, come in... my mother's in

the kitchen," she said as she gestured for us to enter.

"Oh, we must remove our shoes," cried my mother, pausing on the threshold.

The young woman waved a hand. "It's okay. Don't worry—"

"No, no, I know it's an important custom in Taiwanese households," my mother insisted, slipping off her court shoes.

Magnolia gave another brief smile, and this time some genuine warmth entered those dark, almond-shaped eyes. She inclined her head in appreciation, then rummaged in the shoe cupboard next to the door for two pairs of fluffy pink house slippers. Suitably shod in *Hello Kitty*, we shuffled after her down the spacious hall, past the staircase curving to the bedrooms upstairs and the doors leading to the study, TV lounge, and combined sitting and dining room, before finally turning a corner and stepping into the large open-plan kitchen. There was a lovely fragrant smell, faintly reminiscent of tea, that enveloped us as soon as we stepped into the room.

"Ma? Your friend Mrs Rose is here with her daughter," Magnolia said.

Mrs Chu was standing at the stove, stirring something in a pot. Like Magnolia, she was dressed in black, and her grey hair, which had been in a neat bun the night before, was now loose around her shoulders. Also like her daughter, her face was bare of colour, and I began to wonder if having your hair down and wearing no make-up was a Taiwanese tradition observed after a death in the family. Suddenly I felt self-conscious about the pink lipstick I'd applied in deference to my mother, but thankfully Mrs Chu didn't seem to notice as she turned around to greet us. Her face was very pale and her eyes were red-rimmed, but her expression was stoic as she came towards us, with no shimmer of tears or quiver of emotion in her voice. Even so, I recalled the very different, smiling, happy woman I'd met at the party the day before, and I felt a terrible sadness for her. I might not have liked Azalea Chu, but I really liked her mother and would not have wished this tragedy on her.

My mother offered the bouquet of white lilies she'd brought, as well as the pot of home-made chicken soup, and Mrs Chu smiled with quiet gratitude.

"Azalea always like chicken soup," she said. "I will put with other food for her."

"Other food?" said my mother, puzzled.

Mrs Chu gestured to the other side of the room, and we turned to see that a small table had been erected next to the breakfast nook, on the other side of the kitchen. It was something of a makeshift altar, and on it was a framed portrait of Azalea, flanked on either side by burning incense and a potted chrysanthemum. Spread out in front of the portrait were various small dishes of food, cakes, and snacks.

"It's a Taiwanese custom," Magnolia explained, seeing our puzzled faces. "We believe that the spirits of the deceased will return home to say goodbye to their families before they move on to the afterlife. So we open all our windows and doors to allow them back easily, and we make their favourite foods and lay them out for them to enjoy with us one last time."

"Yes, I make Azalea favourite since she was small girl," said Mrs Chu softly. She gestured to the stove and beckoned us over. "I make tea egg."

As we approached and peered curiously into the simmering pot, I realised that it was the source of the wonderful fragrance permeating the room. Soaking in a rich brown marinade were several hard-boiled eggs, still in their shells. What was unusual, though, was that the shells were covered with cracks, as if someone had deliberately tapped the eggs all over. Steam rose from the pot, together with a mouth-watering aroma of roasted tea and spices.

"Wow… it smells incredible!" I said, inhaling appreciatively. "What's in it?"

"It's a family recipe," Magnolia spoke up. "It's basically eggs infused with the flavour of tea and other spices. There's ginger, cinnamon, soya sauce, and star anise, plus a bit of sugar and rice wine in the water. And of course, the Chinese tea leaves. Roasted or semi-roasted black tea is best, like oolong. Not green tea. That doesn't have enough flavour."

"So you boil the eggs in the sauce?" I asked, intrigued.

Magnolia nodded. "They're hard-boiled first, then you crack them gently all over, so that the sauce can soak in through the shells, and then put them back in the marinade for several more hours."

"I also put dry chilli because Azalea like everything spicy-spicy!" Mrs Chu confided, stirring the eggs gently with a ladle. "You try?"

"Oh... I wouldn't... I mean, if you're saving them as an offering..." I stammered.

"No, no, is good. We eat Azalea favourite food—is nice way to remember her," Mrs Chu insisted.

She fished a couple of eggs out of the pot and carefully peeled them before presenting them to us in a bowl. I stared at the eggs, fascinated. The marinade seeping through the cracks in the shells had left an intricate network of delicate brown veins across the surface of the eggs, giving them a beautiful marbled effect.

"Wow... they look gorgeous," I murmured as I carefully lifted an egg out of the bowl and bit into it.

I don't know what I'd expected—probably something along the lines of a typically bland hard-boiled egg—and I was pleasantly surprised. The egg was moist and tender, not hard and rubbery like I'd thought it would be, and there was a wonderful mix of subtle flavours: the savoury-sweetness of the soya sauce mingled with the mellow zing of the cooked spices and the slight kick from the dried chili, all overlaid by the wonderful fragrant aroma of roasted tea. The combination was delicious and I found myself licking my fingers as I finished.

My mother, who had been grappling with the horrifying prospect of having to eat something with her bare fingers, now emerged from her struggles with a brave smile and a full mouth. She swallowed and dabbed her lips carefully with a napkin, before saying warmly:

"They are delicious, Mrs Chu. We would love to have the recipe to try to make tea eggs ourselves sometime."

Mrs Chu nodded. "Already I ask Magnolia help me write in English."

"Oh, yes—I've got the recipe in my handbag," said Magnolia, turning to pick up a leather tote from the kitchen counter. She fished inside and pulled out a piece of paper.

Mrs Chu looked at her in surprise. "You no give to Azalea last week?"

Magnolia shook her head. "No, Ma, I never got the chance."

"Was she planning to add it to the tea bar menu?" I asked politely.

Magnolia shrugged. "My mother thought it was a great idea but Azalea didn't seem so keen. I offered to pop in last week to drop off the recipe but she told me not to bother. I think things were so busy with the grand opening that she wasn't interested in making any changes to the menu—at least until next month."

Mrs Chu looked at her in confusion, obviously not quite following the rapid English. "You say Azalea already make in her restaurant?"

"No, Ma, she hasn't made any tea eggs at the tea bar. She was too busy. She said maybe next month," Magnolia repeated.

A shadow crossed Mrs Chu's face and she dropped her eyes. "Now, no more. Azalea gone."

"I'm so sorry!" said my mother with sudden compassion. She reached out to clasp Mrs Chu's hand. "I do hope the police find the person responsible soon."

Mrs Chu looked back up, her black eyes flashing. "Police no need to look. I know already who kill Azalea."

Chapter Sixteen

"Ma!" said Magnolia in exasperated tones. "You can't say that. You don't *really* know for sure."

"I know," said Mrs Chu emphatically. "Is him."

"Who is this?" I couldn't help asking. "Who do you think killed Azalea?"

Mrs Chu turned to me. "This man name Harry Mah-Kenzee. Azalea tell me he make many trouble for her. Very bad man."

"He's not a 'bad' man," said Magnolia, looking as if she was restraining herself from rolling her eyes. "You don't know what really happened, Ma. You can't believe everything Azalea told you."

"Azalea say he follow her from London," Mrs Chu continued, ignoring her daughter. "Before tea bar open, he come have big fight with her."

Magnolia sighed. "He was just very angry, and probably with good reason. You don't know what Azalea did to him in London. Plus, he didn't *follow* her here—he just happened to get a job as head chef at the Cotswolds Manor Hotel. It was just one of those unlucky coincidences."

"He is big enemy," Mrs Chu insisted.

"Have you told the police about this?" asked my mother. "I'm sure they'll want to know about any enemies that Azalea might have had."

Mrs Chu nodded. "I tell inspector yesterday. Again, also, today when he come."

"Inspector Roberts came to interview

you?" I asked.

"Yes, he come just now. One hour before." Mrs Chu pursed her lips. "But he no listen to me. Even I tell him very serious." She looked suddenly at me. "Jem-Ma—your mother say your boyfriend is policeman, yes? She say he is very big detective in police station."

"Er... yes, Devlin is in the CID," I replied.

"You can ask him to help?" asked Mrs Chu eagerly. "He can go speak to Harry Mah-Kenzee."

"Er... the thing is, Devlin isn't in charge of this investigation," I said awkwardly.

"But he is in police station. He can help, no?" Mrs Chu clutched my sleeve, her eyes wide with appeal. "Please, Jem-Ma. You talk to him?"

"It's just that... Devlin's not really supposed to get involved when he's not the lead..." I trailed off, feeling somehow helpless and ashamed as I saw the hurt and disappointment on Mrs Chu's face.

"Ma, you can't put Gemma in a difficult position like that," Magnolia chided. "I'm sure she would help if she could, but—"

"Look, I'll... I'll see what I can do," I said impulsively.

Mrs Chu's face lit up. "You help?"

"I'll try. I mean, I might not be able to speak to Devlin about it but... but there might be other ways to get information about Harry McKenzie."

Mrs Chu seemed satisfied with that. As the two mothers moved away to discuss the various plates of food on the altar, Magnolia turned to me with an apologetic look and said:

"Sorry about that. My mum's still very old-fashioned sometimes, and she's used to doing things the way it's done in Taiwan. Over there, life revolves around "giving face" and *guanxi*—those are the two most important things in Chinese culture."

"I've heard of 'loss of face' and giving someone 'good face' but I've never heard of *guanxi?*" I said.

"It's hard to explain. There isn't an equivalent English word for *guanxi*. I suppose it's sort of like your 'connections'," Magnolia said thoughtfully. "It's all about who you know and the relationships you have. Everyone's connected in this big network, and the understanding is that friends and acquaintances will 'look after you'. You know, like, say you need to go into hospital, for example. Well, you'd have a word with your friend whose son is a doctor there and it would be his duty to check that you're getting the best care, even if he doesn't know you personally. You might not be on his ward or even have an illness in his area of speciality but he would be expected to look after you. Because of the *guanxi* between you and his mother. Also, it gives his mother—your friend—'good face', because she has a son who can look after *her* friends. See?"

"Yes, I think so," I said slowly. "To be honest, I don't think it's that different here in England or other Western countries. I mean, no one likes to admit it, and maybe it's not so officially celebrated, but the 'old boys' network' is alive and well, I can tell you!"

Magnolia made a face. "Yeah, I suppose it would be called nepotism in the West, and seen as a negative thing. But not in Chinese cultures. It's just the way of life in Taiwan. People are always cultivating good *guanxi*—good relationships—with others, in case they might need help someday. It's a mutual thing, so everyone helps others in the knowledge that they will receive help themselves when they need it, like a sort of unspoken social agreement. That's why my mum immediately thought of asking you: because you have a 'connection' with the police."

"That's okay. I didn't mind," I said. "And I meant what I said. I would really like to help if I can."

"Thank you," said Magnolia. "It would give my mum some comfort and help her cope better."

I glanced across the kitchen. "She seems to be coping very well. I mean—"

"Are you surprised she's not sobbing and wailing because her daughter has died?" Magnolia gave me a cynical look. "That's not the Chinese way. We are always taught to hold back our emotions, especially in public. It does not mean that we don't grieve or feel as deeply as you Westerners—we simply do it in private. To suppress your emotions is a sign of mental strength; to show too much of it is vulgar and could make others uncomfortable."

Wow, I'm beginning to understand

why Mother hit it off so well with Mrs Chu, I thought wryly.

"I can remember being told, ever since I was a little girl, to always keep a neutral face, no matter what I was feeling inside," Magnolia continued. "Even if I thought something was hilarious, I shouldn't laugh too loud, and even if I was devastated by bad news, I shouldn't show it in my expression. I suppose you think that's mad," she added, glancing sideways at me.

I gave a dry smile. "Actually, I understand better than you think. The British are notorious for being reserved and for remaining stoic in the face of disaster—you know, that whole 'keep calm and carry on' thing. Apparently, the band on the *Titanic* kept playing even as the ship was sinking! My mother definitely believes you should never show excessive emotion, so I've been raised in a very similar way to you."

"Oh." Magnolia looked at me for the

first time with genuine warmth. "Yes, I'd forgotten about the British 'stiff upper lip'. Well, it's nice to know that you can relate."

I decided to take advantage of her sudden affability. "Um... you mentioned just now that this Harry McKenzie might have good reason to be angry with Azalea—you sounded almost sympathetic to him. Can you tell me why?"

Magnolia was silent for a moment, as if debating what to say. Finally, she turned her body so that she was facing away from the mothers and lowered her voice, saying, "Look, I know you're not supposed to speak ill of the dead and all that, but my sister Azalea was... well, frankly, she was not a very nice person. Oh, she was beautiful and smart and incredibly talented in business, and she could be really charming too, if she wanted to be—but she was also absolutely cold and ruthless. She always had to win at all costs, no matter what, and she didn't care what happened to others, as long as she got what she wanted. To put it bluntly, Azalea was a Type A bitch."

I blinked, surprised at this vehement description. Magnolia saw my expression and gave a humourless laugh.

"I've shocked you now, haven't I? Especially after telling you all that stuff about not expressing our emotions… I suppose people always expect family members to be gushing with sentimental eulogies after a person has died. Well, I refuse to be a hypocrite. Azalea and I were never close when she was alive and I'm not going to start pretending now that she was the best sister I ever had." She paused, then added in a bitter undertone, "Worst sister, more like…"

"Um…" I hesitated, not quite sure how to respond to these personal revelations. Finally, I opted for the easy route of ignoring them and focusing on the murder. "So... Azalea did something terrible to this Harry McKenzie?"

"Yeah, she pretty much ruined him, just because he owned a popular restaurant down the street from her first tea bar in London. It narked her that he used to get a lot of business—much more than her place. So instead of trying to compete on fair terms, like serving better food or offering better service, she decided to sabotage him. She started rumours in the neighbourhood about people getting food poisoning at his place and used fake online reviews to trash his reputation—"

Suddenly, I realised that this was the same story that Jo Ling had been telling me the night before.

"—didn't help that he went over to her place to confront her and they ended up having a *huge* row. There were loads of witnesses and, bad luck for him, Azalea's friend—you know, that slimy reporter chap Scott—was there that day. He took photos and made it the lead story in the local paper the next day. Well, that played right into Azalea's hands. She went on social media herself with a big sob story about how she's a brave woman trying to make her way in the world and how she was being terrorised by this aggressive man. She really milked the whole 'gender inequality' and 'mistreatment of women' thing, with a bit of racism and discrimination against ethnic minorities thrown in for good measure."

Magnolia gave a cynical laugh that was devoid of amusement. "Of course, the public loved it. You know that whole mob mentality thing on social media, where people jump behind a cause without even bothering to check if the information they're being fed is correct. Everyone started piling onto McKenzie, he lost customers, suppliers... in the end, he was forced to close his place." She shook her head. "You should have seen Azalea's face that day. Never mind that she'd just ruined a man's whole life—all she cared about was that she'd got rid of the competition; she'd *won*."

"Wow…" I said, conscious of a sense of relief that the woman was no longer around to be a threat to my tearoom and then feeling guilty for the sentiment. Pushing the thought away, I said hastily, "But everything you told me actually supports your mother's belief that Harry McKenzie could be the murderer. I mean, if any man had a motive for wanting to harm Azalea, he did."

Magnolia shrugged. "I suppose so. I just… I feel sorry for McKenzie. He was just some poor bloke trying to earn a decent living; he never did anything to Azalea and she went after him and made his life a living hell. It's like, you almost can't blame him, you know?"

"For killing your sister?" I said incredulously. "Are you saying that you think she deserved it?"

Magnolia flushed. "No, of course I'm not saying that she deserved to be murdered! But… you didn't know Azalea," she muttered. "You have no idea what it was like to grow up with her for a sister. She was cruel just for the fun of it. It's hardly surprising that, one day, she'd get payback."

I stared at her, thinking that, in her own way, Magnolia was just as cold as her notorious older sibling. No matter how estranged they were, it seemed to be an extremely cold-hearted way to talk about your own sister's murder.

Before we could talk further, we were startled by a scream from across the room, and I looked up to see Mrs Chu jumping back from my tote bag, which I'd put down on the floor next to Azalea's altar table. Something was moving in the depths of the bag and, the next moment, a little grey-and-white tabby cat squirmed out of the folds of the opening.

She shook herself, then looked around and said brightly: "*Meorrw?*"

"Muesli!" I gasped. "What are you doing here?"

Chapter Seventeen

I realised now why my tote bag had seemed so horrendously heavy—because I'd had a feline stowaway! Muesli had devised a way to make sure that she wasn't left at home and missing out on any excitement: she had crawled into the bag when I wasn't looking and hitched a secret ride.

"*Meorrw!*" said Muesli cheekily as she wriggled free of the bag straps and trotted over to Mrs Chu.

The Taiwanese lady made an exclamation, and for a moment I thought she was frightened. I was just about to reassure her when I saw that her face was creased in an expression of delight, not fear. She bent and scooped Muesli up into her arms and cuddled her close.

"My mum loves cats," Magnolia confided to me, a smile replacing the bitterness on her face as she watched the scene. "She had to rehome her cat back in Taiwan with a friend when she made the move over here and she was really upset about that. I wanted to get her a kitten after she arrived. I thought it would help her settle in better and, you know, keep her company, but Azalea said no way. She didn't want cat hairs on her clothes and furniture."

I glanced back at Mrs Chu, who was now sitting on one of the kitchen stools, with Muesli happily curled up in her lap. The Taiwanese lady was stroking and fussing over the little tabby cat and Muesli was purring like a steam train, her eyes closed in an expression of bliss.

The two of them made a sweet picture and I felt more charitable towards Muesli.

We were interrupted by the sound of the doorbell, and Magnolia returned a few moments later bearing an expensive-looking bouquet of white roses, lilies, and carnations, surrounded by lush greenery.

"They're for you, Ma," she said, handing the arrangement to Mrs Chu.

"Wah! Who sending this?" cried the Taiwanese lady in surprise. Then she found a card tucked amongst the flowers and her eyes widened even more as she read the words inscribed on it. "Is from Mr Wang!" She turned to her daughter. "You see? I say he is not bad. Even he doesn't like Azalea, but he is sending respect to me now."

Magnolia snorted. "He probably just told one of his staff to sort it out. Money's no problem for him, is it? Maybe

Kai guilted him into doing it." Then, seeing her mother's confused expression, she softened her voice and said, "Yes, it was nice of him, Ma."

I looked back and forth between them, filled with curiosity. I wanted to ask who they were talking about, but I caught my mother's reproving eye and swallowed the words. She would have considered it the height of rudeness to pry when the Chus hadn't volunteered to explain. Still, I mulled over the exchange as we sat and chatted for a few minutes longer. Who was "Mr Wang" and why didn't he like Azalea?

My mother rising and thanking Mrs Chu for her hospitality roused me from my thoughts. Hastily, I turned to collect Muesli, only to find that my cat refused to budge from Mrs Chu's lap.

"Come on, Muesli—time to go home now!" I coaxed for the tenth time as I tried to lift her off Mrs Chu's lap.

The little tabby squirmed and wriggled out of my grasp, leaving me huffing with annoyance. I debated grabbing her by the scruff of her neck and just bundling her into my tote bag, but with Mrs Chu watching anxiously, I didn't like to do anything to further upset the poor lady.

"Come on, Muesli," I tried again, making an effort to keep the impatience out of my voice. "Be a good girl... come on..."

Muesli blinked innocently at me—then, to my relief, finally rose to her feet. She stretched daintily, then turned around and plonked herself back down on Mrs Chu's lap with her bum towards me.

"*Muesli!*" I hissed. "Come *on*, we have to leave now!"

"Maybe... maybe she can stay here?" asked Mrs Chu in a hopeful voice.

"Oh yes, darling, that's a marvellous idea," my mother said. "Why not let

Muesli stay the night? She obviously seems very content here and I'm sure she'd bring a lot of comfort to Mrs Chu."

"Yes, my mum would love to have her," said Magnolia quickly. "I'll have to leave and go home soon—I have two little ones and my babysitter can't stay late—so my mum will be left alone here. Having Muesli to keep her company would be great."

"Yes, yes," said Mrs Chu eagerly. "You leave Muss-Lee! I look after—you no worry. I cook many Taiwanese food for her, same like my cat before. I make soup dumpling and pork belly and fish ball. Also soft-soft milk bread. Very delicious!"

I hesitated as three pairs of eyes looked at me expectantly. "Oh... well, if you really don't mind—"

"Is no problem!" said Mrs Chu, beaming. "I make nice bed for Muss-Lee in my room. Tonight, I give her

Taiwanese foot massage."

Bloody hell, at this rate, I want to move in with Mrs Chu.

"Well, okay, but if she gives you any trouble, please don't hesitate to call me, Mrs Chu. I'll come and get her straight away," I said, scribbling my phone number on the kitchen notepad. "And Muesli can be really naughty sometimes, so don't be afraid to tell her off if she does something she shouldn't. She can also be…"

I trailed off as I realised that I was wasting my breath. Mrs Chu was looking down at Muesli with such an indulgent expression on her face that I had no doubt my cat was going to be absolutely spoiled rotten. And from the smug expression on Muesli's face, she knew it!

Still, despite my irritation with the minx, I found that my cottage felt surprisingly quiet and empty without her when I finally got home. *How can one little feline have such a big presence?* I wondered peevishly when I got up the next morning and found myself missing the warm bundle at the foot of my bed, the inquisitive little whiskered face watching me go about my morning ablutions, and even the plaintive wails filling the kitchen as she demanded her breakfast. The ride to my tearoom felt strangely flat without her sitting in my bicycle basket, and once business got going at the Little Stables, I was astounded by the number of customers whose faces fell when they realised that Muesli wasn't there that day. Who knew she had such a big fan club!

Thoughts of Muesli made me think of Mrs Chu and my promise to help with finding Azalea's murderer. It had been a rash promise, and although I didn't regret it, I did wonder now how I was going fulfil it when I wasn't supposed to be doing any investigating of my own!

The Old Biddies wouldn't have let that

stop them, I thought suddenly, glancing over at their usual table by the window. They were not there today—their seats were currently being occupied by a German family—and I wondered where the four nosy octogenarians were. *Heaven knows what they're up to!*

I was grateful when I could flip the "OPEN" sign to "CLOSED" at 5 p.m. and sit down at last to catch my breath and rest my aching feet.

"Bloody hell! It's great to have business back up again, but I'm absolutely knackered!" cried Cassie as she sagged into a chair next to me. "I was supposed to go out on a date this evening but I think I'm going to cancel. All I want to do right now is soak in a hot bath for hours!"

"A date? Who with? Anyone I know?" I asked casually.

"Nah, don't think so. It's this chap I met down at the village pub, actually."

"Oh." I glanced sideways at my best friend. A part of me had half hoped that she might have said her date was with Seth.

Seth Browning was my other closest friend, and the three of us had been inseparable during our university years. One of the best things about my return to England had been resuming the wonderful trio of friendship. Seth had decided to remain in the bosom of academia and had carved out a prestigious career for himself as a researcher and tutor at one of the Oxford colleges. As someone brilliantly clever but painfully shy, life inside the hallowed cloisters of the university suited him. But I knew that he was hoping someone in particular could share that life with him.

Seth had carried a torch for Cassie from almost the first day he'd met her, back when we were all freshers together in Noughth Week, the first week of the

Oxford university term. But he had always been too shy and scared to tell her. I had thought, back at Christmas, that he might have finally got up the courage to declare his feelings. In fact, I was sure I even saw them sharing a kiss under the mistletoe! But things had been decidedly cool between them since the new year had rolled around. In fact, Seth had seemed to be actively avoiding both me and Cassie in the past couple of months, always coming up with an excuse as to why he couldn't join us at the pub or meet us for a meal. And Cassie herself seemed slightly offhand whenever I mentioned Seth. I'd begun to suspect that the events at Christmas had introduced a terrible awkwardness between them and that it was now spilling over into our general friendship. I sighed. I hoped they would both get over it soon and we could return to our old easy camaraderie.

"What about you? Got any plans for

tonight?" asked Cassie, pulling me out of my thoughts.

"Hmm... same as you. A long date with my bath," I said with a chuckle. "Oh, and I'll need to pop over to pick up Muesli from Azalea Chu's place."

"I was wondering where the little monkey was today! How come she's over there?"

I told Cassie what had happened the night before, including my reluctant promise to Mrs Chu, and adding at the end: "I feel bad because I don't really know what I can do. I hate to just let her down, but I did promise Devlin that I wouldn't get involved, and besides, Roberts is impossible to talk to."

"At least he hasn't got anyone tailing you today, so maybe he's dropped the idea of you being a top suspect. The whole thing was such a stupid idea anyway!" said Cassie indignantly. "I mean, *you're* the one who was wronged!

Like I told that journalist chap, it was bad enough that you had to suffer Azalea trying to sabotage your business, without now being accused of her murder as well!"

"What journalist chap?" I asked, sitting up.

Cassie waved a hand. "Oh, this guy that was hanging around the tearoom when I arrived this morning. Said he was some journalist with a popular column in one of the national papers and happened to be in the area when the murder happened. He was obviously sniffing around for a story. He said he'd heard that the police were considering you a prime suspect for Azalea Chu's murder and he wanted your reaction. Well, I told him that you weren't here but *I* could give him some comments!"

I looked at Cassie worriedly. "Was his name Mark Scott?"

"Yeah, that's the bloke. Why—d'you

know him?"

"Not really, but I met him that night at the potluck dinner. He was Azalea's friend, actually." I bit my lip, feeling uneasy. "I'm not sure you should have told him about the sabotage attempts."

"Why not?" Cassie demanded. "It's true that Azalea was trying to ruin your business. I told him that you'd never do anything like commit murder, of course, but if you *had* wanted to wish Azalea harm, it would have been perfectly understandable given the way she'd treated you!"

"You didn't actually say that?" I gasped.

Cassie shrugged. "Something like that. I can't remember the exact words."

"Oh, Cass! You know how journalists twist words around. That's practically like saying I had a good motive for wanting to murder Azalea!"

Cassie looked slightly sheepish.

"Well... now that you put it that way... I didn't really think of it like that. He just got me so wound up, the way he was talking about you—"

"He was probably provoking you on purpose. I'll bet that's his trick for getting people to say things that he can then turn into a sensationalist article."

"Slimy git," Cassie muttered. "I can't believe I fell for it."

I gave my friend a fond smile. In spite of its tendency to sometimes get her in trouble, Cassie's spontaneous, feisty nature was one of the things I loved the most about her. "Never mind. Hopefully you're right, and by now Inspector Roberts has given up his stupid theory about me being a suspect."

Chapter Eighteen

Sadly, it looked like that was wishful thinking on my part, because when I left the tearoom at the end of the day to start my ride home, I found a familiar car on my tail. It was the young DC, trying unsuccessfully to look nonchalant behind the wheel as he followed me down the winding road. I felt a prickle of annoyance, which rapidly changed to a spark of mischief.

So the police want to play games, do they? Fine! I leaned forwards and began pedalling faster, then made a sudden turn off the main road into a smaller lane. The DC had to spin his steering wheel frantically to follow me and I grinned, beginning to enjoy myself. For the next ten minutes, I led him on a merry chase, twisting and freewheeling down the country lanes, through the beautiful landscape of serene pastures and rolling hills that made the Cotswolds so famous, whilst the poor young DC tried desperately to keep me within his sight.

Finally, I began to tire of the game and looped back towards the road that would take me past Meadowford-on-Smythe again and on to Oxford. As I approached the village, I saw a fork in the road and, on a sudden impulse, I took the turning. A few minutes later, I found myself gliding into the car park of the Cotswolds Manor Hotel estate. The car followed, but as it circled, looking for a space to park, I took the opportunity to jump off my bike and wheel it quickly into the main complex of hotel buildings.

Within minutes, I'd found a quiet alley where I could prop my bike against a wall, then I quickly threaded my way through the cluster of buildings until I could peer around a corner and get a view of the car park. I could see the young DC standing by his car, craning his neck in a circle as he desperately scanned the area for a sight of me. Even from this distance, I could see the expression of dismay on his face as he realised that he'd lost the trail. I felt a flicker of pity for him. *Oh dear... someone is going to get a tongue-lashing from Inspector Roberts when he returns to the station!*

I watched the DC for a few minutes more, then I hardened my heart and turned away. Feeling smug, I decided to return to the alleyway where I'd left my bike via a roundabout route. Hopefully, by then, the young DC would have given up looking for me and left the estate, leaving me free to cycle home. It was silly, really, to go to such elaborate lengths—it wasn't as if I was *really* trying to skulk off somewhere in secret!—but somehow, the small act of defiance in sabotaging Roberts's attempts to monitor my movements made me feel a bit better, a bit more in control of the frustrating situation.

I started to follow the detour route, then changed my mind and decided to take a shortcut through the hotel instead. Using a side entrance, I entered the lobby. The place was humming with activity, with guests arriving and checking in, as well as day visitors who had come to enjoy the ambience of the lobby bar, eat at one of the restaurants, play a round at the adjoining golf course, or sample some treatments at the day spa. I had just walked past the reception desk when I caught sight of a man out of the corner of my eye. He had entered via the main entrance and was now hurrying towards me. I made a muffled noise of surprised annoyance. It was the young DC!

Blast! I thought I'd shaken him off!

For a moment, I contemplated running through the lobby to get back to the alley where I'd left my bike, jumping on and pedalling off as fast as I could. It would take him a few minutes to return to his car, start it, reverse out of his parking space, and then come after me—which meant that I would have a good head start. On the other hand, once out of the estate, he would have the advantage and would probably catch up with me easily on the country roads between here and Oxford. I balked at the thought of being hunted down again. Suddenly I was fed up. On an impulse, I stopped and swung around to face him.

The DC stumbled, his face showing almost comical dismay as he skidded to a stop in front of me. Obviously, his training hadn't covered what to do if you walked slap bang into the suspect you were supposed to be tailing!

"Hello, Constable." I gave him a bright smile. "You were at my tearoom the other day, weren't you?"

"Uh… h-hullo… yes… I mean, no… I mean… uh, yes…"

"Have you seen my friends, by any chance? You know—those four old ladies you were talking to the other day."

He gulped, his Adam's apple jerking frantically. "Th-they're here?" he whispered with a panicked look around.

"Well, they should be. We arranged to meet for tea in the hotel lobby." I made a big show of looking over his shoulder. "Ah! I think I see them now…"

He let out a whimper of fear and bolted with a hasty: "I… I have to go now! Duties back at the station!"

I chuckled to myself as I followed him to the main entrance and watched him race across the car park. A few minutes later, his car roared out of the estate, leaving a cloud of exhaust fumes behind it. *Okay, that was a bit mean*, I admitted to myself, grinning. *But it certainly worked a treat!*

Turning back, I resumed my original shortcut route through the lobby to get to the alley where I had left my bicycle. As I strolled past the plush, comfortable seats of the lobby lounge, I saw a large stand in the corner with a display promoting the new *degustation* menu in the hotel's main restaurant. There was a photo of a man in a white chef's uniform and hat, standing with his arms crossed, next to the list of menu items. I stopped and stared. It was the man I'd seen outside the Yin-Yang Tea Bar on the night of the potluck dinner—the one who had torn down one of the promotional posters and trampled on it furiously. He looked very different in this picture, his rather jowly face wreathed in a proud smile rather than an angry scowl, but it was undeniably the same man. I went closer to the stand, my eyes zeroing in on the words:

"Our fresh and exciting degustation menu has been personally designed by our award-winning head chef Harry McKenzie and promises to be a gift for your tastebuds!"

Harry McKenzie. The man whose restaurant business had been ruined by Azalea Chu. The man that Mrs Chu was convinced was a "bad enemy". The man I'd seen in a fit of rage outside the tea bar, just a short time before Azalea had been murdered. Was it all a coincidence?

I started as a voice spoke at my elbow and I turned to see a middle-aged woman in the hotel's mauve uniform standing next to me.

"Hello—were you interested in our new *degustation* menu?" she asked brightly.

"Oh… um… yes, it looks very

interesting."

"Have you tried a tasting menu before?"

"No, not really."

"Oooh, then you must definitely try this one!" the woman exclaimed. She glanced around, then stepped closer, saying in a conspiratorial voice: "You know, I used to think they were just a pretentious gimmick myself, but then I tried a *degustation* meal last year—it's one of the staff perks here, you see; we get to sample the new menus they're developing—and, oh my goodness, *what* an experience! All those different flavours... and then the wines that complemented the dishes... I got quite tipsy, I can tell you!" She giggled.

I smiled, amused by her loquaciousness. "That does sound like a lovely experience," I agreed.

"And of course, taking your time over the food rather than wolfing it all down is *sooo* much better for your digestion, isn't it? Patrick—that's my husband, well, he's not really my husband. I mean, not officially, like. I suppose they call them 'partners' nowadays, but we've been together so long, we're practically like an old married couple!" She giggled again. "Anyway, as I was saying, Patrick is normally a 'meat and two veg' man. Won't put anything other than ketchup on his food! But even he said the *degustation* experience was bloody good. You could bring your fella and make a night of it, like we did."

"That's a nice idea," I murmured as I eyed her speculatively. It was obvious that she was one of those people who loved a good natter, and it seemed silly not to take advantage of the opportunity. *Besides, having a bit of a gossip isn't the same as snooping or interfering in an investigation, is it?* I told myself. *I can't help it if people around me like to talk and I just happen to listen...*

"So... um... I read that this menu has been specially designed by your head chef?" I said, indicating the poster.

"Yes, Harry—I mean, Mr McKenzie is a marvel!" she gushed. "He has the most wonderful talent for combining flavours and textures and coming up with mouth-watering combinations. You know, things you'd never think would taste good together, and then you try it and you think: blimey, that's delicious! We're really lucky to have Harry as head chef here. He oversees all the hotel's different eating establishments, you know."

"Has he been working here long?" I asked.

"Just under a year. But he's had many years of experience working in hospitality," said the woman quickly. "In fact, he used to run his own restaurant in London."

"Oh?" I paused, then said innocently, "You know, I thought his name sounded familiar. Wasn't there some scandal associated with his restaurant—?"

"Oh, yes, it was terrible! But it wasn't his fault!" said the woman, her eyes sparkling at the prospect of more juicy gossiping. "He won't talk about it much but I heard all about it from Rachel on reception who had it from one of the sous chefs. She was going out with him at the time, see—the sous chef, not Harry—and he used to tell her all sorts of stories about what goes on in the kitchens. They're not together anymore, though, more's the pity. She's seeing this chap from Oxford now. Came to attend a conference here at the hotel, and apparently they got talking when he was checking in and—bang!—it was like love at first sight. Not that you're supposed to believe in that sort of thing but—"

"Er... so Rachel told you about Mr

McKenzie?" I interrupted gently, keen to bring the conversation back on track.

"Oh yes, that's right! She said that Dave—that was her sous chef fella—had been keeping up with the whole thing when it was happening. The stuff on social media, plus the gossip in the industry, you know. And he said that Harry had been completely shafted by a woman who owned a fancy 'tea bar' down the road from his place in London. She sabotaged his restaurant and—" She broke off and gasped. "Oh my God, I've just realised! It's not her, is it? The woman who was murdered the night before last? The police didn't release much information in the press conference and everyone here's been speculating about it here at the hotel. Some thought it was a customer who had been killed, and others said it was the owner... and I've just remembered now that I heard the owner of our tea bar first started in London. Is it the same woman?" She looked at me eagerly.

"Um…" I wondered how to answer. If the police hadn't confirmed the identity of the victim, should I be revealing any more information? "I've heard the same rumours as you," I said at last, adding in a gossipy tone: "If the victim *was* the owner and the same woman who was harassing Mr McKenzie in London, do you think the police would suspect him? I mean, it sounds like he would have a good motive, wouldn't he?"

The woman's eyes widened with delight. "Blimey, I hadn't even thought of that! Yes, you're right—Harry could be a suspect!" she said with relish. "Yeah, when you think about the way she treated him and how much he lost— everything he had was invested in his restaurant, you know—well, anyone would want revenge for that."

"But do you think Mr McKenzie could be capable of murder?" I asked in a mock whisper. "I mean, what's he like?"

"Well, he *does* have a terrible temper. Rachel told me that her sous chef fella said if things went wrong in the kitchen, Harry could really lose his rag. But that's fairly normal, isn't it? I mean, you're always seeing these chefs on telly screaming and shouting at everybody."

"So Mr McKenzie doesn't get aggressive or anything like that?" I prodded.

"I think he's thrown a plate across the room once or twice, but he's never hit anyone or anything," said the woman, sounding disappointed.

"What about the other staff in the kitchen? Are any of them afraid of him? Do any of them think that Mr McKenzie could be capable of murder?"

The woman started to answer, then she froze, her eyes rounding in horror as she looked at something beyond me. Puzzled, I swung around to see what she was staring at and found myself facing a large ginger-haired man in a chef's uniform, his face dark with anger.

It was Harry McKenzie.

Chapter Nineteen

"H-Harry!" stammered the woman. "We were just talking about—er… I mean, we were just talking. Just… er… chatting, you know." She plastered a bright smile to her face. "Anyway, I… I must dash! I'll leave you two to get acquainted. Er… Harry can tell you more about the *degustation* menu, miss." And with a guilty look at me, she hurried away.

Harry McKenzie ignored her. Instead, he loomed over me, his face flushed and angry.

"Who the hell are you, coming here

and accusing me of murder?" he demanded.

"I wasn't accusing—"

"You were talking about me just now. I heard you!" he said, jabbing a thick finger at my face. "You were trying to imply that I'm aggressive towards my staff!"

"No, I was just asking—"

"Are you a reporter? Paparazzi? You rats are always trying to dig up dirt for a scoop... Wait a minute, are you trying to frame me for the murder?" he said suddenly, his eyes narrowing. "You're trying to find details that you can twist, aren't you, so that you can make up a fake story and get everyone to believe that I killed that Chu woman—"

"No!" I cried. "It wasn't like that! We were honestly just having a chat about the murder because it's in the news and... and yes, okay, your past connection with Azalea Chu did come up, but I wasn't trying to—"

"Don't lie! I heard you," he cut in. "You were asking if I was aggressive and if my staff are scared of me, and if anyone thought I could be a murderer. You bloody cow! I'm going to call hotel security and have them notify the police. The press have no right to harass—"

"No!" I cried, horrified at the thought of this incident reaching Inspector Roberts's ears. "No, no, I'm not paparazzi or anything like that! I'm not associated with the media at all; in fact, I'm sort of affiliated with the CID—" I stopped, dismayed at what I'd just blurted out. "Er... I mean, not officially, just..."

"What's this? Either you're with the police or you're not. Well, are you?" McKenzie demanded.

I gulped. If I said "yes", was he more likely to be placated? At all costs, I had to prevent him from calling security and contacting the police!

"Y-yes," I said. "I... I'm sort of a... er... freelance consultant for the CID. I've helped them with several investigations in the past." *Which isn't a lie*, I told myself. *It's true—I have helped the CID with several murder cases.*

Harry McKenzie eyed me suspiciously but I could see that he seemed to be calming down, his colour lessening. "So am I a suspect in the case?"

"Well... um..." I took a deep breath, then said, parroting the well-worn police phrase: "We're exploring all lines of inquiry. In cases such as these, it's normal to... er... check up on all contacts in the victim's background. And you can't deny that you do have a history with Azalea Chu," I continued boldly. "It's on the record."

"What should be on the record is how *she* treated me," he said, scowling. "That witch ruined me! She used all sorts of underhanded methods to sabotage my business, and then manipulated things to make it look like *I* was the villain in the story!" He paused, then added, "But before you think that gives me the perfect motive to murder her, let me tell you that, in a way, Azalea did me a favour."

"A favour?" I said in surprise.

"Yeah. She gave me the excuse I needed to finally shut my restaurant. I'd always dreamed of opening my own place, but once it got going, I quickly realised that I wasn't cut out for running a business," he said grudgingly. "Half the time—bloody hell, most of the time!—I was dealing with unreliable suppliers, staffing problems, juggling the inventory, doing the bloody accounting, trying to come up with marketing ideas... instead of being in the kitchen, where I really wanted to be. And even with all that, it was still a struggle to turn a profit!" He shook his head, his voice bitter. "I wish someone had told me, before I started, that businesses in the hospitality and catering sectors are three times more likely to fail than businesses in general."

He looked up and met my eyes. "To be honest with you, the writing was on the wall even before Azalea came on the scene. But I'd invested too much in my place, given up my whole life for it, and I couldn't bear the thought of quitting. So when she actually forced me to close, it was almost a relief. It gave me the out that I needed." He gestured to the lobby around us. "And then I got a job here as head chef and it's been the best thing to happen to me. Now I get to do all the things I really love—cook and design dishes, plan exciting menus—while somebody else deals with all the headaches of running a business." His expression hardened. "So you see? I had no reason to harm Azalea. You could almost say that I'm grateful to her."

"You didn't look that grateful two nights ago," I said dryly. "I saw you outside the tea bar. You looked livid when you were tearing down one of the promotional posters."

"Oh, that." McKenzie looked both sheepish and annoyed. "Yeah, well… Look, I'm human, okay? Even though it all turned out for the best, it doesn't change what Azalea did to me. She put me through hell. So, yeah, it still narks me when I think about it. And when I saw all the fuss being made about the 'grand opening' and realised that she was opening another tea bar… well, I just lost it for a moment. But that doesn't mean that I would commit murder!"

It was a convincing story, and as I pedalled away from the hotel complex a short while later, I had to admit that I was inclined to believe him. If nothing else, Harry McKenzie seemed to be living his perfect life now, with his fresh start and new fulfilling career—would he throw that all away just for a moment of petty revenge?

Of course, people did do rash things in the heat of the moment, and it was obvious from the gossip via my "chatty friend" that the head chef had a volatile temper. Someone who threw plates across the room when he was infuriated certainly wasn't in control of his emotions! So could McKenzie have killed Azalea in an impulsive fit of rage? He would certainly have been well placed to do the deed. As a member of staff, he would have been familiar with the various buildings and access points around the hotel estate; in fact, his own experience with restaurant kitchens would have meant that he knew about back alleys and rear service doors as alternative means of entry

And yet... I frowned. It just didn't seem in character. Azalea Chu had been ambushed in the kitchen, so whoever had murdered her would have had to sneak into the tea bar via the back alley and then hide in the kitchen and lie in wait for her to come in. That didn't sound like someone acting impulsively at all. Besides, if McKenzie really *had* been planning to kill Azalea, would he have done something as stupid as show himself in front of the tea bar only a couple of hours before—in full view of anyone watching—and tear down her posters aggressively?

No, the most likely answer was that Harry McKenzie wasn't the murderer, in spite of what Mrs Chu thought. But if that was the case, then who *had* killed Azalea? I felt a wave of frustration as I realised that because I didn't have access to the progress of the investigation, like I usually did when Devlin was on the case, I had no idea who else the police were considering as suspects. *Well, aside from myself,* I thought sourly. Surely the husband was on the list, though? Surely even Roberts couldn't ignore the statistical fact that more often than not, spouses and partners were involved in a murder?

I realised suddenly that I'd been pedalling on autopilot and paying scant attention to where I was going. Now I saw that I was on the outskirts of Oxford, and I slowed as I debated whether to go home first or head straight over to Mrs Chu's to pick up Muesli. Deciding on the latter, I turned onto the road leading to the leafy streets of North Oxford and, a few moments later, pulled up in front of the familiar Victorian townhouse. The front door was wide open this time, and I could hear the sound of voices and the clink of crockery drifting out of the open doorway. I walked in to find almost a house party inside. There was no music, of course, but there was a warm hubbub from the group of people—mostly women— congregated in the sitting room and adjoining dining room.

Everyone seemed to be eating and drinking, and the large dining table was overflowing with food and beverages. I saw a few faces which seemed familiar— probably OISS members I'd seen at the potluck dinner—as well as several East Asian ladies around Mrs Chu's age. Then I saw one face I did recognise: Jo Ling. She was dressed in work clothes and standing next to a dainty older lady who bore a remarkable resemblance to her. They were both part of a crowd surrounding the sofa suite, all watching something avidly. Curious, I went closer and stood on tiptoe to peer over the heads.

I don't believe it...

Mrs Chu was sitting on the sofa with Muesli on her lap, and around them were several middle-aged ladies, each holding a bowl and a pair of chopsticks. As I watched incredulously, they took it in turns to pick up a tasty morsel from their bowls and feed it to my tabby cat, who lolled on her back, her four paws waving in the air and a self-satisfied expression on her whiskered face. Every time she took a lovingly offered piece of tuna sushi, minced beef, or steamed fish, there were coos of appreciation and smiles all around, and when she put out a paw to grab a pair of chopsticks and pull the proffered titbit closer to her mouth, the crowd laughed delightedly and practically burst into applause.

Unbelievable, I thought, mentally rolling my eyes. Muesli had barely been there twenty-four hours and already she had amassed a fan club, with adoring attendants hand-feeding her delicacies and lavishing attention on her every whim. *How do cats do it?*

Then I glanced at Mrs Chu and saw the way a smile would light up her face each time Muesli did something cute, briefly replacing the shadow of grief lingering there—and I felt a grudging appreciation for Muesil's ability to help the Taiwanese lady cope with the tragedy of her daughter's death.

I heard my name being called and looked up to see Jo Ling making her way around the circle towards me.

"Hi, Gemma! I think your cat has personally converted half of the OISS community into pet lovers," she said, chuckling. "Even my mother started talking about maybe getting a kitten and she hates animals." Then she sobered and said, lowering her voice, "I suppose you've heard that Dev is off the Azalea Chu case?" She pulled a face. "That slimy git Roberts is in charge. Honestly, if I had a quid for every time he's hassled me about post-mortems, I'd probably be able to buy a luxury yacht by now!"

"*Have* you done the autopsy on Azalea yet?" I asked.

"Yes. This morning. It's what it looked like: death from blunt force trauma to the head. Her skull was partially crushed, actually, from a large, heavy item striking it with great force. There are no signs of a struggle, so I would say that she was surprised by the attack and probably went down without even seeing her attacker. Someone crept up and struck her from behind."

I winced. I might not have liked Azalea Chu but nobody deserved such a violent end. "Do you have any ideas what the weapon could have been?"

Jo's eyes gleamed. "Actually, I do have a theory."

Chapter Twenty

I looked eagerly at Jo as she began to explain:

"There was an impression on the skin around the head wound and I've matched the indentations to the kind of patterns seen on the embossed surface of a cast-iron teapot."

"A cast-iron teapot?"

"Yes, you know, a bit like that one…"

Jo indicated a cabinet at the side of the sitting room, and I glanced across to see a selection of ornamental teapots on display. I followed her as she led the way across and lifted one teapot from the centre of the display. It was made of heavy cast iron, in a dull grey-black colour, but with a fading coat of teal-blue lacquer clinging to the intricately embossed surface.

"This is a *tetsubin*—it's a type of Japanese tea kettle invented in the seventeenth century," Jo told me. "They were originally used to boil water over charcoal stoves, to brew tea with, and they retain heat really well, so your tea stays hotter for longer. Some people say that the cast iron also improves the taste of boiled water, so the tea brewed in this tastes mellower and sweeter. I have to say, I can't notice a big difference myself. Maybe I haven't got a discerning enough palate." She grinned, then indicated the embossed surface of the teapot. "You see these dot patterns on the surface? This is the traditional style of decoration often found on these pots. They're all cast by hand, and these patterns are manually stamped into the moulds by master craftsmen in Japan."

"I saw teapots like these at Azalea's tea bar," I said, remembering the afternoon tea set menu that Cassie and I had sampled.

"Yeah, but those were probably cheaper imitations," said Jo. "Most of the cast-iron teapots you see in the West, especially in Chinese and other Asian restaurants, are not proper *tetsubin* pots. I mean, they look similar on the outside and they *are* made of cast iron, but they've got an enamel coating on the inside, so you can't really use them over a fire, and they're also usually mass-produced in factories, not crafted by hand. They're really popular now, you know, even in trendy Western establishments, and with general tea drinkers, so they're sold everywhere. But anyway, even the cheaper models all have the same embossed pattern on the outside—and that's exactly the pattern I found imprinted into the skin around Azalea's head wound. I think the murderer may have used one of her own teapots as the weapon." Jo hefted the *tetsubin* experimentally in her hand. "These cast-iron teapots can weigh up to four pounds and, being made of hard metal, one could do a lot of damage if brought down with force on someone's head."

She handed the teapot to me, and I made a hearty noise of agreement as I felt the sudden weight of it drag on my grip.

"Have they checked all the teapots at the tea bar?" I asked.

Jo nodded. "I asked the SOCO team and I also checked myself. One of their teapots *is* missing," she said triumphantly.

"So you think the murderer ran away with the weapon?"

"That's what it looks like. I've told Roberts that he needs to concentrate his efforts on finding that missing teapot. It could lead us straight to the murderer."

"But if these teapots are so popular nowadays, how would you know that it's the right one?" I asked. "Even if the murderer decided to keep it, he'd make sure to clean it, wouldn't he?"

"DNA evidence is very hard to remove," said Jo grimly. "Even if he scrubs like mad, he won't be able to remove all traces of skin and hair and other material. Especially with this kind of surface…" She indicated the elaborate etchings on the metal pot, which gave it an uneven exterior covered with numerous grooves, pits, and raised bumps. "With proper forensic examination, I should be able to get a match."

We were interrupted by several voices calling to us, and I looked up to see that Mrs Chu and her friends seemed to have noticed my arrival at last. They pulled me into the circle and began plying me with questions about Muesli, who sat with a smug expression on her little face.

"How old? How old is Muss-Lee?"

"Um… she's a rescue cat so I'm not really sure. I think she might be around three years old."

"You have her from baby?"

"No, I adopted her about a year and a half ago."

"She kill rats for you?"

I looked at my spoiled moggie and swallowed a laugh. Muesli probably couldn't kill a toy mouse if it dropped on her head! "No, not really. Luckily, I haven't seen any rats where I live."

"Where does she sleep at night?"

"She sleeps on my bed."

"When she makes a baby, can you give me?" one woman asked eagerly.

"Er… well, Muesli's been neutered—she had an operation," I explained. "So she can't have babies. But you can go to the rescue shelter and adopt another cat," I added quickly. "There are lots of cats needing good homes and many of them are just like Muesli."

There were murmurs of excitement around the group, and several ladies began discussing a joint trip to the local animal shelter.

Mrs Chu sidled up to me. "Muss-Lee can stay here again tonight? No go home?" she asked hopefully.

"Oh… er…" I stared at her pleading eyes. "Well… um… isn't it a pain for you?"

"Pain? I don't have pain," said Mrs Chu, puzzled. "I am very good health."

"No, sorry… I meant, isn't it a trouble for you?" I explained.

She beamed and shook her head. "No, no—no trouble! Muss-Lee very good!"

"Oh. Well… um… sure, she can stay another night," I said uncertainly. Then

I took a deep breath and said: "Mrs Chu... I saw Harry McKenzie today."

The Taiwanese lady stiffened and her eyes searched mine fearfully. "Yes? You speak to him?"

I nodded. "I asked him a lot of questions. I don't think he killed Azalea," I said gently. "It's true that he was very angry about what she did to him—er, I mean, about their business problems—but there is no reason for him to want to hurt her now." I told her about McKenzie's fresh start and his grudging gratitude towards Azalea.

Mrs Chu's shoulders slumped. "But if Harry Mah-Kenzee not the bad one, then who?" she asked despairingly.

I thought back to the Old Biddies' conviction that Azalea's husband was involved. "Mrs Chu... can you tell me about Azalea's husband? What is he like?"

"Kai? He is nice boy. His mother is

English, his father from China. Very good family, you know. Very rich. Very powerful in China." She smiled. "Kai is good husband for Azalea."

"But... I thought they were getting a divorce?" I said.

An expression of chagrin crossed her face and she sighed. "Yes, they have many big fight. I don't know why. I ask Azalea but she no tell me. She make Kai leave house before I come from Taiwan."

"Is Kai still in Oxford?" I asked.

Mrs Chu nodded. "Yes, yes. He is dentist. He has clinic."

"A dental practice in Oxford?"

She nodded again. "He is very good dentist. I don't know why Azalea fighting with him." She sighed. "Maybe is because of father. Mr Wang not happy Kai choose Azalea."

My ears pricked up. "Mr Wang? Is that

the person who sent you those beautiful white flowers the other day?"

Mrs Chu brightened. "Ahh... yes, yes. Is him."

"Er... Magnolia seemed surprised by the gift?" I prodded.

"Magnolia no like him. She say he always insulting our family. But I think he is not bad man. Just he don't want Kai marry Azalea."

"Oh? Why is that?"

Mrs Chu shrugged. "Mr Wang is important man in China. Big name. Many *guanxi.* He want Kai marry girl from China. He say daughter-in-law from Taiwan make him lose face. They are fighting many time, but Kai no change mind. He say he love Azalea, want to marry her." She smiled again. "Kai very good boy."

It was obvious that she adored her son-in-law and I chose my next words carefully. "Mrs Chu, what is Kai like when he gets angry?"

"Kai never angry. He is nice boy."

"Yes, but even nice people get angry sometimes, don't they? I mean, he must have been very upset with Azalea because of their fights—"

"You think Kai is the one killing Azalea?" She stared at me, aghast.

"Yes—no… I mean… it's a possibility," I stammered.

"No, no! Kai is nice boy! He love Azalea."

He might not love her so much anymore, especially after the way she's treated him, I thought grimly. Out loud, I asked, "Can you tell me where his clinic is?"

She gave me an address just off one of the main streets in central Oxford, then she looked at me anxiously. "You think is true? You think Kai is bad?"

I didn't know how to reply. In the end,

I said lamely: "I don't know, Mrs Chu. Sometimes… well, sometimes people can do bad things, even if they're not really bad people." Seeing the look in her eyes, I reached out impulsively and touched her arm. "But I will try my best to find out. I will get the truth about Azalea's murder. I promise."

Chapter Twenty-One

When I arrived at my tearoom the next morning, I was surprised to find Cassie in a flaming temper. She was in the kitchen, pacing back and forth next to the wooden table in the centre, fuming and gesticulating, whilst Dora listened sympathetically. For a moment, I thought she must have fallen foul of incompetent traffic police again when leaving her house that morning, then I realised that she was waving something in one hand and pointing to it with loathing.

"...a total wanker! I can't believe how

he's twisted my words and completely changed the meaning. I swear if I ever see him again, he'll be sorry! I've half a mind to report him to the—Gemma!" She broke off as she saw me. "Er… hi. Good morning."

"Doesn't sound that good from your point of view," I observed. "What's wrong, Cass? Why are you so angry?"

"Because of this!" Cassie slammed the newspaper she had been holding down on the table in front of me.

My eyes widened as I took in the front page. It featured a large professional photograph of Azalea Chu standing in front of her newly opened tea bar, one hand casually resting on a hip in the standard pose used by models and celebrities when fronting the cameras. In the corner was a smaller inset image, which showed a blurry picture of me, hovering between two tables at the Little Stables, a tray in my hands and a harassed expression on my face. It was not a flattering picture and had obviously been taken from a distance, probably through the tearoom windows by a furtive photographer.

What really made me suck in a breath of dismay, though, was the headline that dominated the page:

SHE TRIED TO RUIN MY BUSINESS... I'M GLAD SHE'S DEAD!

~ Local tearoom sleuth is top suspect in grisly murder ~

Underneath the picture was a short article by Mark Scott and I felt my horror and indignation growing with every line I read:

...last week, residents of the Cotswolds were rocked by the death of Azalea Chu, a top entrepreneur who launched a successful new concept 'tea

bar' in London a few years ago and had just opened a second establishment on the outskirts of Meadowford-on-Smythe. She was found in the latter's kitchen, brutally murdered by a violent blow to the head. Police have launched an investigation into the killing and top among their list of suspects is Gemma Rose, the jealous owner of a rival tearoom situated on the other side of the village.

A source confirmed that the two women had been embroiled in a bitter fight over customers, with Rose claiming that Chu had tried to ruin her business through deliberate sabotage. Rose herself is no stranger to murders. The 'tearoom sleuth' boasts an enviable reputation for solving cases faster than the police and has even offered her services as a freelance consultant to the Oxfordshire CID. This time, however, she might find herself on the wrong side of the magnifying glass...

I stopped, unable to continue reading, and looked up to see Cassie's contrite face.

"This is awful!" I cried. "It makes me sound so... so—and what's this about 'jealous owner of a rival tearoom'? I wasn't jealous of Azalea!"

"It's just sensationalised rubbish," said Cassie. "He just put that in there to imply that envy might have been your motive."

"And all that stuff about boasting that I can solve cases faster than the police— I never said any of that!" I said indignantly. "It makes me sound so horribly arrogant."

"It's the kind of sordid soap-opera drama that people like to read," Dora spoke up, adding loyally: "But it's not undeserved praise. You *have* solved several cases faster than the police, Gemma."

I groaned. "Oh God, what if Inspector Roberts sees this?"

"I'm so sorry," Cassie said, hanging her head. "I honestly had no idea that bastard Scott would twist my words like that! I never told him that you were 'glad' that Azalea was dead or any of the other things he wrote."

I gave her hand a squeeze. "It's all right, Cass. I know you didn't mean it." I sighed. "They do say 'today's news is tomorrow's fish 'n' chip papers', or something like that—don't they? Let's hope that this blows over quickly and everyone just forgets about it."

Unfortunately, Meadowford was a small place and news travels fast; before long, it seemed like every customer in the tearoom had a copy of the paper and were eyeing me covertly over the top of the pages and gossiping with the others at their table. I tried my best to ignore the whispers and stares, although it was a strain, and I was relieved when the lunch rush was finally over and I could retreat into the kitchen, leaving Cassie to serve the remaining tables.

I was just helping Dora transfer a batch of freshly baked teacakes onto a rack to cool when Cassie popped her head around the side of the kitchen door.

"Hey… do you mind popping into Oxford?" she asked me. "We've got a catering order that needs to be dropped off in the centre of town. I'd do it but the chain on my bike is acting up and I'd rather use it as little as possible before taking it in for repairs tomorrow."

"Oh, of course," I said, glad of an excuse to leave the tearoom and all the curious eyes for a bit. "Will you be okay to hold the fort alone, though?"

"It's not too busy at the moment—it's that lull between lunch and teatime. That's why I thought it would be good timing for you to pop out."

I nodded and hurried to collect the order of freshly baked scones and other goodies and stow them in the basket at the front of my bicycle. I cycled into Oxford and made the delivery in record time. However, as I was starting back, I decided that, rather than brave the traffic in the congested streets, I would wheel my bicycle on foot out of the city centre and remount when I got to the quieter outer roads. Aside from not having to fight my way between double-decker tour buses, coach services, local cars, and taxis, it would be nice to take the chance to stroll through the historic city.

I felt the familiar waves of nostalgia wash over me as I walked past the iconic colleges with their "dreaming spires" and the quaint cobblestoned streets between the famous landmarks that topped every tourist's photo bucket list. It had been nearly ten years since I'd walked through these streets, wheeling a similarly old bicycle as a student—on my way to a lecture, perhaps, or hurrying back to college to finish an essay for a tutorial. Oxford had changed a lot since my student days, and yet it was also one of those places that felt like it never changed. For those who had once lived and studied here, the university city had a certain timeless quality, a sense of stepping back in time whenever you returned and were offered a glimpse into a moment in your past.

Like this street corner... how many times had I stopped here to wait to cross the road? I paused and looked thoughtfully up at the honeyed stone wall next to me. I knew it belonged to one of the constituent colleges but I couldn't remember which. One of the unique features of Oxford University was that it did not have a separate "campus"—something which confused many of the tourists and visitors searching for a definitive location of the famous institution. In a way, the city *was* the university campus and vice versa. The buildings of the University were interwoven and threaded into the very foundations of the city, the parts belonging to "town" and "gown" often standing side by side. This meant that the colleges themselves were intermingled with shops and council offices, markets and pubs, and the map of the city was, in fact, a directory of the various departments, faculties, research laboratories, and residential colleges of the university.

I racked my brains now for my memory of that map and the relative positions of the different colleges, trying to remember which one was situated on this corner. *Is this Trinity? Or maybe Balliol…?* Then I caught sight of the main college gate a short distance down the street, flanked by a pair of huge wooden doors. One of the doors was open but the entry was barred by a stand with a sign reading:

Pendlebury College
Closed to visitors

Pendlebury... Almost without realising it, I walked down and paused in front of the gate. Fragments of the conversation I'd had with Professor Gillian Bennett at the potluck dinner echoed in my mind: "...*the youngest daughter, Freesia, who is currently in her second year at Pendlebury and is probably my most promising student...*"

So this is Freesia Chu's college, I thought, staring at the sign. The memory of the mysterious figure I'd seen outside the kitchen windows on the night Azalea was murdered flashed through my mind. I'd been trying not to think about it, but now it popped up, vivid and insistent, before I could mentally look away: *Could it have been*

Freesia? Had she been running away from the scene of the crime?

Someone tapped me on the shoulder, interrupting my thoughts, and I turned to find a man holding a large DSLR camera standing next to me, flanked by a woman and two teenage children.

"Excuse me, miss, but are you a student here?" he asked eagerly

Feeling flattered that I could still pass as a student, I gave an embarrassed laugh and said, "Well, I *am* a graduate but—"

"Cool! Do you mind if we get a picture with you?" he asked, brandishing his camera. Without waiting for me to answer, he started to shift my bicycle into position. "We'd love a pic with a 'real' Oxford student... if you could stand here... like this... you know, in front of the gate, with your bike... like you're going off to a lecture or something... yeah, perfect! Now, Emma, you come and stand next to her here... and Ben— no, no, not there... here... and Claire, honey, you go on the other side...”

Bewildered, I found myself being shuffled and arranged with the other members of his hapless family as he darted between us, pushing and prodding like a manic sheepdog working a flock. Finally, he seemed to be satisfied and stood back with the camera to his eye. The shutter clicked rapidly several times, then he exclaimed: “Awesome! Now how about a shot next to—”

The tourist was interrupted by the appearance of a bearded man in a black suit stepping out suddenly from between the gates. I recognised the newcomer instantly as a college porter—the guardians of student life at Oxford. College porters officially provided a combination of security and concierge services but most also acted as a friendly avuncular (or materteral!)

figure to the resident students.

Now, he put a protective hand on my shoulder as he asked, "Is there a problem?"

"Oh no, no problem." The tourist spoke up before I could answer. "We were just getting some photos with one of your students. Hey! I was wondering if we could get one inside—in one of them 'quadrangle' things?" he asked boldly, peering through the half-open gates.

The porter glowered. "The college is closed to visitors. Now, if you'll excuse us…" He turned and swept me with him as he retreated once more behind the college's high walls.

When we were out of sight behind the gates, he turned to me and said: "Can't stand those cocky buggers. Shouldn't be hassling the students. You should have called me if he was bothering you…"

For a moment, I felt flattered that he,

too, had mistaken me for a student. Then I reminded myself that Oxford had lots of mature students and members enrolled in graduate programmes, so the assumption wasn't necessarily a comment on my youthful looks!

Still, I decided to take advantage of the mix-up and I said with a grin, "Thanks for rescuing me. I didn't mind, really, but he *was* a bit pushy!" I paused, then, on an impulse, asked, "Do you know Freesia Chu, by the way?"

"Ah, Freesia! Of course. Lovely girl." A fond smile spread over his face. "Came in the other week with some dumplings her mother had made." He smacked his lips at the memory, then looked speculatively at me. "You a friend of hers? Don't remember seeing you together. Come to think of it, are you a member of this college? Don't think I've seen you before."

"Er… no, I'm not. I just came to find Freesia. She… we were supposed to meet by the Bod," I said, improvising quickly and pleased at how easily the old nickname for the Bodleian Library had slipped off my tongue. "But she didn't turn up and I thought she might have forgotten. I wanted to return some of the notes she lent me. She'll need them for her own essay."

"Ah." He relaxed and nodded. "Well, you can leave them in her pigeonhole, if you like."

He gestured towards the Porter's Lodge next to us, in which there would be a wall covered with rows upon rows of wooden cubbyholes, each one corresponding to a current member of the college. Popping into the Porter's Lodge each day to check your pigeonhole for mail, packages, handwritten notes from friends, and messages via the university's internal system used to be a time-honoured tradition for all students in my day.

But maybe less so now, given all the

mobile phones and messaging apps everyone's got, I reflected. Aloud, I said to him, "Oh... um... I'd rather give them to Freesia in person. There were a couple of things I wanted to ask her as well. But I can't remember where her room is now—can you remind me?" I asked ingenuously.

For a moment, I thought he was going to refuse or grill me further, and I squirmed slightly. I wasn't sure why I had launched into this litany of lies about my relationship with Freesia. It would have been easy enough to just present my university alumni card and gain access to the college that way. But if I had done that, it wouldn't have been the same as saying that I was Freesia's friend, and I wasn't sure if the porter would have been as happy to give me the details of her room.

To my relief, he didn't question me further but disappeared into the Porter's Lodge to check his records, then popped his head back out a moment later and said:

"Chapel Quad, Staircase 5, Room 12. The code's 012022 to get in." He nodded towards the side of the Lodge, where I could see several bicycles leaning against the wall. "You can leave your bike here and pick it up on your way out."

Chapter Twenty-Two

I made my way slowly through the college. Pendlebury was not one of the biggest or grandest of the Oxford colleges, but it was still impressive enough by any standards, with several quads enclosing manicured green lawns and buildings dating to medieval times. Like many of the colleges in the university, Pendlebury had expanded through the centuries by acquiring new land and buildings, so that it was now a sprawling hotchpotch of different historical architectural styles. Most of the buildings were in the neo-classical style, but its most distinctive feature was still its oldest structure—a Saxon tower built in the eleventh century, which dominated the main quad and was probably a remnant of the monastic institution that the college had originally grown from.

I circled the tower and found the college chapel tucked behind it, easily recognisable by the set of beautiful stained-glass windows above its entrance. Stepping into the small adjoining quad, I looked around. Doors were set at intervals along three sides of the quad, with each leading to a cluster of student rooms opening off the landings on each floor. Staircase 5 was the first one on my left and I let myself in, then began climbing the creaking wooden staircase. It was narrow and steep, and I found myself puffing slightly by the time I reached the third landing.

I paused to catch my breath, then froze as I heard the sound of crying. I realised that the door nearest to me was slightly ajar and, as I hovered outside, I caught a glimpse of the interior of the room through the narrow gap. There was the usual single bed alongside the wall, with a cluttered desk, a shabby armchair, a bookshelf overflowing with books and knick-knacks, and a faded rug taking up the rest of the space in the room.

There were two figures sitting side by side on the bed. One of them was Freesia Chu and she was trying to talk between choked sobs as she angrily brushed tears from her eyes. The other figure was Professor Gillian Bennett; the older woman had her arms around the girl and was patting her back, like a mother comforting a hurt child. There was so much tenderness in the scene that I felt almost like I was intruding on an intimate moment.

Freesia's anguished voice drifted out to me:

"*...no, no, it's not... hate having to*

pretend... fake happy family... all a big lie!"

Professor Bennett murmured something in a calmer tone. I couldn't hear what she said and she was quickly cut off by Freesia again:

"I don't care! I don't regret doing it—"

The Oxford don interposed again. This time I caught some words: *"...shouldn't have been there... if no one else saw, then hopefully the police won't suspect..."*

Freesia's voice, shrill with emotion, drowned hers out: *"The police don't know anything! They have no idea—and don't tell me you're not supposed to speak ill of the dead. She was a witch and she didn't care how much she hurt others as long as she won! Karma is real, you know, and maybe... maybe Azalea got what she deserved!"*

Suddenly, the door burst open and I

jumped back as Freesia Chu stumbled out. Her long black hair was tangled around her head, her eyes wild and bloodshot, and her face twisted in an agonised expression. She pushed past me and flung herself down the staircase, clattering down the steps at such a speed that it was a wonder she didn't trip and fall. Somehow, she made it to the bottom safely and disappeared out into the quad.

I barely had time to register all this before Professor Gillian Bennett came rushing out of the door after her.

"Miss Rose!" She stopped short as she saw me. She was dressed as elegantly as at the potluck dinner, although her grey-streaked blonde hair was now tucked up in a French knot.

"Oh! Er... hi," I said, feeling ashamed and embarrassed, even though I hadn't been eavesdropping on purpose. "I... um... I happened to be in town and... um... well, I was... um... talking to Mrs

Chu last night and she was very worried about Freesia, so I thought, since I was passing the college..." I trailed off, the garbled lies sounding weak even to my own ears.

Professor Bennett, however, didn't seem to be focusing on my lame explanation. Instead, she looked at me anxiously and said: "Did you hear what Freesia said just now...?"

"Yeah, I did," I admitted.

"It's not what you think!" she said quickly. "I know it's tempting to jump to conclusions, but Freesia is not involved in her sister's murder." She gave a forced laugh. "You know how things can be taken out of context and misconstrued..."

I hesitated. I could see that she was expecting, hoping that I would adopt the famous British habit of studiously ignoring or brushing over an embarrassing situation, so as to avoid a socially awkward moment. I had to admit that the force of my upbringing almost had me stammering a polite rejoinder and hastily changing the subject. Then I stiffened my spine and said:

"Well, it's hard to see how things can be misconstrued when Freesia said she didn't '*regret doing it*' and also said her sister '*got what she deserved*'."

"No, no, you *have* misconstrued it!" Professor Bennett insisted. "She wasn't talking about not regretting the murder—she was talking about not regretting her writing!"

I stared at the Oxford don. "Her what?"

Gillian Bennett nodded, eager to explain: "As you know, Freesia is a writer, and writing is how she processes her thoughts and emotions, how she makes sense of her experiences in the world. She has a journal app on her phone, and that night at the potluck dinner, after she had an… er… upsetting conversation with Azalea, she was so angry afterwards that she wrote quite a… er… graphic fantasy in her journal. She was just venting, really; you know, the way we all do to friends and family sometimes, making threats about what you're going to do to someone. Except that she wrote it, instead of speaking it.

"But it was all just hyperbole, really. There's no real intention of ever doing such things," she added hurriedly, seeing my expression. "In real life, Freesia couldn't hurt a fly. But like a lot of writers, on paper, she can imagine a more empowered, more heroic version of herself."

Of all the explanations and excuses I'd come across, this was a new one. I looked at her sceptically. "If it's simply fiction, then why were you worried about the police suspecting her?"

"Because if the police see that entry,

they will completely misunderstand things! Policemen have no imagination, and they wouldn't be able to understand the important distinction between a creative catharsis and a written confession." Professor Bennett added quickly, "Anyway, Freesia has an alibi. She was very upset after the conversation with Azalea, and I spent some time with her, offering a sympathetic ear and a shoulder to cry on. So I can vouch that we were together at the time the murder occurred."

I frowned. *If Freesia was with Gillian Bennett the whole time, does that mean that she wasn't the furtive figure I saw through the kitchen windows? But then, who could it have been, if it wasn't her?*

"Are you sure you were with her the *whole* time?" I asked. "You didn't, like, leave her for a minute to go and get her a drink or something? Freesia could have slipped into the kitchen while you were away and—"

"No! She was with me and I'd thank you not to make suggestions like that to the police!" snapped Gillian Bennett. "Look, I *know* Freesia had nothing to do with the murder, and I don't want the poor girl to be hounded unnecessarily. The last thing she needs—the last thing the whole family needs—is for her to be treated as a suspect in her own sister's murder case. If you really cared about Mrs Chu, you wouldn't be doing anything that might bring police attention on Freesia."

She took a step closer, her voice passionate. "Do you realise what would happen if they started investigating her? Even if she's eventually proven to be innocent, mud sticks, you know, and gossip in college communities can be vicious. And what about the media? I don't want to see Freesia ostracised by her own peers or have her future prospects tainted by a criminal association. She has so much potential—you don't understand just how talented she is—and she needs our support and understanding, so that she can realise the brilliant future ahead of her!"

Professor Bennett paused, breathing hard, and seemed to collect herself. She took a deep breath, then said in a more conciliatory tone: "Now, if you'll excuse me, I need to go and find Freesia and make sure she's all right." She started towards the top of the stairs, murmuring distractedly. "Hopefully, she'll have gone to the graveyard—"

"The graveyard?" I said, startled.

She gave me a wan smile. "Oh, it's not as gruesome as it sounds. I should probably have said 'churchyard'. It's that place in the middle of St Giles. It's one of Freesia's favourite spots in Oxford. She says it's very peaceful sitting among the gravestones."

"Oh... right... I know the place," I said,

recalling passing it many times during my student days. It was a pretty green oasis in the middle of the inner-city suburbs, but still, it seemed an odd choice for a "favourite" spot in Oxford!

I watched Professor Bennett descend the staircase and disappear out into the quad, my thoughts troubled. Her words about protecting the Chu family had brought a flicker of guilt, and I thought uneasily of Mrs Chu's trust in me. Sighing, I began to descend the staircase myself. Just as I reached the bottom, however, I bumped into a dark-skinned young man coming in. He paused and stepped aside to let me pass, then did a double take.

"Wait—you're that... you're the owner of that tearoom, right?" he said, smiling.

I looked up in surprise and eyed him properly for the first time. He looked vaguely familiar but it took me a moment to place him. It was the young man who had been with the Indian family that had come to my tearoom recently.

"Oh! You came into the Little Stables recently with your parents, sister, and grandmother," I said.

He grinned. "Yeah. I'm Sanjit. Nani—that's my gran—she still talks about your Victoria sponge cake, you know. And Dad still keeps saying he's never tasted better scones."

I flushed with pleasure. "Thanks. I'm really glad your family enjoyed the visit. Are they still here?"

"No, they just came to visit for a few days. I'm the first one in my family to get into Oxford so it's a really big deal for them, especially for my nani."

I smiled at him. "They must be really proud. And you're one of the first men to be enrolled at Pendlebury too, aren't you? A double achievement," I said with a teasing laugh.

He chuckled. "Yeah, you know, I was

a bit worried about that. You wonder if you're going to walk into some kind of man-hating, feminist coven or something... but actually, everyone's been great. They're all really welcoming... and they've all been like: great to have you here!"

I wondered cynically if "everyone" included Professor Gillian Bennett. Thoughts of the Oxford don led me to Freesia, and I said on an impulse:

"You don't happen to know Freesia Chu, do you?"

A wary expression came over his face. "Yeah. A bit. Her room's actually across the landing from mine. Why?"

"Oh... I just wondered... um... Have you heard what happened to her sister?"

He nodded soberly. "Yeah. Really awful."

"Well, you know... some people think Freesia might be a suspect," I said in a suggestive tone. I half expected him to leap to her defence or at least to express disbelief at the suggestion, but to my surprise, he shifted uncomfortably and said, "Yeah, there's been a lot of talk in the college too."

"Really?" I raised my eyebrows. "You mean, people think she *could* be capable of murder?"

He shrugged, looking even more uncomfortable. "No, no, they're not saying that exactly but... well... Freesia's known for being really *intense*, you know? And she can, sort of like... well, flip out, sometimes."

"Flip out?" I looked at him sharply. "Do you mean she gets aggressive?"

"Look, she hasn't done anything to me," he said hastily, putting his hands up in a defensive gesture. "But one of my friends sort of had a 'thing' with her during Freshers' Week. There are all these events to welcome the new students, you know—bops and dinners and stuff like that—and everyone gets totally hammered. And then... people snog and sometimes things go a bit further... you know...?" He made an awkward, embarrassed gesture with his hands. "Anyway, my friend told me that afterwards, Freesia started acting really weird, like they were a serious couple or something. She wouldn't leave him alone, and when he was like: no, I'm not ready for a relationship—she went a bit nuts. He said she went to his room and started screaming and crying." He shook his head in bewildered disbelief. "They only spent one night together. It was just a shag! He never promised her anything."

"Did she get violent with him?" I asked.

"No, no, I don't think so," he said. "I mean, Nigel said she threw a couple of books at him but not, like, really to hit him, you know? I think Freesia's just a bit volatile and, like, really intense about everything. She's always been nice to me, though, whenever we've met in the staircase or around the college," he added hastily. "I mean, I think she's 'all right'. I just think she needs to chill out a bit, maybe, and not take everything so seriously or... she might do something she regrets, you know?"

Chapter Twenty-Three

I wasn't too surprised to get a phone call from Mrs Chu just as I was leaving the tearoom later that day, begging me to let Muesli stay another night. In spite of my misgivings, I relented. Somehow, I didn't think my little cat would mind staying longer in her "Taiwanese lap of luxury". Besides, if I was honest with myself, I wanted to avoid having to go over that night and thus face Mrs Chu again—especially when I was feeling so torn about the case myself.

I had to admit that there had been a great sense of relief when Gillian

Bennett had insisted that she could vouch for Freesia having been with her the entire time, and that therefore the mysterious figure in the back alley couldn't have been the youngest Chu daughter. But it didn't make it any easier for me to grapple with the guilt of not telling the police what I'd seen. I knew it was wrong to withhold information from the police, especially in a murder investigation, but at the same time, if I *did* tell them, then it was true that it would point the finger of suspicion at Freesia. Even with Gillian Bennett providing an alibi, the police would still turn the investigative beam on her, and I was uneasy about how Inspector Roberts would treat the girl, not to mention the consequences of all the negative attention. I thought of what Professor Bennett had said about malicious gossip and the harassment of the media and winced inwardly. Having known what it was like to be hounded as a murder suspect myself, I wouldn't have wished that experience on anyone—and especially not a sensitive and emotionally fragile young woman who had just suffered a loss in the family.

What about Devlin, though? Shouldn't I at least tell him? I wondered guiltily. But I knew that he would be annoyed with me for "interfering" in the investigation, especially after he had warned me not to get involved. He might even insist that I tell Roberts... I recoiled at the thought. *No, I don't need to bother Devlin*, I decided. *It's not as if there's any actual lead to the real murderer, after all. Freesia is just a red herring.*

My cottage was situated by Folly Bridge, at the south end of the city, and I normally cycled through central Oxford on my way home after work. Tonight, though, with no cat to feed and the prospect of an empty house and solo evening ahead, I found that I was reluctant to go straight home. Instead, I slowed as I reached the centre of the city and dismounted my bike, wheeling it through the streets, which were now empty of tourists. The smell of cooking wafted out from a nearby restaurant, and I felt my stomach rumble.

Maybe I'll get a takeaway, I mused. It had been a long day and it would be nice not to have to cook. I paused on the corner of Carfax, the junction of the four main streets through Oxford and officially the "heart" of the university city, and considered my options. *Hmm… Indian? Thai? Chinese?*

Then I blinked as I caught sight of four figures trotting importantly down the opposite side of the street. *The Old Biddies! What are they doing in town?* I wondered. *Is it a bingo night? Or one of their community group events? But surely none of those would be taking place here…?*

My gaze sharpened as I saw them stop outside an office building on the High Street and huddle together, as if in urgent conference. Then they pushed open the discreet door leading into the building and disappeared inside.

Before I realised what I was doing, I'd crossed the street and made my way to the same door. There was a brass plaque next to the door, etched with various professional names. One of them jumped out at me:

DENTAL SURGERY

Dr Kai Wang

BDS (Lond.), MFGDP(UK)

I stared at the name. *Kai Wang?* Was this Azalea's estranged husband? True, Wang was a common Chinese surname, but it was surely too much of a coincidence to find someone called Kai

Wang who also happened to be a dentist with a clinic in central Oxford, just as Mrs Chu had described? It had to be him! Besides, why else would the Old Biddies be skulking around outside his clinic? *But what* are *they doing here? Are they up to their old snooping tricks again?* Trying to ignore the familiar sense of foreboding, I chained my bike hastily to a nearby railing, then pushed open the door and followed them inside.

A few moments later, I stepped into a small waiting room. The lights were dimmed and the seat behind the reception desk was empty, and I would have thought that the clinic was closed if it weren't for the sound of male voices coming from a room out of sight down a corridor. The Old Biddies had been sitting on the upholstered chairs lining one wall and they sprang up as they saw me.

"Gemma! What perfect timing," declared Mabel. "You're just the person to help us!"

"Ooh yes, she can do the searching," cried Florence.

"I thought *I* was doing the searching," said Ethel in indignant tones. "We agreed that I have the best eyes without specs."

"Yes, but Gemma is younger and she can move a lot faster, dear," said Florence.

"I'm sorry—what?" I looked at them in bewilderment. "What are you talking about?"

"We're carrying out an undercover operation, dear," said Glenda with a giggle. "We're shadowing Azalea Chu's husband and we are sure he has the murder weapon hidden somewhere in this clinic!"

"It should be easy to find since it's rather unusual," Mabel added. "It's a cast-iron teapot which he used to hit Azalea on the he—"

"How on earth did you know that the murder weapon is a cast-iron teapot? No, never mind… don't answer that," I said with a sigh. It had been a stupid question. The Old Biddies had probably known the contents of the post-mortem report before Jo Ling even completed it!

"If we can find the teapot, it'll prove that the husband is guilty," said Glenda eagerly.

"We're sure he's keeping it hidden in the back office," said Mabel. "So we've come up with a cunning plan: while we distract Dr Wang, you will creep into his office and search through his things for the teapot—"

"What? I will do no such thing," I cried.

"If *she* won't, I can still do it," Ethel said eagerly. "I can move fast. I won the Most Nimble Octogenarian Award at the village fair last year, you know."

The other three Old Biddies ignored

her. Instead, they looked reproachfully at me.

"You have to help us, Gemma. We've been following Dr Wang for the last two days and this is our best chance," insisted Mabel.

"No way! I'm not going to creep into some man's private office and rifle through his things—and neither should you! Do you realise how much trouble we'd get into if we're caught?" I shuddered at the thought of Inspector Roberts finding out. This was exactly the sort of thing Devlin had warned me about. "We should all leave now," I said firmly, trying to take hold of Glenda's arm. "Come on, if we go now, he won't even realise we've been—"

I was interrupted by the sound of the voices down the corridor suddenly rising in anger. It seemed that the two men were having an argument of some sort, although, as the voices got louder, I realised that they were speaking in

Mandarin and therefore the exchange was completely unintelligible to me.

"What are they saying?" asked Glenda eagerly. "It sounds like a dreadful row."

Florence looked around. "Does anybody speak Chinese?"

"I once looked through a Chinese phrase book when I was working at the library," Ethel offered. "But all I can remember is '*Ni hao*'—'hello'—and '*wo mílu*'—'I'm lost'. Oh, and '*Ni pífu hen yang*', which means 'your skin is itchy'," she said proudly.

"*What—?*" I looked at her, baffled. "Why on earth would you need to learn that—"

"Shh!" Mabel hissed. "Listen..."

One of the voices, which had sounded very halting when speaking in Mandarin, switched suddenly to English.

"*...Ba, ni bu míngbai wo de xin—look, I know I disappointed you when I* *married Azalea. And maybe you were right. Maybe it was a mistake. Azalea wasn't... okay, I was blind about her... but even if she was an angel, you would have hated her! And for such a stupid reason—"*

The other voice cut him off sharply in Chinese.

"—so what?" cried the first voice in exasperation. *"Not everyone cares about politics—"*

There was an angry exclamation, then the sudden staccato of footsteps coming down the corridor. The next moment, a middle-aged Chinese man stepped out of the corridor and into the waiting room. He was very distinguished-looking, dressed in an expensive, tailored three-piece suit, with silver-streaked black hair combed back from an austere face. He had an air of cold authority about him, and he barely gave us a glance as he strode past and disappeared out the door of the clinic.

We'd barely had time to digest his appearance before a younger man, dressed in traditional white dental scrubs, came rushing out of the corridor after him.

"Pa! Wait, I—" He broke off as he saw the Old Biddies and me.

There was an awkward silence for a moment, then he assumed an expression of polite interest and came forward to greet us. He was very slender and good-looking in an almost feminine way, with black hair purposefully grown long and styled to frame his face, and slightly almond-shaped black eyes. In fact, he looked more like a K-pop star than a dentist. *This must be Kai Wang, Azalea's husband*, I thought, recalling Mrs Chu telling me about his mixed Anglo-Sino heritage. And the Chinese man who had just left... I recalled Kai shouting "Pa!" as he came running out of the corridor. Had that been his father—Azalea's erstwhile father-in-law?

Kai Wang gave us a cordial smile. "I'm afraid the surgery is closed now. Perhaps you'd like to make a booking for—"

"Oh, doctor!" cried Glenda, flinging herself forwards and fluttering her eyelashes with all her might. "You must help me! I have the most dreadful toothache!"

"Yes, me too!" Florence chimed in. "My dentures seem to have got stuck."

"And me," said Ethel. "I think my gums have receded entirely."

"I need to have a word with you too, doctor," said Mabel briskly. "What do you think about eating more fibre to combat bad breath?"

Kai reeled back. "Er… um… I'd like to help you, ladies, but—"

"Oh, marvellous. We'll take it in turns to pop onto the chair. Is your room this way?" said Mabel, grabbing the dentist's elbow and swinging him around.

The other Old Biddies grabbed his other arm, and between them, they began frogmarching him down the corridor. Just as they disappeared into the treatment room, Glenda dropped back and waved to me frantically.

"His office is the next door along," she said in a loud whisper, pointing excitedly. "As soon as we have him distracted, you can sneak in there and start searching."

"No, wait, this is mad! I can't—"

"We're relying on you, Gemma! Don't let us down!" she hissed before disappearing after the others.

I was left on my own in the corridor. From the treatment room came the sounds of feeble protests, the random whirring of machinery, and squeaking chair hinges. Then I heard Kai say weakly, "So... um... who would like to go first?"

Shifting my weight from foot to foot, I

hovered uncertainly in the corridor, wondering what to do. I knew what I *should* do—which was turn around and march straight out. It was crazy to even consider following the Old Biddies' suggestion. But on the other hand... what if they were right and Kai Wang *was* involved in the murder? This was an opportunity to snoop that would probably never come up again.

Besides, I told myself, if I left them to it, that wouldn't mean that the Old Biddies would abandon their ludicrous plan. They would simply figure out a way to search the office themselves, which could turn out even worse. Who knew what they might do or what danger they might put themselves in? At least if *I* did the searching, I could hopefully "contain" the situation and make sure that we all got out of here as soon as possible.

Making up my mind, I tiptoed down the corridor—darting past the open treatment room door so as not to be seen—and paused just outside the next door, which supposedly led into Kai Wang's back office. When I stepped inside, I found that it was really not much more than a large storeroom, with metal shelving units bursting with box files, office supplies, and dental equipment, and a small desk and sofa wedged in the far corner.

What made it feel even smaller was the clutter in the room. As I took in the lumpy pillow and rumpled blanket tossed at one end of the sofa, the empty packets of pot noodles and microwave meals, and the used towels and haphazard piles of clothing shoved against one wall, I recalled the gossip I'd heard about Azalea forcing Kai not only out of his marital home but also his new rented flat. It looked like, rather than continuing an expensive hotel stay, he had decided to camp out in his own clinic for the time being instead.

So he's been reduced to squatting in his own office, because of a mean trick played by Azalea, I thought. *When you think of all the other vindictive things she's done to him... surely that's more than enough reason for Kai to be very bitter?* But the question was—was he bitter enough to commit murder?

The faint whine of a dental drill coming from the room next door reminded me that I had limited time, and I hurriedly began my search. The shelves looked too organised to hide anything easily, so I focused on the desk and sofa, and the jumble of Kai's personal belongings against the back wall. Everything was a mess, which made it harder to comb through things systematically, although at least it also meant that any evidence of rifling was less obvious. I had just finished searching the desk and sofa and was turning my attention to the heap of clothing and other personal effects, when the storeroom door opened with a creak of its hinges.

I jumped and swung around, my heart pounding, only to exhale in relief as I saw the Old Biddies framed in the doorway.

"What are you doing here? I thought you were distracting Kai—" I broke off, frowning. "Wait a minute… where is he?"

Glenda beamed. "Oh, don't worry. We've made sure that he's comfortable."

"What d'you mean 'comfortable'? What have you done to him?" I asked.

"A little snooze won't harm him," Mabel declared.

"What? What are you talking about? What have you done to Kai?" I asked frantically.

Without waiting for them to answer, I rushed next door, with the Old Biddies at my heels. In the treatment room, I was met by the sight of the dentist flopped face down over his own dental chair, his cheeks squashed against the leather upholstery as he snored softly. Beside him, I could see a small cannister mounted on a trolley with a long tube and a face mask attached, and the letters "N_2O" on a label affixed to the side of the can.

I stared in horrified disbelief. "You've gassed him with nitrous oxide?"

"Oh, it's perfectly safe, dear," Florence assured me. "It just makes you feel calm and relaxed. My nephew, who lives in America, says that dentists there use it all the time to help anxious patients. It's not used so much here in the UK; we were lucky that Dr Wang had some."

"*Lucky?*" My voice was shrill with exasperation. "I can't believe you did this. I mean, this isn't just 'calm and relaxed'—you've completely knocked him out!"

"I did tell them," Ethel piped up, throwing a reproachful look at the others. "I said laughing gas can have that effect on some people."

"Yes, well, it was a bit unexpected but rather a good thing, actually," said Mabel with a satisfied look at the sleeping dentist. "With Dr Wang out of the way, it means that we can help you with the search. Speaking of which, we should be getting on with that. Come along!"

With that, she marched out of the treatment room, with the other Old Biddies trotting after her.

"Wait… you can't just… stop! We can't just leave him like that!" I spluttered, rushing after them.

I found them back in the storeroom, already enthusiastically rummaging through the pile of Kai Wang's personal belongings. Florence was looking through the dentist's toiletry bag, Mabel was inspecting his underwear, and Glenda and Ethel had seized a bundle of clothes and were pulling it back and forth between them, like two children playing tug of war.

I waded into the fray, hissing: "Stop it! This is crazy... You can't just—"

The bundle between Glenda and Ethel unfurled suddenly, sending both little old ladies staggering back, as a tangle of clothing fell to the floor. Something tumbled out from amongst the soft folds. We all stopped and stared.

It was a cast-iron teapot.

Chapter Twenty-Four

"Aha!" said Mabel, pouncing forwards with glee. "We told you that we'd find the murder weapon here!"

I stared at the teapot with wary disbelief. I couldn't quite accept that the Old Biddies' far-fetched assumption could actually be a reality. *Could they be right after all? Could Kai Wang be the killer?* It was certainly true that this was a *tetsubin*-style teapot, moulded from cast iron and with a pattern of raised dots etched onto its outer surface— exactly the kind of thing that could have caused the imprint Jo Ling had found on the murdered woman's skull.

Then I thought of the furtive figure I'd glimpsed through the kitchen windows. I had always assumed that it was a woman, but could it have been Kai Wang instead? With his slender figure and delicate, almost feminine features, not to mention that longish, sleek black hair, it would have been easy to confuse him for a female, especially in dim lighting and from a distance.

I looked again at the teapot and realised—with a skin-crawling revulsion—that part of the side was covered by a red stain, a dark crimson smear that looked exactly like dried blood.

The significance of it hit me and I jumped forwards to grab Mabel's hand just as she was bending to pick the teapot up. "Don't touch that! If it really *is* the murder weapon, then you mustn't contaminate it with your fingerprints or anything!" I looked distractedly around.

"We need to try and wrap it up safely in something, so we can take it to Forensics—"

The storeroom door creaked again, and this time all five of us jumped and whirled around. My heart sank as I saw Kai Wang standing in the doorway. His clothes were dishevelled, his eyes slightly bloodshot, and he looked shaken and bewildered.

"What... what happened? What are you doing in here?" he asked, stumbling into the room. His gaze took in the mess of clothes and personal belongings strewn on the floor, and his expression turned indignant. "You've been going through my things!"

"Yes, and we'd like an explanation for *that*!" said Mabel before I could reply. She pointed accusingly at the cast-iron teapot on the floor. "You used it to kill your wife, didn't you, Dr Wang?"

"I—what? No!" cried the dentist, his

face screwing up in horror. "How could you think such a thing?"

"Hasn't Azalea been making your life a misery? Isn't she the reason you're living here like a homeless tramp?" asked Mabel.

He flushed dully. "I… well, yes, Azalea did make things very… er… difficult for me but… but that doesn't mean that I wanted to kill her!"

"We wouldn't blame you if you did," said Ethel kindly, patting his arm. "She treated you so very dreadfully."

"Yes, you had a very good motive," said Glenda, like a teacher commending a student for a clever idea. "Anybody in your situation would have wanted revenge."

"I'm sure people would be very understanding if you admitted that you're guilty," said Florence encouragingly.

"But… but I'm *not* guilty!" cried Kai. "I

had nothing to do with Azalea's murder."

"How do you explain *that* then?" asked Mabel, pointing to the teapot again. "Azalea was hit on the head by a cast-iron teapot exactly like that one, and the murderer took it with him. Now, *you* have a good reason to hate Azalea and you've got the murder weapon. Surely that's just too much of a coincidence?"

"Look, I don't know about the teapot that was used to kill Azalea, but I can tell you that it's not this one!" said Kai, starting to look angry. "The teapots used at her tea bar are cheap, factory-made imitations. *This* is the real thing. This is an authentic *tetsubin* tea kettle, cast by hand, from the Morioka Prefecture in Japan, and I've had it since before I married Azalea. It was one of the things I insisted on taking with me when she kicked me out of the house."

The Old Biddies exchanged uncertain looks. I could see that their conviction was starting to waver, and I began to have doubts myself. Somehow, Kai Wang sounded so genuinely indignant that it was hard not to believe him.

"What about the stain on the side of the teapot?" I spoke up. I indicated the dark red smear that covered one side of the engraved cast-iron surface. "That looks a lot like dried blood."

"That's not blood—that's lacquer!" said Kai impatiently, bending to seize the teapot and thrusting it at me.

The Old Biddies clustered around and we all peered at the surface of the *tetsubin*. My heart sank. It was true. Up close, I could see that the cinnabar-red colour covering the etched surface had a glossy, smooth texture and a saturated intensity that could only have come from a deliberate application. Due to age, it had worn away in some places, leaving only part of the cast-iron surface covered, and thus giving the impression of a smear or a stain. I suddenly recalled standing with Jo Ling next to Mrs Chu's display of teapots and admiring the *tetsubin* in her collection. It had been a dull grey-black colour, but there had been a fading coat of teal-blue lacquer clinging to the intricately embossed surface.

We looked sheepishly back up at the dentist, who seemed to be coming out of his gas-induced fugue and finally grasping the situation. He scowled as he looked around the room.

"This is outrageous," he fumed. "How dare you come in here and snoop around like this? And to accuse me of murder! The police have interviewed me already and confirmed my alibi. I can prove that I was here at the clinic on the night Azalea was killed. I have a good mind to call the police and—"

"Oh no… no, no, there's no need for that," I cried. "It's just a slight misunderstanding, really—"

"*Slight* misunderstanding?" seethed Kai Wang. "First you barge into my clinic and trick me with fake dental problems... then you ransack my office... and then to top it all, you have the gall to accuse me of murdering my wife?"

"Well, she was your *estranged* wife, really," Mabel pointed out.

"Yes, but I still loved her!" burst out Kai, his face anguished. "In spite of everything she did to me, in spite of the fact that *she* was the one who had the sordid affair with her own brother-in-law, I still cared about her and—"

"Wait—what did you say?" I cut in. "Azalea had an affair with her brother-in-law?"

Kai looked at me impatiently. "Yeah. Her sister Magnolia's husband. Didn't you know? And she wasn't even sorry! When I confronted her about it, she just laughed in my face. That was why I wanted a divorce. I couldn't continue our marriage after she'd broken my heart like that."

I stared at him as a new idea whirled in my head. The stealthy figure I'd seen through the kitchen windows on the night of the murder—my first thought at the time was that it was Freesia. With Gillian Bennett vouching for the girl, I realised that it couldn't have been her after all. But now I wondered if it could have been *Magnolia* instead? Both sisters looked incredibly alike, with their slender, petite figures and long, silky black hair. In fact, I recalled how, that first time I visited Mrs Chu's house with my mother, I'd almost mistaken Magnolia for Freesia when she opened the door.

Oh my God, what if we've been barking up the completely wrong tree? I thought, glancing at Kai Wang's irate face. *And now we've wrongfully accused an innocent man, trespassed in his office, searched his personal belongings without a warrant, and gassed him with nitrous oxide!*

As if sharing my thoughts, the Old Biddies began edging their way towards the door.

"Er… well, it's been lovely meeting you, doctor," said Mabel. "But it's getting late now and it's time us pensioners were home in bed." She hustled the other Old Biddies out into the corridor. "We'll just leave you young people to chat—"

Oh no, they're not doing it again! I thought furiously. *Getting me in trouble and then abandoning me to deal with the mess!*

I began to make my own way towards the door, pausing only to glance over my shoulder at Kai and say hastily: "Well, um… sorry again for the… er… mix-up! I'm sure you'll want to be getting home after a long day—" Belatedly, I remembered that he was sleeping at the clinic and I winced. "—I mean… er… getting some rest. Anyway, I'd best be off. Thanks for… for everything. Good night!"

I hurried out into the corridor. It was empty, as was the waiting room. The Old Biddies must have already left the clinic. Marvelling at how fast four little old ladies could move, I followed in their footsteps and a moment later found myself standing outside in the street. I peered in all directions, up and down the High Street, but there was no sign of the four octogenarians anywhere. Deciding that I didn't dare hang around myself, in case Kai came out chasing after me, I grabbed my bike and took off, pedalling quickly.

I was just breathing a sigh of relief as I turned off the tow path by Folly Bridge when I caught sight of a vehicle parked in the cul-de-sac where my little rented cottage was situated. It was a black Jaguar XK. *Devlin's car.* My heart skipped a beat. Normally, I would have been delighted at the thought of an impromptu visit from my boyfriend, but right at this moment, with the uncomfortable memory of the scene with Kai Wang still fresh in my mind, Devlin was the last person I wanted to see. He knew me too well and had an uncanny ability to sense my deepest thoughts and emotions. It wouldn't take much for him to guess that something was up.

Even as I had the thought, I saw his tall figure emerge from the shadows by my front door and come to meet me as I slowed the bike and dismounted.

"Devlin!" I said, hoping that he thought my breathless voice was due to the exertion of the ride and not to nerves. "What a nice surprise!"

"Hi, Gemma." He didn't lean forwards to give me a kiss and I noticed uneasily that he had a frown between his eyes. "I was just beginning to get worried. I tried you at the tearoom but Cassie said you'd left ages ago. Then I rang your mobile but nobody answered."

"Oh... I must have had it on silent by mistake," I said as nonchalantly as I could.

"Cassie said you were planning to come straight home and I thought you would have arrived before now." He didn't ask where I'd been, but the question was implicit.

"Um... I... er..." I faltered. I hated lying to Devlin but there was no way I could tell him about my recent escapade with the Old Biddies. Then I hit upon a possible explanation. "I stopped off at Mrs Chu's house on the way back. You know, Muesli's been staying with her for a few days and I went to pick her up."

Devlin glanced at the empty basket attached to the front of my bicycle. "But you don't have her."

"Yes, well... Mrs Chu wanted to keep

her a bit longer." I tried not to squirm under Devlin's searching gaze. "Anyway, what are you doing here?" I gave him a bright smile, trying to inject a note of teasing into my voice. "Don't tell me they've let you out early for a change?

He didn't return my smile. "I'm actually here for a work-related reason." His blue eyes were hard as he said: "Gemma, what were you doing spying on Harry McKenzie?"

Chapter Twenty-Five

"I... I didn't—"

"He says you were talking to other hotel staff behind his back, implying that he could be responsible for Azalea's death, and when he confronted you, you started questioning him about his movements on the night of the murder!"

I swallowed, quailing under Devlin's accusing gaze. "That isn't quite how it happened," I said weakly. "I mean, I wasn't spying on him on purpose. I just happened to get chatting to one of the hotel staff about the menu that McKenzie had created, and then the conversation led to the scandal around his failed restaurant and... well, since Azalea was the person who had sabotaged his business and also the person who had just been murdered, it was natural to speculate about him as a possible suspect." I gave him a cajoling look. "Come on, Devlin—I'll bet lots of people all over Oxford have been gossiping about the case. If they'd known McKenzie's history with Azalea and what a strong motive he had, they would have been asking questions too!"

"Yes, but they wouldn't have been impersonating CID while doing it," said Devlin curtly. Seeing my suddenly guilty expression, his mouth hardened and he continued: "McKenzie rang the station today to make a complaint about the CID and how one of our 'freelance consultants' has been harassing him."

"No..." I gasped.

"And you're lucky that the call was put through to me," said Devlin grimly. "I was left with the enviable job of placating McKenzie while at the same time being forced to confirm whether you *were* affiliated with the CID."

"What... what did you say?" I whispered.

"What choice did I have? I told him yes," said Devlin, his voice furious. "Bloody hell, Gemma, this is exactly the kind of thing I was warning you about the other day! You put me in a position where I was forced to lie to cover up for you—meaning I've now done exactly the kind of unethical thing that Roberts is always accusing me of. If he hears about this, it will give him exactly the ammunition he needs to block my promotion—maybe even get me suspended!"

I hung my head, unable to meet his eyes. "I'm sorry! I honestly didn't set out to snoop on McKenzie. I just happened to get into conversation with that woman—the hotel staff member—and then one thing led to another..."

Devlin was silent.

I swallowed, then touched his arm hesitantly. "I'm sorry, Devlin. Really, I am! You know I wouldn't consciously do anything to get you in trouble. I really didn't mean this to happen. If... if there's anything I can do to help or fix things, just tell me!"

I saw his blue eyes soften slightly. He sighed. "Just... stay out of the investigation, Gemma, okay? I was able to protect you this time but I won't always be there. And Roberts is already got it in for me. He's desperate for anything he can use to sabotage my career in the CID."

"I know," I said in a small voice.

Devlin sighed again. "Look, I know you just want to help—and the Old Biddies too—and I've always appreciated your efforts in the past. But things are different this time and I just can't afford to give Roberts any more leverage against me." He gave me a wry look. "I just hope there's nothing else you've been doing with those meddling old hens that I don't know about."

I gulped, thinking uneasily of the recent escapade at the dental clinic. *What if Kai Wang makes a complaint to the police as well?* Then I thrust the thought away. The dentist had seemed like a fairly mild-mannered sort of man. He hadn't even wanted revenge on Azalea after all the things she'd done to him. Surely he wasn't going to make a fuss over a little "misunderstanding"?

"Gemma?"

I started and hastily refocused on Devlin. "Yes... I mean, no... We won't... I'll speak to the Old Biddies and make sure that they understand." I wrapped my arms around his neck and pressed a kiss against the side of his jaw. "And I'm sorry again, Devlin."

His arms had slid unconsciously around me as I leaned into him, and although he still looked stern, I could sense that he was mellowing.

"Do you… do you want to stay over tonight?" I asked shyly. "Have you eaten yet? I can rustle us up something to eat and then maybe we could watch a movie and…"

He gave a regretful smile. "Sorry, Gemma, I wish I could, but I've been assigned to a homicide case out in Blackbird Leys and there's a stake-out planned tonight. It'll probably go on until the early hours of the morning."

"Oh." I tried not to show my disappointment.

This was yet another example of Devlin having to put his job before our relationship—something that seemed to be happening all the time now. I couldn't remember the last time we'd gone on a "date" or spent a romantic evening together. *By the time he's promoted to Chief Inspector, I'll probably have to get arrested just to see him*, I thought peevishly.

Then I felt ashamed. Devlin had always been supportive when it came to my tearoom, never complaining when I had to put work before a social life. I knew that I should do the same in return. It was just a lot harder when his hours didn't follow that of a normal working day but seemed to spill over and dominate his entire life.

"Well… I suppose you'd better get going then," I said with a little sigh, starting to pull back.

Devlin's arms tightened around me and he looked silently at me again, but this time, there was a very different gleam in his blue eyes.

Glancing towards the door of my cottage, he grinned and said: "Well, the night is still young and I don't have to be at my stake-out for a few hours yet. And you know, now that you mention it, I think I'm beginning to develop a ravenous appetite..."

***

I arrived at work the next morning resolved to do as Devlin had asked and stay out of the investigation. *I'll have to go and pick up Muesli today, but after that I'm not going to contact the Chu family or pay any more attention to Azalea's murder,* I told myself. As for the Old Biddies... as soon as they had settled at their usual table by the window, I went over to join them with a tray laden with goodies. I was hoping that a bit of Dora's delicious baking might make them more amenable to the remonstrations I would have to deliver.

"Ooh... teacakes!" said Ethel, her face lighting up as I set the tray down.

"Mm, hot toasted teacakes with lashings of butter... they have to be one of the most delicious things in the world," Florence declared, rubbing her hands in anticipation.

"Do these have spices?" asked Mabel, eyeing the plate suspiciously. "I can smell cinnamon and mixed spice. A proper teacake doesn't have any spices added, otherwise it would be a hot cross bun."

"Oh, Mabel..." Glenda remonstrated. "You know there are slightly different recipes for teacakes all over the country. There isn't one 'proper' way to make them. Some people bake them with spices, some without. Some people use mixed peel as well as dried fruit, others only sultanas—"

"Personally, I think a bit of spice is very nice," said Florence, leaning towards the tray to sniff appreciatively. "Hot cross buns have a lot more spices in the recipe, plus they're usually a lot sweeter, with the sugar glaze on top. I think teacakes have the balance just right."

"Are you joining us, Gemma?" asked Ethel, looking at me.

"Er..." I glanced around the tearoom. It was relatively empty and Cassie was tending to the other customers. I smiled. "Yeah, all right. Why not?"

I pulled an extra chair over and joined the Old Biddies at their table. Although I often grabbed a bite to eat in between serving orders, and I'd sampled all of Dora's creations, I had never had the chance to sit down in my own tearoom and sample the baking in a "proper" manner. Now, I savoured the novelty of the experience as I helped myself to one of the toasted teacake halves, slathering some butter on it before biting into the soft, chewy bun.

Like a lot of British baking, teacakes had a slightly misleading name. They weren't cakes at all but a type of lightly spiced, sweet yeast bun, often filled with juicy dried fruit, like currants and sultanas, although there were other variations depending on the region. The buns were baked into little round, domed shapes, but to eat them, the best way was to split them in half and pop them under a grill (or over an open fire if you were of a romantic bent) so that they became soft and puffy, with crisp golden edges. Topped with oozing melted butter and accompanied by a hot cup of tea, teacakes were one of the ultimate comfort foods.

I was enjoying myself so much that I almost forgot the reason I had come over. But as I swallowed the last crumbs of teacake and put down my cup of tea, I reluctantly launched into an account of my conversation with Devlin the night before.

"...so you have to stop all your snooping and shadowing and whatever else you're doing," I said as I finished. "We can't meddle in this investigation anymore."

"We weren't *meddling*," said Mabel indignantly. "We were doing important detective work."

"Yes, if we hadn't gone to the clinic last night, we would never have found that cast-iron teapot," said Glenda.

"But it doesn't matter!" I said, exasperated. "That teapot wasn't the murder weapon anyway and Kai Wang didn't kill his wife. He has an alibi, remember? He said the police had already checked him out."

"Pah! The police!" Mabel gave a contemptuous sniff. "The police can't investigate their way out of a paper bag. Besides, it was just a cursory check, alongside the rest of the Chu family. They didn't pay special attention to Dr Wang and they could have missed—"

"Wait—did you say they checked the

alibis of the entire Chu family?" I broke in. "Do you know that for sure?"

"I trust my sources," said Mabel loftily.

It never ceased to amaze me how the Old Biddies managed to keep their arthritic fingers in every pie, their hearing aids switched on to every juicy titbit of information. This wasn't just a case of a mole at the police station—this was an entire network of prying eyes and poking noses that stretched from the highest offices of the Oxford City Council to the lowliest teenage gangs on the local housing estates.

"So do you know what the alibi of the middle sister is?" I asked eagerly. "Magnolia—where was she when Azalea was murdered?"

"Surely you don't suspect her?" said Florence.

"Why not?" I asked. "You heard what Kai said last night: Azalea had been having an affair with her brother-in-law, Magnolia's husband. And when I met Magnolia at Mrs Chu's the other day, I already got the impression that there was very little love lost between the two sisters. In fact, Magnolia outright called Azalea a 'Type A bit—'" I broke off, belatedly remembering who I was talking to and hurriedly amended it to: "—er, a vicious cow. So if she found out that Azalea had been shagging her husband and was probably not very remorseful about it either, judging from what Kai said about her laughing in his face... well, that's the ultimate in sisterly betrayal, isn't it?"

"But would she murder her own sister?" said Ethel doubtfully.

"You were happy to accept that Kai would murder his own wife. I don't see much difference," I said. Turning to Mabel, I added, "That's why it's so important to know what Magnolia's alibi is."

"She told the police that she was out at a restaurant with her husband, Dax—"

"Her husband's called Dax?" I said disbelievingly. *Bloody hell, what with Azalea, Magnolia, Freesia, Kai, and now Dax... did anyone in this family have an ordinary name?*

Mabel nodded. "Dax Hutton. He's a doctor working at the John Radcliffe," she said, naming Oxford's biggest hospital. "Magnolia said he was called back to the hospital during their dinner; she finished the meal on her own and then returned home."

"Can anyone confirm that?" I asked.

"Well, the babysitter said Magnolia came home around ten thirty."

"But when did the husband leave for the hospital?" I persisted. "Because Azalea was probably murdered just before ten o'clock, which means that if Dax left early enough, Magnolia could have had ample time to drive to the tea bar, do the deed, and then return home."

And could she have been the figure I saw through the kitchen windows? I wondered. *But... what about the jumper?* I distinctly remembered the figure wearing a bulky knit jumper—exactly like the one I'd seen on Freesia just a short while earlier that evening.

"Hmm... we'll have to check about the husband," mused Mabel. She shared a speculative look with the other Old Biddies. "Edna's great-niece might do. She works as a nurse at the JR and she might be able to ask the A&E staff when Dr Hutton came back in that night—"

"What about Irene's grandson?" suggested Glenda. "He isn't a doctor—I think he's a physiotherapist—but he does go up to the JR regularly to see patients." She giggled. "Very good-looking lad. Recently divorced, you know, and I heard that he's got all the girls after him. He could be like James Bond and use his charm to—"

"Oh! Oh, I know!" cried Ethel excitedly. "How about Beverley's neighbour? She told me that he has to go up to the hospital every week for dialysis treatment. Maybe he could sneak off when nobody is looking and—"

"Stop! Stop!" I cried, listening to their plans with growing horror. "This is crazy. You can't ask *any* of them! It's exactly what Devlin said we mustn't do, remember?"

"Well then, how are we going to get any answers?" demanded Mabel.

I bit my lip, then I sighed: "I guess we can't. I think we're just going to have to let it go."

The Old Biddies looked aghast. "You mean... we just give up trying to find the murderer?"

I took a deep breath, then nodded.

"We mustn't do anything that could get Devlin in trouble. And that definitely means that asking your friends and neighbours to snoop at the hospital is *off* the cards."

The four old ladies looked so crestfallen that I felt sorry for them.

"Look, it's not as if the whole case is going to be abandoned," I reminded them. "The police are still working on the investigation."

"But the police don't know what they're doing," protested Mabel. "That Inspector Roberts is the biggest ninnyhammer in the county!"

Silently I agreed, but I put on a determinedly bright smile and said, with more conviction than I felt, "Oh, he's not that bad. I'm sure he'll solve the case in the end. Meanwhile, we can get back to our 'normal' lives—me running the tearoom and you enjoying morning teas and bingo and visits to the garden centre and… and all the other fun stuff you OAPs get up to. It'll be nice not to have to stress about solving a murder for a change, won't it?"

From their glum expressions, the Old Biddies obviously felt as excited about getting back to "normal" life as I did.

Chapter Twenty-Six

The Chu residence looked quiet when I arrived that evening, with no sounds of conversation, eating, or drinking coming from within, and the front door firmly closed for a change, although a white cloth still hung over it. However, when I rang the bell, I discovered that Mrs Chu wasn't alone after all—my own mother opened the door and beamed when she saw me.

"Darling! What perfect timing—I was just telling Mrs Chu all about your new Flexible Knee Pads," said my mother.

"What knee pads? I don't have knee

pads."

"Oh, you will, darling. I'm going to get you a pair as an early birthday present. Then you'll be able to kneel anywhere without hurting your joints. Helen Green showed me the most marvellous online shopping site where one can purchase things to make daily life more convenient. And they even deliver straight to your door! They have a fabulous range of items, like the EasyGrip Toothpaste Squeezer and the Long Reach Lotion Applicator for those who have trouble reaching around, and Comfort Wrap Terrycloth Slippers with cushioned insoles … oh, and even a device which lets you put on stockings without having to bend over—isn't that helpful?"

"EasyGrip? Comfort Wrap? Mother, these all sound like things for old people," I said suspiciously.

"Nonsense, darling. Young people can find such things useful too. The Relaxing

Read Tablet Pillow, for instance, enables you to prop your iPad close to your face, even if you're in bed, and it comes with a side pocket for glasses and a washable cover! I wasn't sure which colour you'd like, so I ordered one in pink and one in blue..."

"What? But I don't want a Tablet Pillow, in pink *or* blue!"

My mother continued as if I hadn't spoken: "—and Mrs Chu says she'd like one too, which is perfect as they're running a promotion at the moment. If I put in an order by this weekend, I can claim a free Pendant Magnifier Necklace! It's the cleverest thing, darling—it looks so stylish, nobody would realise that your jewellery is also a handy magnifier. You'll never be left stranded at a restaurant, unable to read the menu again!"

"Mother, I don't have a problem reading menus," I groaned.

"But you will someday, darling, and it's always good to be prepared."

I sighed and gave up. "Er... have you seen Muesli? I've come to pick her up."

"Oh yes, she's in the living room with Mrs Chu. Come in, darling..."

My mother led me into the house, and I found Mrs Chu in the same place I'd seen her last, sitting on the sofa with Muesli sprawled on her lap. My little tabby cat opened one eye as I came into the room, then stretched luxuriously and closed it again. *So much for thinking that Muesli might miss me and be feeling homesick*, I thought dryly.

"Ahh... Jem-Ma!" Mrs Chu smiled and attempted to rise.

"No, no, it's okay—no need to get up," I said, returning her smile and sitting down next to her.

"You are hungry? You eat already?" asked Mrs Chu. "I have very nice Chinese chicken soup—you want?"

"Oh… that sounds lovely but I'm not hungry at the moment."

"You very thin!" said Mrs Chu, eyeing me disapprovingly. "Have to eat more. Same I always tell Azalea—" She broke off suddenly, her face clouding with sadness.

There was a strained silence, which was broken by my mother clearing her throat and saying brightly: "How about a cup of tea? Mrs Chu has shown me how to brew tea Taiwanese style."

I really just wanted to grab Muesli and leave but that seemed too abrupt and rude, so I agreed. I hoped that Mrs Chu would accompany my mother to the kitchen, but the latter insisted that she could manage on her own and left us alone in the living room.

"Um… has Muesli been good?" I asked.

Mrs Chu beamed. "Yes! She is very *gwai*—very good girl." As she spoke, she stroked my little tabby lovingly, running her fingers over Muesli's ears and then sliding them under the cat's jaw to rub her chin. Muesli opened her eyes and gave an appreciative chirrup. Mrs Chu laughed. "She like this face massage. I do for her all the time."

"*Meorrw!*" said Muesli, looking at me meaningfully.

I pulled a face at her behind Mrs Chu's back. *Oh, no, you little minx—don't think you'll be getting twenty-four-hour chin rubs when you come home.*

Mrs Chu turned to me: "Jem-Ma, you speak to Kai?"

I had been dreading the subject and hoped that talking about Muesli would keep her distracted. No such luck. Shifting uncomfortably in my seat, I said:

"Yes, I've spoken to Kai but he's not... He has an alibi for the time of the murder. That means he was somewhere else. He couldn't have done it," I explained.

Mrs Chu relaxed. "You see? I told you—Kai is good boy." She looked at me expectantly. "Last time you say you will find out what happen for me. But now you say cannot be Harry Mah-Kenzee and cannot be Kai... so who is kill my daughter?"

One of your other daughters. The thought jumped into my head and, for a horrified moment, I thought I had voiced it out loud. I looked at Mrs Chu speculatively. I was almost tempted to start asking her about Azalea's relationship with Magnolia. Then I stopped myself. *You're not getting involved anymore, remember?*

Taking a deep breath, I said: "Mrs Chu, I'm really sorry but... I don't think I can do much more. The police are still investigating the case, of course, and I think we need to leave it up to them. I'm... I'm sure they'll find out who killed your daughter."

The words sounded lame and trite—like a weak excuse or fob-off—and I had to brace myself against the dejected look in Mrs Chu's eyes. I was grateful that my mother returned at that moment with a tray of tea. We sat and sipped and made polite conversation for ten minutes, then I rose and said:

"Well, I'd better be getting home now. Thank you for the tea, Mrs Chu. I'll just get Muesli…"

I leaned forwards to pick up my cat, but the little tabby jumped off Mrs Chu's lap and darted out of my reach.

"Muesli! Come here," I admonished, reaching for her again.

"*Meorrw!*" said my tabby cat, twitching her tail and giving me a defiant look. Then she turned her back on me and trotted out of the room, her nose in the air.

"Muesli!" I yelled after her.

Excusing myself to Mrs Chu and my mother, I followed my cat out into the hallway and was just in time to see the tip of her tail disappearing up the stairs.

I stuck my head back into the sitting room. "Mrs Chu—Muesli has just run upstairs. Is it all right if I go up to get her?"

"Ah! Yes, is no problem," said Mrs Chu, making a move to get up. "You want I come?"

"No, no, I'll be fine. I'll just be a few minutes," I assured her, before turning and hurrying up the stairs.

At the top, I paused on the landing to get my bearings. Several open doors led off a short corridor, and I hurried past each, pausing to peer inside for a wayward feline. Most of the doors led to bedrooms, with one opening into an upstairs bathroom and toilet. I hated the thought of trespassing in private bedrooms, and I was glad that I could easily see from each doorway whether Muesli was inside.

The first three were empty, as was the bathroom, but when I reached the master bedroom, I found my quarry at last. Muesli was sprawled across the bedspread of the huge king-sized bed, looking smug. She rolled onto her back when she saw me, showing her white furry belly and giving me a cheeky look.

I glanced around the room. From the clutter of expensive cosmetics and perfume on the dressing table, the designer handbags and other accessories thrown carelessly across chairs and dangling from hooks, and the framed photographs gracing the bedside tables, I guessed that this had been Azalea's bedroom. It looked like someone had started sorting through her personal effects, with the wardrobe door thrown open and a chest of drawers emptied of its contents, which had been piled haphazardly on the bed. Muesli was now lolling next to the pile and, as I watched, she reached out insolently with her claws to pluck at a silk camisole strap. She yanked it towards her, then curled around it and began kicking enthusiastically with her back legs, as if disembowelling prey.

"Hey, stop that!" I cried in horror as I imagined her claws tearing the delicate fabric of the camisole.

I rushed across the room. Muesli waited until I was almost on top of her before uncurling suddenly, letting go of the camisole, and springing to her feet.

"*Meorrw!*"

"Come here," I growled as I made a grab for her.

But she was too fast for me. She jerked sideways, just evading my hands, then leapt across the pile of clothes. Infuriated, I lunged after her, clutching wildly. My awkward position made me lose my balance and I fell sideways into the middle of the clothes, toppling the heap and sending most of it onto the floor.

"Oh bugger!" I fumed.

I shot a dirty look at Muesli, who was now sitting by the doorway to the ensuite, nonchalantly washing a paw.

"Just you wait…" I muttered as I turned my attention back to the clothes.

Getting down on my knees, I began to gather the scattered items from the floor. Thankfully, aside from the silk camisole, most of the pile seemed to be made up of fairly robust items of clothing: T-shirts, sweaters, and hoodies. Nevertheless, I shook each one out, then folded it carefully before replacing it on the bed. I was picking up the last piece when I stopped as I noticed something on the floor next to my foot: a crumpled piece of paper.

There was blurred writing on the paper's surface, and from its ragged appearance, it looked like it had been soaked and then dried again. Probably one of the many pieces of paper which we tend to shove into pockets and then forget about, so that they end up in the washing machine and then get a cycle in the tumble dryer. I wouldn't have thought much of it, except that a few of the blurred words jumped out at me:

... WILL MAKE YOU REGRET...

I hesitated, then picked up the piece of paper and tried to unfold it, handling it gingerly as it was so fragile. It crumbled beneath my fingers even as I tried to spread it out flat, and I cursed under my breath as I lost a large part of the note. But the remaining scrap had enough writing left to show a disturbing message. The ink had faded but I could still read the words:

...YOU TAIWANESE WHORE... GET WHAT YOU DESERVE... THINK YOU LIKE A TASTE OF INDEPENDENCE? ...WILL MAKE YOU REGRET IT...

A sound behind me made me swing around, and I saw Mrs Chu standing in the bedroom doorway, looking quizzically at me.

"Jem-Ma? What you doing?" she asked.

"Oh, Mrs Chu..." I sprang to my feet, my right hand clenching reflexively around the note. Then I winced as I realised what I'd done and felt the note disintegrate completely. *Bugger!* I looked down. Tiny scraps of paper littered the carpet around my feet like ashes. There was no way I could ever hope to piece together that note again.

"You have problem?" asked Mrs Chu in concern, coming towards me.

"Oh no... no, problem," I said, feeling

a bit stupid. "Sorry... um... I was trying to catch Muesli and I knocked the clothes off the bed by mistake. I was just picking them up..."

I realised that I was still clutching the last piece of clothing I had picked up. As I turned to place it onto the top of the pile, I paused and looked at it properly for the first time. It was a bulky, cable-knit sweater in a soft powder blue, but what really held my attention was the fact that it looked awfully familiar.

Isn't this the jumper that I saw Freesia wearing on the night of the murder? And it was also the same jumper I had seen on the figure running away from the kitchen that night, I reminded myself, frowning. I had assumed at first that Freesia and that furtive figure had been one and the same. But if the girl had an alibi—if she had been with Gillian Bennett the entire time—then it couldn't have been her. So could it have been Magnolia instead? But that would mean that Magnolia had to have somehow been wearing her younger sister's jumper...

I realised that Mrs Chu was talking to me and hastily refocused my attention on the Taiwanese lady.

"This morning, I have nothing to do. I think maybe good come tidy up Azalea room," Mrs Chu said with a sigh. She looked sadly at the pile of clothes on the bed. "You know, long time before in China, when somebody die, supposed to be burn their clothes. Even now, still, in the countryside, some place are doing like that. But now in the city, no more follow that old tradition. In Taiwan also, we are doing more modern way. Usually, we give the clothes to charity." She indicated the pile. "Azalea have many nice things. Will be good to give to charity."

"All these clothes are Azalea's?" I said. I held up the blue jumper. "This one as well?"

"Yes, I buy for her."

"Um… do you know if Magnolia borrowed it recently?" I asked.

She looked at me quizzically. "No. Why she borrow?"

"Oh, it's just…" I paused, wondering what to say. I could hardly tell her my suspicions about her daughter and the link to the mysterious figure I'd seen! "I thought I might have seen her wearing it sometime," I said at last.

It was a lame reply since the only time I'd met Magnolia in person was the time my mother and I had come to pay our condolences, and both mother and daughter had been dressed for mourning. Still, thankfully, Mrs Chu didn't question me. Instead, she said:

"No, is not this one. Magnolia has one also."

"She's got one as well?"

Mrs Chu nodded. "I buy for all three

girls," she explained. "Very good sale. Shop is closing down. This material very nice quality, you see? The knitting work very good, so I buy three—one for each daughter."

I stared at her. "So Magnolia has one exactly the same?"

She nodded again, looking puzzled at my interest. "Yes, same like this. Is lucky they have three same size." She paused, then held the jumper out to me. "You like? Can give you Azalea one. You are also similar size."

"Oh, no, no," I said hastily, taking a step back. "But... but thank you very much. It's a beautiful sweater. I just don't really need one... er... I think it would be more appreciated if you donate it to charity," I added, not wanting to hurt her feelings.

"*Meorrw! Meoooooorrw!*"

We looked down to see Muesli rubbing herself against Mrs Chu's ankles, obviously deciding that it was time she was the centre of attention again.

"Oh! Muss-Lee, you are hungry?" Mrs Chu gave Muesli an indulgent look. "I make some Taiwanese sausage for you?"

"That's really kind of you, Mrs Chu, but Muesli and I really must be going home now," I said, quickly bending to scoop up my cat before she could get away again. I held her squirming body firmly against my chest. "Thank you again for looking after her—"

"No, no, is thank you to you," Mrs Chu said. "Is nice to have Muss-Lee. Make me not so sad." She took a deep breath. "Tomorrow, they are giving me Azalea body. They finish autopsy now. Police say I can take her back to Taiwan. For doing funeral."

"Oh... I didn't realise you'd be burying her back there".

"Yes. I already speak to *feng shui*

master in Taiwan. He help me choose best day for funeral. Is very important, so spirit can leave properly."

I left the Chu residence a few minutes later with Muesli safely stowed in her cat carrier. She grumbled loudly as I loaded her into the front basket of my bicycle, but I barely paid attention to her as I mounted and started off home. Although Devlin's admonishing words echoed loudly in my mind, I found it hard not to mull over the mystery of Azalea's murder. In particular, I was thinking of that blue knitted jumper: now that I knew all three daughters had possessed the same garment, it meant that Magnolia *could* have been the mysterious figure I'd seen, after all.

But just because she owns the same jumper and she had good reason to hate Azalea doesn't automatically mean that she's the murderer, I reminded myself. There's still the issue of her alibi...

Chapter Twenty-Seven

I was still mulling things over the next morning as I lay in bed, trying to decide whether to rise. It was a Monday—the only day of the week that the tearoom was closed and my usual day off—and I normally luxuriated in sleeping in late. This morning, however, I found myself wide awake well before my normal alarm and, despite my best efforts, unable to go back to sleep. After tossing and turning for ten minutes, my thoughts constantly returning to the investigation, I gave up and sat up in bed.

Muesli opened one eye from where she was curled at the foot of my bed and regarded me balefully. She was still sulking after discovering that her dinner the previous night was not the smorgasbord of handfed delicacies she had come to expect but a bowl of boring cat food.

"*Meorrw!*" she said irritably, twitching her tail.

"You go back to sleep then, grumpy puss," I said, grinning as I got out of bed.

I'll go out for a walk, I decided. There was always something lovely about being out just after dawn. Quickly, I showered and dressed, then left my cottage. Instead of heading into town, I turned and strolled down to the towpath by the river. This was a section of the famous Thames, although—in typical quaint Oxford fashion—it was known as the "River Isis" for the duration it flowed through the university city. I stood on the towpath and looked back towards Folly Bridge, which spanned the crossing that was probably the original ford over which oxen were driven, and which had given Oxford its name. Everything seemed still and tranquil in the early morning light, with the city just waking up and the sounds of traffic and human activity distant and muted.

The towpath ran along both sides of the river, with the section on the other side, beyond Folly Bridge, leading south to the town of Abingdon. It was a lovely walk along a beautiful stretch of the river made famous by *The Wind in the Willows*, but it would take over three hours and I hesitated, not sure I should devote that much of my one day off to mindless meandering. Finally, I turned and walked in the opposite direction instead, heading west along the winding section of the river, to where it was joined by Castle Mill Stream. This was a much more suburban area, with rows of small terraced houses lining the banks instead of woodlands, hedgerows, and pretty country pubs, but it was still very pleasant. I passed several people cycling and jogging along the path, and as I moved sideways to allow one particularly enthusiastic runner to pass, I did a double take. It was Lincoln Green.

"Gemma!" he said in delight, spotting me at the same time. He came to a stop, huffing and puffing beside me. "Fancy meeting you here."

"Hi, Lincoln—I didn't realise you go running in the mornings?"

"I don't usually. At least, I haven't been, but I've decided it's high time I made more effort to exercise properly. You know the sad cliché of doctors always telling patients to do things that they're guilty of not doing themselves?" he said with a sheepish smile. "It's hard for me to find the time in the evenings, though, as I'm often working late at the hospital, so I thought I'd try to get a run in first thing. Usually I just do a quick jog near home, but one of my colleagues was raving about the towpath down here, so I thought I'd give it a try." He looked at me curiously. "What about you? Is this part of your usual morning routine?"

I gave a laugh. "I wish. Normally at this time, I'm manically rushing around, trying to leave the house in time for work! But Monday's my day off so things are a bit more relaxed. I usually have a long lie-in, but I woke up really early today and just couldn't get back to sleep."

"Busy mind?" said Lincoln sympathetically. "My mother mentioned that your mother told her you've been having some business troubles at the tearoom?"

"Yes, but things have improved, thank goodness. We're not completely back to normal but hopefully getting there. It was—" I hesitated. "Well, it was actually

Azalea and her tea bar that caused a lot of our issues. However, it did force us to pull our socks up, with regards to marketing and some of the other areas we'd been slacking on. We're getting a new, professionally designed website and revamping our menu, and making some other changes that I think will improve a lot of things at the tearoom, so it ended up being a silver lining in the end. Also, since the murder, with the tea bar closed, a lot of the customers have returned—not that I'm glad or anything," I added hurriedly. "It was a terrible thing to happen."

Lincoln's expression sobered. "Yes. It was a dreadful end to that night. It's all everyone's been talking about at the hospital all week, especially following on the heels of all the gossip about Dax's affair."

My ears perked up at the name. *Isn't Magnolia's husband called Dax?* It was an uncommon name. And I recalled the

Old Biddies telling me that he was a doctor at the John Radcliffe Hospital. It had to be the same person.

"Dax?" I asked Lincoln.

"Oh, sorry—Dax Hutton. He's one of the emergency doctors in A&E."

"Are you friendly with him?"

"Well, I wouldn't say we're great mates or anything, but I work with him from time to time. They often have to send people up to us in Intensive Care or call one of us down to A&E to make an assessment."

"What's he like?" I asked.

Lincoln gave a shrug. "He seems a nice enough chap—at work, anyway. But I suppose you never really know what a person is like in their private life, do you? That was a pretty shoddy thing he did, having an affair with his sister-in-law." He glanced sideways at me. "You know that he's married to Azalea Chu's sister? Well, now with Azalea's murder in the news and people joining up the dots, tongues all over the hospital are wagging again."

"Did everyone know about his affair?" I said in surprise. "I wouldn't have thought something like that would be public knowledge, unless a person was having an affair with someone at work."

Lincoln grinned. "Hospitals are a hotbed of gossip. Rumours and hearsay spread through wards faster than a gastro bug. And in this case, even those who didn't know Dax got to know about his affair because of the whole bedpan incident."

"What bedpan incident?"

"His wife turned up at the hospital last month and caused a huge scene. It seems that she'd just found out about the affair and she was absolutely livid: stormed into A&E and started screaming at Dax in front of all the other doctors and nurses and patients. I wasn't there but I heard from a couple of nurses that she launched herself at Dax and started smacking his face and trying to claw his eyes out. It was like something out of a soap opera! They had to call Security in the end to escort her from the premises, but not before she'd grabbed a full bedpan and emptied its contents over Dax's head."

"Ugh!" I winced. "That's disgusting."

"Mmm... but very dramatic and memorable. You can just imagine how that kind of story would get repeated all over the hospital and beyond. People seem to be split between seeing her as a vicious shrew who'd overstepped the mark or cheering her on as a wronged wife who wasn't afraid to stand up for herself and get revenge."

The question is, did Magnolia's thirst for revenge stop at humiliating her husband? Or did she decide to punish her sister too? I wondered. "Have you met Magnolia—Dax's wife?" I asked out loud.

Lincoln shook his head. "I hadn't really met any members of the Chu family before that event at the tea bar last week. Although I *had* heard Jo mention the name a couple of times when she was complaining about her mother pressuring her to befriend the Chu girls. I didn't give it much thought, though. I certainly hadn't made the connection with Dax until all the gossip came out after the murder."

I hesitated, then asked: "Lincoln... um... Dax Hutton went back to the hospital on the night of the murder, didn't he?"

"Yes. I was surprised when I heard that. I didn't think he was rostered on that night," said Lincoln. "In fact, I distinctly remember meeting him as I was leaving the hospital that evening and he told me that he was looking forward to a couple of nights off."

"He was supposed to have been out at a restaurant with Magnolia, but she told the police that he left the meal early as he'd been called back to the hospital."

"Hmm… that's odd. They would have had other doctors working the night shift in A&E and would have been unlikely to bother him."

I frowned. "So in that case, why would he have gone back?"

"Does it matter?" asked Lincoln, looking puzzled. "As far as I understand, he's not a suspect in the murder investigation. The police have confirmed that he was in the hospital at the time of Azalea's murder, so he has a solid alibi."

I didn't answer his question. Instead, I asked, "Lincoln, do you think you could find out when Dax returned to the hospital that night? Is there like a sheet where doctors sign in or something?"

He laughed. "No, we don't clock in and clock out like in a factory, although it certainly feels that way sometimes." He looked at me curiously. "Why do you want to know?

"Well…" I chose my words carefully. "There seems to be a period of time between when Dax Hutton left his wife and when she returned home. Depending on how long that period of time was, she might have been able to do different things."

"What sort of things?"

"Things like murdering her sister in revenge for Azalea sleeping with her husband."

Lincoln's eyebrows shot up. "You think Magnolia could be the murderer?"

I shrugged. "You know what they say: *Hell hath no fury like a woman scorned.*"

Lincoln shook his head in disbelief. "But… murder? Of her own sister? It seems a bit extreme. Have you discussed your suspicions with the police?"

I made a face. "Devlin isn't handling the investigation this time. There's a tosser named Roberts who's the lead investigator on the case and he's completely useless. I mean, he thinks that *I'm* a suspect—can you believe it? He's been having me tailed and wasting time and police resources on all sorts of dead ends."

"Well, if you can't speak to him, surely you can still speak to Devlin? He *is* still in the CID—he could probably check the police interviews and alibi statements for you, even if it's not officially his case."

"The thing is..." I shifted my weight. "Well, Devlin doesn't want me to get involved this time." Quickly, I explained about Devlin's difficult situation with Roberts, as well as his warning to me not to do any investigating on my own.

"So you see, if I ask him, he'll know that I'm still... 'interested'. But I was thinking, since you're at the hospital, maybe you could just ask around and get the information for me...?" I gave Lincoln a disarming smile and looked at him hopefully.

Lincoln looked uncomfortable. "Er... I might be able to, but Gemma... maybe that's not such a good idea."

"Why? Will you get in trouble?"

"Oh no, it's not that. It's just... well, Devlin is a great chap and I have a lot of respect for him. If he thinks you should stay off the case, then... then maybe you should just do what he says."

I stared at him, feeling peeved. I realised that in the past, whenever things had been difficult with Devlin, I had always been able to go to Lincoln and rely on him to act as my "alternative knight in shining armour". He'd always good-humouredly gone along with my plans and enthusiastically participated in any sleuthing I proposed. I'd never expected to meet a day when Lincoln would take Devlin's side of things!

This is what happens when you put two English men in drag and let them loose with a couple of beers, I thought wryly, recalling the raucous male bonding session I'd witnessed at the tea bar that night. Now the old potential rivals had turned into new best friends!

"I'm sorry, Gemma," said Lincoln awkwardly. "I'd like to help, really, but in this case, I really think that you're best to follow Devlin's advice and leave things well alone."

I sighed as I watched Lincoln jog away a few minutes later. Maybe he was right. After all, I'd told myself that I wouldn't get involved in the case anymore, and I had admonished the Old Biddies for wanting to do exactly what I was trying to ask Lincoln to do now. It was frustrating and it went against all my instincts, but maybe I really had to let things go this time.

Chapter Twenty-Eight

I took a deep breath and reluctantly pushed open the door to the police station. This wasn't what I'd envisaged myself doing on my day off. Still, after a restless morning trying to force my thoughts away from the Azalea Chu murder, I'd finally decided that I couldn't just forget it and get on with my life. If I didn't do something, I'd never have any peace. And since I couldn't do any investigating on my own, the only other option was to swallow my pride—and my frustrations—and take my suspicions to Inspector Roberts.

"Well, well, if it isn't 'O'Connor's Girl'," the duty sergeant greeted me with an affectionate grin. He was a regular at the front desk and was my biggest fan—ever since I'd brought in a batch of scones and shared them around the police station. "If you're looking for Devlin, I'm afraid you've missed him, luv. He left for Blackbird Leys about half an hour ago."

"No, actually, I was hoping to speak to Inspector Roberts."

The duty sergeant pulled a face. "What d'you want to speak to *him* for?"

I gave him a rueful smile. "Believe me, if there was any way I could avoid it, I would."

The duty sergeant pointed down the corridor. "He should be in the CID offices. You know the way—" Then he broke off and pulled another face. "Actually, if you don't mind, I think you'd better wait here while I ring through and announce you officially. Probably not a good idea just to wander in like you normally do. Roberts is a big stickler for following all the protocols, if you know what I mean, and he's been on the warpath lately."

"Oh, trust me, I do," I said. "And that's no problem at all. I'm perfectly happy to play everything strictly by the rulebook."

By the time I was installed behind a table in a cramped, airless interview room, with Inspector Roberts facing me on the other side and a tape recorder activated between us, I was really beginning to appreciate just how much leeway I was normally given. Whenever I'd had to deal with other officers in Devlin's unit, they'd usually greeted me with the friendly deference of a fellow colleague, and the few times I'd been in the interview rooms in the past, it had always felt more like a casual chat than an interrogation. Now, I sat upright in the hard chair, trying not to fidget as

Roberts deliberately let the silence stretch between us. I had informed him, as soon as he'd led me into the room, that I had important information about Azalea Chu's murder, but instead of responding, Roberts had simply sat back and glowered at me.

I knew what he was doing. It was the age-old technique of unnerving your opponent by purposefully not saying anything and letting the silence become oppressive. Humans are hardwired to reach out, to communicate, and for most people, the urge to fill the conversational gap often meant that they blurted out things they didn't intend to.

Well, he's going to find that that old trick won't work with me, I thought, crossing my arms and leaning back in my chair in a determinedly casual pose.

Roberts scowled as the silence stretched on, then finally fiddled with the thick folder he had brought in with him and pulled out something which he slapped on the table between us. My heart sank as I saw what it was: the front page of the local paper with Mark Scott's article about Azalea Chu's murder and me.

"I suppose I should be honoured to be paid a visit by the 'tearoom sleuth with an enviable reputation for solving cases faster than the police'," he said in bitterly sarcastic tones.

I took a deep breath, reminding myself not to be baited by him, and said in a cool voice: "I came because I have some important information about Azalea Chu's murder, which may help your investigation."

"Oh really? You think I need help, do you? Well, let me tell you, Miss Rose, I don't need your 'freelance consultant services'." He nearly spat the words.

I made a sound of irritation. "Look, I never said any of those things in that article, okay? You should know by now that the media often take liberties with the truth. Mark Scott, the journalist, made most of that up, just so he could milk a bit of melodrama. But I'm genuinely here because I have some information which may be helpful." When he made no response, I asked bluntly: "Who have you got as your top suspect for Azalea's murder?"

Roberts's lips curled back in a sneer. "That's none of your business! I hope this isn't some ploy to try and fish for information. Let me tell you, whatever you may be used to with O'Connor, I'm a different—"

"I'm not fishing," I said impatiently. "I'm asking because I think I know who the murderer is and I need to know if you suspect them as well."

"Oh, you know who the murderer is, do you?" said Roberts with a derisive smile. "What did you do—read it in your daily horoscope?"

"No, I worked it out using logic!" I snapped. Then I took a deep breath, reminding myself not to let him get to me, and said in a calmer voice: "I think it's Magnolia, the middle sister."

"Magnolia?" Roberts gave a bark of laughter. "She's got a solid alibi. We've checked her whereabouts on the night of the murder: she was out having dinner at a restaurant in Oxford with her husband, and then her babysitter confirmed that she went home afterwards."

"Yes, but she said her husband left early to go back to the hospital," I persisted. "So depending on when he left, there could be a gap of time in which Magnolia's movements are unaccounted for. Do you know what time he left the restaurant? Come to that, when did *she* leave? Have you interviewed the restaurant staff?"

"I don't need you to tell me how to do my job!" growled Roberts. "And yes, I did know that Dr Hutton left the meal early and returned to the hospital." He leaned forwards suddenly, narrowing his eyes at me. "What I'm more interested in is how *you* knew."

"What do you mean?" I asked, surprised at the sudden change in subject.

"That interview with Magnolia Hutton was confidential information. So unless you had access to the case files, how could you have known details like what she told us about her husband's early departure?" he demanded. "It was O'Connor, wasn't it? He's been snooping in my files and passing on information to you, hasn't he? *Hasn't he*?"

"What? No!" I cried, alarmed at the way he had jumped to the wrong conclusions. "This has nothing to do with Devlin! I haven't discussed the case with him at all!"

"Then how did you get this

information? How could you know what Magnolia told the police about her alibi?"

"I... I have other sources," I faltered, knowing how ridiculous that sounded but not knowing what else to say.

"'*Other sources*'?" Roberts snarled. "What do you take me for? Do you think this is a Hollywood movie? If you think it's funny to muck me around—"

"No! I'm serious... I... the four old ladies that I'm friends with—well, they have a lot of contacts across Oxfordshire, and they managed to get information about Magnolia's interview, including the details of her alibi."

"Do you expect me to believe that a gaggle of old-age pensioners can get access to confidential police information just because they like to gossip with their friends?" said Roberts scathingly.

"But it's true!" I cried. "Mabel Cooke and the others—they're well known for their amazing ability to find out the most obscure information through their network of family and friends. I know it sounds crazy, but if you were more familiar with them, you'd know that—"

"You're right, it sounds crazy. What's more, it sounds like a pack of lies made up by someone desperate to hide the truth: which is that you got this information from O'Connor. Don't try to deny it. Lying won't protect him now. I'm going to make sure that the DCC and the rest of the committee know exactly what O'Connor's been up to—"

"No! Please, Devlin had nothing to do with this—I promise!" I gasped, horrified at how the situation was unravelling. "I'm telling you, this has nothing to do with him. Devlin hasn't been involved in any way nor done anything to help me—" I stopped short as I suddenly recalled Harry McKenzie's complaint and Devlin covering up for me. *Oh my God, if Roberts should ever find out about that...*

Taking a deep breath, I said in a

trembling voice: "Look, I… I admit I've been doing a bit of… er… investigating on my own. But honestly, that was all off my own bat and had nothing to do with Devlin. I promise!"

Roberts didn't seem to be listening. He had risen and said, in a cold voice: "This interview is terminated"—before turning off the recorder and going to open the interview room door. He looked at me pointedly.

I rose from the chair, gathering the shreds of my dignity, and walked past him with my head held high. I kept my expression neutral as I allowed him to escort me out of the station, but inside I was seething with anger and despair. I couldn't believe that I had gone to Roberts with my suspicions, just as everyone had recommended, and not only had I not succeeded in convincing the police to take Magnolia seriously as a suspect, but I'd given Roberts new ammunition with which to attack Devlin!

Finally, I raised my head and realised that I'd been walking aimlessly along the pavement for a while. The police station was far behind me and I was almost in the centre of Oxford. I paused at the side of Cornmarket Street, the pedestrianised shopping strip that ran through the heart of the city, my mind a mess of thoughts and emotions. It was just past noon and the university city was heaving with tourists and office workers out for their lunch break. I supposed that I ought to go and get some lunch, but I found that my appetite had deserted me.

As I stood there undecided, I glanced up idly, tracing the tops of the buildings that were visible to me from this part of the city. I could see some of the famous spires and towers that gave Oxford its iconic skyline, including the distinctive square shape of Pendlebury College's Saxon tower.

Pendlebury. Freesia Chu's college...

My thoughts drifted back to that day when I had inadvertently eavesdropped outside the youngest Chu daughter's room. The snatches of conversation I'd overheard came back to me, especially Freesia's shrill voice:

"... don't tell me you're not supposed to speak ill of the dead... She was a witch and she didn't care how much she hurt others as long as she won... karma is real, you know... maybe Azalea got what she deserved..."

But it was the other voice—Professor Bennett's—that I found myself focusing on now. She'd been struggling to get a word in edgewise and her calmer, lower tone had been hard to hear compared with Freesia's histrionic outbursts, but I did remember hearing her say: *"...shouldn't have been there... if no one else saw, then hopefully the police won't suspect..."*

Now I pondered those words. What had she been talking about? Or rather, *who* had she been talking about? Who "shouldn't have been there"? I'd assumed at first that it was Freesia she was referring to, but now, for the first time, I wondered if she could have been talking about Magnolia instead. And what if Freesia's distress hadn't been for herself, as I'd assumed, but rather for her sister? What if she suspected that Magnolia was involved in the murder and was scared of the police finding out? Had she taken advantage of her tutor's soft spot for her and asked Gillian Bennett to cover up for Magnolia, to lie to the police?

I felt a quickening of excitement. *I need to speak to Gillian Bennett again*, I thought, turning in the direction of Pendlebury College. Then I paused as I thought of the recent scene with Roberts at the police station. Going to speak to the Oxford don now would be seen as exactly what I *wasn't* supposed to be doing: "meddling" in the investigation.

What does it matter? I thought resentfully. *I tried to do the "right" thing but all I got for my troubles was to make things worse! Roberts is going to believe the worst of me and Devlin, and jump to the worst conclusions, no matter what I do!*

Well, if I was going to be hanged for a sheep as for a lamb, then I might as well make it bloody worthwhile!

Chapter Twenty-Nine

This time I had no trouble getting into Pendlebury College. The friendly porter I'd met the previous time waved to me as I entered the gates and obligingly directed me to Professor Bennett's rooms. Although one of the founding principles of Oxford University was having its faculty live among the students, in modern times, members of the teaching faculty and governing body often did not live in their affiliated colleges (bar the head of the college, who had a dedicated residence within the college walls). But perhaps because she was single and childless, Gillian

Bennett was one of the exceptions. She occupied a suite of rooms just off the main quad and, as I made my way there, I hurriedly rehearsed what I'd planned to ask her. When I knocked on her door, however, I was disappointed to find that there was no answer. The sound of footsteps made me turn around and I found a young female student hovering behind me. She was holding a sheaf of papers in one hand and looking at me impatiently.

"I don't think she's in," I said, indicating the closed door. "I knocked but there's no answer."

"Oh, Prof Bennett never locks her door," said the girl, stepping past me to reach for the doorknob. "She says her door is always open to us and we're welcome to go in and wait for her, or leave her a note, if she's not there."

She strode boldly into the room, and, after a moment's hesitation, I followed. It was a stereotypical Oxford don's room, with dark wood-panelled walls, shelves bulging with textbooks, and faded armchairs arranged facing each other in front of the fireplace, ready for the next tutorial. In the corner was an old-fashioned mahogany pedestal desk, cluttered with books and papers, and the student tossed her essay onto a teetering pile atop its surface before strolling out again.

After she'd gone, I hesitated, then slid into one of the armchairs. I was instantly hit by a wave of déjà vu: how many times had I sat in a chair like this one, clutching my returned essay and waiting nervously to hear if my rushed efforts had managed to produce a coherent enough treatise to earn my tutor's approval?

Together with Cambridge, Oxford was one of the last places in the world to still embrace the "tutorial system". This meant that—instead of being taught in classes and seminars—each week, students were assigned a topic and expected to research and write an essay of several thousand words on the subject. There were still lectures, of course, and, for those studying medicine and the sciences, practical sessions in laboratories, but the weekly tutorials formed the backbone of student education.

Thus, once a week, you met one on one with your tutor to discuss and dissect what you had learnt in the course of your research and writing. It was an idiosyncratic way of teaching, where the aim was to foster "independent critical thinking" and to encourage the ability to consider all opposing arguments on their own merits, and then form your own conclusions. *There is no black and white, we were told—only shades of grey—and it's important to understand and appreciate them all.*

I had to admit that at eighteen, I didn't have much appreciation for the higher aims of the educational approach at Oxford. My weekly essay assignment simply seemed a tiresome burden amongst the more fun activities of student life, from the clubs and societies to the parties and socialising. And unlike some of my more disciplined and organised fellow students, who carefully spread out their workload across the week and always had their essays completed well before the deadline, I usually ended up partaking in the time-honoured tradition of the "Oxford essay crisis".

I could still vividly recall the numerous times I'd sat down the night before my essay was due, brimming with confidence over my ability to read twenty-three academic articles and five textbooks (oh, and maybe that research reference I'd borrowed from the library as well)—in time to dash off two thousand words of thoughtful dissertation before sunrise. Of course, what usually happened was that I spent the next sixteen hours in a state of jittery panic, guzzling gallons of coffee whilst madly typing a hopefully-not-too-obvious regurgitation of the handy summary I'd found in one of the textbooks... I would then emerge, pale and bleary eyed, at dawn, to make my way to the tutorial, only to find, to my squirming horror, that the very textbook which I'd plagiarised—*ahem*, I mean, which had inspired my essay—had, in fact, been written by my tutor, the country's leading expert on the topic...

All those memories washed over me now as I sat in that sagging armchair, and despite the fact that nearly a decade had passed, it all felt so real that I almost expected my tutor to walk in any minute and ask if I'd like a glass of sherry! Feeling a bit silly, I sprang up from the chair and crossed over to the desk. There was an empty notepad lying on the central leather blotter and I seized this on an impulse. Picking up a pen, I began scribbling a note:

Dr Professor Bennett,

I need to speak to you urgently regarding Azalea Chu's murder and what you told the police about that night. Can you give me a ring asap? I can pop back to Pendlebury to see you any time that's convenient later today/tonight. Thank you.

I tore the page out of the notepad and read it over again, then signed my name and added my mobile number. Then I hesitated, wondering if I should try to find an envelope to put it in. I turned slightly to look around the side of the desk, then gave a muffled scream as my body brushed up against another.

I gasped and whirled around to find a young woman standing behind me. It was Freesia Chu.

"Oh God! You scared me to death," I said, clutching my chest.

She said nothing, but just continued to stand there, and I shifted uneasily under the intense scrutiny of those black, almond-shaped eyes.

How long has she been here? I wondered. The door to the rooms had been left open and she had come in so noiselessly that I hadn't heard her at all. *Did she see me writing the note? Had she been reading it over my shoulder?*

"Um… hi, Freesia." I stammered. "I was looking for your tutor but… er… Professor Bennett doesn't seem to be here, so I was just leaving her a note."

She made no response, her face remaining impassive, her eyes still watching me.

I cleared my throat and said, with an attempt at a breezy smile: "Well… um… anyway, I suppose I'll catch her later…"

I realised that I was still holding the

note in my hands and agonised briefly over what to do. The last thing I wanted now was to place it on Gillian Bennett's desk, with Freesia Chu standing there watching me. On the other hand, not leaving it would be even more conspicuous. Finally, I settled on a compromise, carefully folding the note over several times before tucking it under a corner of the leather blotter. Then I murmured a goodbye and hurriedly left the room, feeling Freesia's eyes boring into my back until I had turned the corner out of sight. I breathed a sigh of relief when at last I stepped back out into the quad. *Bloody hell, that girl is seriously creepy*, I thought as I made my way out of the college.

With nothing else to do, I was forced to return home, despite the nagging feeling of "unfinished business" and a sense of ominous foreboding that I couldn't quite shake off. I arrived back at my cottage to find that Muesli had finally roused herself from my bed and was downstairs in the kitchen, staring balefully at the cat food in her bowl.

"*Meorrw!*" she said as soon as she saw me. "*Meorrwwww!*"

"It's no use complaining. You're not going to get handmade sushi or Taiwanese sausage or any other fancy gourmet food... so you'd better get used to it," I told her irritably.

Muesli made a noise that sounded uncannily like "*humph!*" and stalked out of the kitchen with offended dignity. I was about to follow when my phone rang. I dug it out of my pocket and glanced at the screen: it was Devlin. My heart skipped a beat—not in romantic anticipation, like it normally did, but rather with nervous apprehension.

"H-hello?"

"Gemma."

Instantly, I knew from the tone of his

voice that things were bad.

"Er… hi, Devlin… how… how're things?" I asked brightly.

"You tell me," he said in deceptively soft tones. "I've just had a call from the Super saying that the DCC would like to see me tomorrow… to discuss concerns raised about my code of conduct, ethics, and professionalism. It seems that Inspector Roberts has put in a report detailing how I'd 'illicitly accessed files on the Azalea Chu case and shared confidential information with members of the public, in particular with my girlfriend, who has since used that information to take action in ways which could seriously jeopardise the murder investigation'."

I bit back a groan. "Devlin, I can explain. It's just Roberts being a jerk. I went to see him this morning to tell him my suspicions about Azalea's sister and he immediately jumped to conclusions! He wouldn't believe me when I told him that I found out about the sister's alibi from the Old Biddies and their sources. He thought that I must have got the information from you. I *told* him that you had nothing to do with it but he just refused to listen—"

"Why did you even go to speak to him?" demanded Devlin. "You know what Roberts is like. You know that he was just looking for any excuse to discredit me—you practically handed him my head on a plate!"

"I was only doing what everyone kept telling me to do!" I said defensively. "You all kept telling me to let the police do the investigating, so when I had information that could be crucial to the case, I went to share it with Roberts."

"I wasn't telling you to share your theories and deductions with the police—I was telling you to stay completely out of it!" said Devlin. "You shouldn't have had anything 'crucial' to share with Roberts, because you shouldn't have even been involved in trying to gather information in the first place."

"Don't be ridiculous!" I cried, feeling my own temper rising. "Police appeal to the public for information all the time! Am I supposed to ignore something which could help the case, just so I don't step on Roberts's fragile ego?"

"It's one thing if police put out a public appeal for information but that wasn't the case here. Roberts didn't ask for public help; he patently doesn't want anybody muscling in on his patch, and then you waltz in there and start telling him what to do—"

"I didn't tell him what to do," I said indignantly. "All I did was urge him to seriously consider Magnolia, Azalea's sister, as a suspect because of the holes in her alibi."

"You should have trusted that the police *would* investigate her and left things well alone," snapped Devlin.

"But what if Roberts is so bloody incompetent that he *doesn't* investigate her properly? What if he ends up totally missing all the vital clues?"

"You know what your problem is, Gemma? You don't trust anybody, and you're so uptight about micromanaging everything that you always have to stick your own oar in—"

"That's not true!" I cried angrily. "This isn't about micromanaging anything. This is about not letting a murderer get away! You used to care about that, Devlin O'Connor—you used to want to seek the truth at all costs, remember? Or do you care more about playing politics now just to get a promotion?"

"I care about keeping my job so that I can continue to seek justice on behalf of those who need it," said Devlin in a coldly furious voice. "Sometimes you have to lose a battle to win the war,

Gemma. I can do more good to mitigate the incompetence of people like Roberts if I remain in the CID."

"What? What are you talking about?"

"I'm talking about the fact that my meeting with the DCC tomorrow is to discuss the recommendation that I be suspended from all duties, pending an internal investigation into my integrity as a police officer."

I gasped. "No! They can't do that!"

"They can and they will, unless the DCC can be convinced otherwise," said Devlin grimly. "Your actions could mean that I never investigate another case again."

Chapter Thirty

I felt sick after ending the call with Devlin—sick with dread and worry for him, but also sick with anger and indignation for myself, and most of all, filled with a burning resentment towards Inspector Roberts. It seemed so wrong and unfair that he should be able to behave so badly and get away with it!

I moved restlessly through the house, trying not to think about the recent call but unable to really concentrate on anything else. I tried sitting down to deal with a backlog of emails, endeavoured to tackle a list of neglected bills and paperwork, and made a half-hearted attempt to sort through a pile of laundry, but gave up each time after a few minutes. Finally, I wandered into the kitchen, thinking that perhaps a cup of tea and something to eat might soothe my troubled emotions. I normally brought home some of the unused food from the tearoom each day, and I opened the pantry now, searching hopefully for a leftover scone or an odd bun. But there was nothing in the bread bin except a few lonely crumbs. I sighed. If there was ever a time I needed the comfort of home baking, it was now!

Then, as my eyes spied an old packet of flour shoved behind the bread bin, I perked up. Why did I have to rely on leftovers? Why couldn't I make some fresh scones myself? Okay, I knew I wasn't the best at baking, but I'd watched Dora make scones dozens of times and I'd even helped her on occasion. Surely it wasn't that hard?

Eagerly, I began to scour my kitchen for the necessary ingredients. One of the great things about scones was that they only required basic pantry items to make: just flour, butter, sugar, salt, milk, eggs and baking powder. I had everything... except eggs. I stood looking at my assembled ingredients on the counter and debating what to do. Of course, I could just make scones without eggs—many modern recipes omitted them, claiming that they made the taste too rich—but for some reason, I felt a need to cling to the traditional way of doing things, as if this insistence on baking scones "properly" could somehow help the mess in the other parts of my life.

So I found myself, fifteen minutes later, browsing the shelves of the nearest supermarket. Half my mind was absently reading the labels on the different cartons of free-range eggs whilst the other half was still ruminating over the call with Devlin, still feeling distressed and infuriated despite my best efforts. I'd just finally selected a carton when I heard a familiar voice behind me.

"Well, hullo there, Gemma—how nice to see you!"

I turned to find Mr Prendergast standing in the aisle behind me. He was dressed in an old-fashioned mackintosh, with a grey felt hat on his head and a newspaper tucked under one arm

"Hello, Mr Prendergast," I said, pleased to see a friendly face and keen to have someone distract my thoughts. "I didn't realise you lived in Oxford. I thought you lived near Meadowford-on-Smythe."

"I do, but I'm in town for a few days to stay with a friend," he replied, adding with a twinkle in his eye: "But I would still have been sitting at that tearoom of yours this morning if it weren't closed today." He threw a rueful glance at the newspaper tucked under his arm. "In fact, I'm sure I would have fared better with today's crossword if I could have had my daily cuppa and a nice bit of baking from the Little Stables' menu. I tried a café in the Covered Market but it wasn't quite up to snuff."

I laughed. "Well, I'm glad we're ahead of the competition, in the cruciverbal stakes, if nothing else."

"Oh, you're ahead of them in more ways than one, my dear," declared Mr Prendergast. "By the by, do you remember the clue that had us stumped the other day? The original clue was: '*Nosiness victim, visual sweep*', two words. We worked out that the first word was 'cat' but we couldn't think of the second. Well, I finally thought of the answer: 'cat scan'."

"Oh... duh!" I said, giving myself a mock smack to the head. "Yes, of course, to scan something is to do a quick visual sweep. Why didn't I think of that?"

"It took me a few days," said Mr Prendergast, chuckling. "I'm grappling with a new one now, though. I don't suppose you have any idea what this might be referring to?" He paused to unfold his newspaper and read out loud: "*British panacea, metaphorical facial humiliation (3, 3).*"

"*British panacea, metaphorical facial humiliation...*" I repeated slowly.

"Yes. It's two words. Three letters each."

I thought for a moment. "A 'panacea' is a cure for all ills, isn't it?"

He nodded. "Yes, a remedy for all problems. It comes from the Latin word which means 'all-healing'. In fact, Panacea was the Greek goddess of healing."

"What's a British solution for all problems?" I asked, half talking to myself. Then I chuckled suddenly and looked up at him. "Ooh... do you think it could be 'tea'? Isn't that what people always tease the British about—that we think everything can be fixed with a cup of tea?"

"Tea?" He raised his eyebrows. "By Jove, you could be right! I kept thinking of medical terms and trying to come up with a British-invented cure, but your lateral-thinking approach is much better. Yes, 'tea' would fit. But that leaves the second word once again... Teabag? Teacup? Teapot—oh no, those would all be counted as one word. In any case, none of those match '*metaphorical facial humiliation*'."

There was silence as we both pondered the clue.

Finally, Mr Prendergast gave a sigh and said, "Ah well, I'll keep thinking about it. But thank you for your help, my dear—at least you've set me on the right track!"

"I'll keep working on it too," I promised. "We can compare notes the next time we meet."

He smiled and tipped his hat to me, then continued on his way. It was only a short encounter but I found that I left the supermarket a few minutes later in much better spirits myself. Aside from the pleasure of Mr Prendergast's company, the small victory over one of the crossword clues felt like a rare positive achievement, after all the frustrations and antagonism I'd been dealing with in the past few days. I had even been able to forget, for a short while, all about Azalea Chu's murder and Devlin's anger and predicament at the police station.

When I arrived back at my cottage, I met Muesli's grumpy "*Meorrw!*" with a cheerful "Hello", then went into the kitchen. But before I could start unloading my shopping, there was a knock on my front door. I opened it to find the journalist Mark Scott on my doorstep. He was clutching a foolscap folder bulging with papers under one arm and holding a voice recorder in the other hand.

"Miss Rose!" he said brightly. "I've been hanging around hoping to catch you and I just saw you come home..." He leaned forwards, flashing his teeth in a persuasive smile, and raised the voice recorder to my face. "I hear you've been busy working on the Azalea Chu case. Any chance of a few sound bites?"

"I can't believe you have the cheek to ask that, after that article you wrote about me," I said, looking at him in disgust.

"Aww, come on... you can't say I didn't make you sound good in that article," he said, grinning unashamedly.

"I don't need you to make me sound good," I said tartly. "I need you to report facts accurately. I never said half those things you claimed I said in the article!"

Scott shrugged. "Hey—sometimes, in the interests of good writing, you need to take a bit of creative licence, you know? Besides, the *gist* of everything I said was true, and that's what's important, isn't it?"

I pressed my lips together, refusing to engage with him.

"Come on…" he wheedled. "If you give me some 'real' comments, that means I won't be obliged to… er… get 'creative' again, eh?"

"I have nothing to say to you," I said, making as if to shut the door.

"Wait—" Scott put out a hand to stop me and, as he did so, the folder slipped from under his arm and fell to the ground, spilling its contents everywhere.

"Ahhh… bugger!" he growled, bending down to start the laborious process of collecting all the scattered papers.

I stood watching him for a moment, then—unable to help myself—I sighed and crouched down to help him. It was mostly sheets of scribbled notes and printed text, together with a variety of newspaper and magazine clippings and some photographs. These seemed to be mostly of Azalea Chu, I realised, and as I picked one up, I looked at it curiously.

It showed Azalea—a much younger, fresh-faced Azalea—standing in a crowd of people, all gathered behind a picket fence. From their ages, clothes, and hairstyles, I guessed that they were all students. Azalea was standing with two other girls of similar age, and they all looked to be chanting something. One of the other girls was holding up a sign which read "FREEDOM FOR COUNTRIES SEEKING INDEPENDENCE!" whilst the other girl held up two fingers in a peace sign and Azalea jubilantly waved a flag high above her head. I frowned as I looked closer. The flag looked familiar—

I remembered seeing a miniature version proudly adorning the mantelpiece in Azalea's house, each time I'd been to visit Mrs Chu.

"What flag is that?" I asked Mark Scott.

He paused in the act of picking up a sheaf of papers and glanced at the photograph. "That? It's the flag of Taiwan." He smiled—the first genuine smile I'd seen him give—and said, with nostalgic affection in his voice, "Azalea was fiercely patriotic, you know. The whole Taiwanese identity thing was really important to her; she would start arguing with anyone in the street on the subject. It's how we met, actually. I was writing for one of the university student papers then, and I was doing a story on student protests... Anyway, Azalea marched right up to me and demanded that I write a piece for her." He shook his head, chuckling. "It was a bloody cheek but I couldn't help admiring her *chutzpah*. We ended up at the pub, talking for hours, and we were friends ever since. We used to meet up every so often and..."

He continued talking but I was no longer listening. Instead, I was staring at the photograph and thinking about his comment about Azalea being "fiercely patriotic". My mind jumped backwards to that meal I'd had with Devlin and my parents, when my mother had first mentioned her new friend Mrs Chu and explained her background. I recalled my father explaining the political controversy surrounding the lady's native island:

"*...there is still the thorny question of its status as an independent nation. China claims that it is a renegade territory, whereas Taiwan considers itself a separate country...*"

Then I thought back to the night before and the crumpled note I'd found in Azalea's bedroom. It had contained menacing words, including "Taiwanese whore" and a taunt about "independence".

I interrupted Scott: "Listen, do you know if Azalea ever received threats because of her political activities?"

Chapter Thirty-One

Mark Scott looked at me in surprise. "Yeah, actually, she did. Several times, in fact. She could be pretty vocal about Taiwan, you know, especially on social media, and she got a fair amount of backlash. In fact, she received several anonymous notes in the past few weeks, warning her to shut up on the subject, but she always just laughed them off... Why?" His eyes gleamed. "Are you thinking there might be a political motivation for her murder?"

"No, no," I said hastily. "I was just... er... curious. Um... anyway, I've got some shopping I need to put in the fridge so... if you'll excuse me..."

I managed to duck back into my cottage and shut the door in his face before he could stop me. Then I turned and leaned my back against the door, trying not to listen to Scott's pleading and cajoling on the other side. Finally, he gave up and left. I blew out a sigh of relief and tilted my head back, resting it against the door and staring up at the ceiling.

Have I been looking in the wrong direction all this time? I had always thought that Azalea had been murdered for "personal" reasons: a thirst for revenge, perhaps, or an act of emotional retribution, but what if I had been completely misled? What if there had been a *political* motive behind her murder?

Mr Wang—Kai's father—had been opposed to his son marrying Azalea and, from all accounts, had intensely disliked his daughter-in-law. I had just assumed that it was a personality clash, but now I wondered if her political activities could have been the bigger reason. In fact, now that I thought about it, I remembered the night that the Old Biddies and I had sneaked into the dental clinic, and inadvertently eavesdropped on a heated exchange between son and father. I'd overheard Kai say in English: "...*even if she was an angel, you would have hated her! And for such a stupid reason... Not everyone cares about politics...*"

But his father obviously did. For a man with Mr Wang's social status and connections back in China, having such a daughter-in-law could have meant serious loss of "face"—something that was incredibly important to the Chinese.

But surely not important enough to commit murder? I wondered incredulously. Even as I asked myself the question, I was already thinking of how easy it would have been for someone of Mr Wang's wealth and power to organise the killing. Had he hired thugs to try and intimidate Azalea with threatening messages? And then, when she ignored the warnings, had he decided to move on to murder? It seemed too far-fetched, too ridiculous—and yet it was well known that people could feel extreme emotions, commit extreme acts in the name of their political beliefs...

So did that mean that the furtive figure I'd glimpsed through the kitchen windows had been a hired killer? I frowned. *But what about the blue jumper?* Well, if Mrs Chu could buy three of the same items, who was to say someone else couldn't have bought the same item from the same shop? True, it was odd, but maybe by some mad coincidence, the contract killer hired by Mr Wang *had* gone to the same sale and bought the same jumper...

I sighed and pushed away from the door. My head felt like it was swimming with all these new theories and possibilities, but meanwhile, I reminded myself, I still had fresh milk and butter sitting on the kitchen counter, waiting to be put in the fridge.

I walked back into the kitchen and stopped short as I saw my phone sitting on the counter. Belatedly, I realised that I'd forgotten to take it out with me. I glanced at the screen. There was a missed call and one message. Curious, I listened to the voicemail. It was Professor Bennett and she sounded uncharacteristically flustered:

"Hello, Gemma—this is Gillian. Gillian Bennett. I'm sorry to have missed you. I didn't return to my rooms until just now. I'm happy to meet but I'm afraid it can't be tonight as I've just found a message left by Freesia Chu. The poor girl sounds very distressed about something and

says she needs to see me urgently, so I have to find her and I might need to spend some time with her. Perhaps it would be better if we arranged to meet tomorrow?"

I sighed. *Oh well, I suppose one more day won't matter.* Putting my phone back down, I began to unload my shopping. Aside from the eggs, I'd also picked up some more milk and fresh butter, a loaf of bread, a couple of packets of instant soup, and a bar of chocolate. Muesli wove herself between my legs as I stowed things away in the pantry.

"Meorrw?" she said, looking meaningfully at her food bowl which she had finally, grudgingly, emptied. *"Meorrw?"*

"No, you're not getting any more food until suppertime," I said sternly. "I think you've doubled your weight since going to stay with Mrs Chu."

"*Meeeeeorrw!*" said Muesli petulantly. She stretched up and batted at the egg carton which I'd placed temporarily at the edge of the counter as I turned to open the fridge door.

"Oi! Stop that!" I admonished, grabbing the carton. "You horror! You could have knocked that over and then all the eggs would have smashed on the floor! And on you too," I added. "Yes, you're standing right beneath it, and half the eggs would probably have cracked over your head. You would have ended up with egg on your face litera—" I broke off suddenly.

Egg on your face... to be embarrassed... humiliated... 'metaphorical facial humiliation'... I gasped. "Oh my God! That's the answer to the second clue! It's 'egg'!" I whooped. "I solved it, Muesli, I solved it!"

"*Meorrw?*" said Muesli, looking quizzically at me.

I calmed down, feeling a bit silly. "Yes, well… so the whole answer to Mr Prendergast's last clue is 'tea egg'."

How weird! I thought. What a strange coincidence that that term should be in the crossword. I'd heard of the Baader-Meinhof phenomenon—when something new you'd never experienced or heard of before suddenly starts cropping up everywhere, straight after you've just encountered it. It was supposed to be a "frequency illusion"—a sort of cognitive bias, caused by your brain noticing a "new" thing more, now that it can recognise it, and thereby giving the false impression that you're encountering it more often. Still, even knowing that, it was hard not to feel like it was some kind of deliberate weird coincidence. I'd never really heard of this unique Chinese snack before, and now, suddenly, I was tasting them at Mrs Chu's house and finding them featured in a random crossword!

Then I stopped, staring blindly down at the carton of eggs I was holding in my hands, whilst my mind's eye saw a different scene entirely: the kitchen at the Yin-Yang Tea Bar on the night I had found Azalea's body... the gleaming stainless-steel surfaces, the carefully ordered condiments and food supplies... the central island with the various pots and bowls, filled with meat, vegetables, and tofu soaking in fragrant marinades... and one pot filled with eggs. I hadn't paid much attention at the time—the discovery of Azalea's body had wiped all other thoughts from my mind—but now that I recalled the scene, I realised that the pot had held *tea eggs*. Yes, I could see it clearly in my mind's eye now: the beautiful, delicate marbled pattern on the surfaces of the hard-boiled eggs marinating in the fragrant tea broth...

Then my memory jumped to that day

in Mrs Chu's kitchen and Magnolia answering her mother's enquiry about whether Azalea was including tea eggs in her restaurant menu:

"No, Ma, she hasn't made any tea eggs at the tea bar. She was too busy. She said maybe next month…"

My thoughts began racing. If Magnolia had been the murderer, she would have been in the kitchen that night and she would have seen the pot of tea eggs on the central island. She couldn't have failed to—they were right next to where Azalea had collapsed. Which meant that she had to have known that Azalea was already cooking tea eggs at the restaurant… which meant that she wouldn't have answered her mother as she had. Not unless it was an elaborate double bluff, of course—pretending that she didn't know, just to show that she hadn't been there—but somehow I doubted it. It had been a casual, matter-of-fact response to her own mother, not a calculated reply during a police interview. No, the simplest answer was often the right one, which meant that Magnolia didn't know about the tea eggs... which meant that she couldn't have been at the tea bar that night...

Which means that she can't be the murderer, I realised reluctantly, annoyed to admit that Inspector Roberts had been right, after all. But then what about the stealthy figure I'd seen? Could it really have been a contract killer hired by Mr Wang? Or... had my first instincts been right and it had been Freesia after all? But Professor Bennett had insisted that she was with the girl, I reminded myself.

Unless Gillian Bennett is lying, I thought suddenly. I had always just taken it at face value that the Oxford don was telling the truth. But what if her fondness for Freesia and protective maternal instincts had induced her to provide the girl with a *false* alibi? After all, I had been willing to accept that she might have been persuaded by Freesia to cover up for Magnolia... well, why not for Freesia herself? I recalled the Oxford don's passionate defence of the girl and her belief in the sacrifices that were necessary in order to allow rare talent to flourish. I could easily see her helping to cover up Freesia's crime so as not to harm her "brilliant potential and bright future", especially when she already disliked and resented Azalea Chu for controlling her younger sister's life.

I flashed back suddenly to the creepy way Freesia had stood behind me in Professor Bennett's rooms, watching me write that note, reading the message over my shoulder... She'd known that I was asking questions and guessed that Gillian Bennett might be challenged on her alibi.

"Oh my God..." I whispered as I thought of the voice message left by the Oxford don, saying that the youngest

Chu daughter wanted to see her urgently.

No, it was not a political murder, after all, but a very personal one. And if Freesia had killed her sister, then her tutor was the only person who could incriminate her—unless she was silenced first.

Gillian Bennett's life could be in danger.

Chapter Thirty-Two

What should I do? I wondered, pacing the kitchen. My first impulse was to grab the phone and call the police, but the memory of my interview with Roberts that morning was still sharp in my mind. I could almost hear his voice, sarcastic and sneering: "So this morning you thought it was one sister, and now you think it's the other? This is why we don't leave murder investigations to amateurs."

No, it was a waste of time calling the police—time that could make a difference to Professor Bennett's life. But the only other option was to warn her myself. I glanced at the clock, then checked my phone again. The Oxford don's message had come in just over ten minutes earlier. Quickly, I searched and dialled the number for Pendlebury College. Someone in the Porter's Lodge answered and put me through to Professor Bennett's rooms, but the phone rang and rang unanswered. Frustrated, I hung up.

Gillian Bennett might have only just left her rooms to search for Freesia. If I hurry, I might still be able to catch her before she leaves the college and warn her that she could be in danger.

Whirling, I ran out into the hallway and grabbed my bike which was leaning against the wall by the front door, barely avoiding trampling on Muesli, who jumped out of my way with a startled *"Meee-orrw!"* as I rushed past. Once on the streets, I pedalled feverishly, heading up St Aldates and crossing over

Carfax into Cornmarket Street, ignoring the rule that cycling was forbidden in the central pedestrianised stretch of the city. Thankfully, dusk was coming and the streets were emptying of tourists and workers, but even so, I had to concentrate to maintain my speed and not crash into any of the people walking down the shopping strip. I approached the end of Cornmarket with relief and turned the bike sharply into one of the side streets, just on the corner of St Michael's Church.

It felt like forever but it must have only been a short while later that I pulled up, panting heavily, in front of Pendlebury College. I dismounted, hastily propped my bicycle up against the wall, and was relieved to find that my porter friend was on duty. He looked up in surprise as I rushed, panting and wheezing, into the Porter's Lodge.

"My goodness, where's the fire?" he asked jovially.

"Have you... have you..." I gasped and swallowed, struggling to catch my breath. "Have you seen Professor Bennett?"

"Yes, you just missed her actually," said the porter. "Funnily enough, she was in a great tearing rush too. I was standing by the gate and she barely said hello to me as she went past. Think she was searching for someone—kept looking up and down the street."

"Do you know where she went?" I asked.

"Sorry, luv, no idea." He paused for a moment, his brow furrowed. "I think she was heading north up St Giles the last I saw her."

I thought quickly. Gillian Bennett had obviously been searching for Freesia; where was she likely to have gone? Then I remembered the time I'd inadvertently eavesdropped outside Freesia's room. That time, the girl had stormed out and the Oxford don had also gone to search for her. She had mentioned something then about expecting to find the girl at her favourite spot in Oxford...

The churchyard on St Giles, I remembered suddenly. It was a secluded green space, filled with ancient gravestones amidst trees and shrubs, which was attached to a twelfth-century church located at the point where St Giles, the wide boulevard that ran north out of Oxford, split into two roads. The churchyard was particularly popular with tourists and local workers as a sunny spot to have lunch. Right now, though, it would be dark—would Freesia still have gone there?

Well, it was the best guess I had. Thanking the porter, I dashed out of Pendlebury's main gate and started north up St Giles. Within a few minutes, I had arrived at the crossing which led across to the churchyard, islanded in the V of the split where St Giles divided. The church itself was alight—there seemed to be an evening service in progress—but next to it, the graveyard was dark and silent.

I glanced up and down the street. Traffic was light now and there were no cars approaching. Without waiting for the pedestrian crossing to signal a safe walking interval, I dashed across and entered the churchyard. Shadows leapt in front of me, black and eerie, and I hesitated for a moment, peering into the darkness between the shrubs and trees. Had I been wrong? The place seemed empty.

Then I heard a sound—something like a muffled cry—and my eyes caught a flicker of movement a few hundred yards away. My heart pounding, I plunged across the thick grass, skirting the jutting headstones, and rushed towards the cluster of yews beyond which I'd seen the blur of motion. As I rounded the stiff, upright branches, I realised that the dense, dark foliage had hidden a small open space beyond, in which a lichen-covered stone chest tomb lay surrounded by tall grass and wildflowers. The glow from the distant streetlights penetrated enough for me to make out the two figures by the tomb. One was Gillian Bennett, the other was Freesia, and they appeared to be locked in a struggle.

"Stop! Stop!" I cried, flinging myself forwards and grabbing Freesia's arm, yanking her away from the older woman. "It's too late, Freesia! I already know the truth and I'll make sure the police arrest you!"

"Let go of me!" snarled Freesia. She wrenched her arm free and glared at me. "What the hell are you talking about?"

"It's no use pretending. I know you did it. You murdered Azalea," I said bluntly. "Silencing Professor Bennett isn't going to prevent the truth from coming out."

"I wasn't trying to 'silence' the prof or anything!" cried Freesia angrily. "Are you bonkers? I was just, like, giving her a hug, okay?"

I glanced at the Oxford don. She had fallen back against the chest tomb and was now leaning heavily against it, her face pale and drawn.

"It's... it's not what you think," she said weakly.

I looked at her with pity. Surely she wasn't so blinded by misplaced maternal love that she would still be willing to cover up for the girl, even now?

"And that's bollocks about me killing my sister," continued Freesia. "There's nothing to show that I have anything to do with her murder!"

"Oh, don't think getting your tutor to cover up for you will save you," I retorted. "Everyone knows that alibis can be faked and people can lie. Besides, there's other evidence against you—like an eyewitness account."

"Whose eyewitness account?"

"Mine. I saw you through the kitchen windows. You were in the alley behind the tea bar."

Gillian Bennett drew her breath in sharply and made a sound of dismay. Freesia flushed and her eyes darted nervously left and right, as if she was trying to decide how to reply. Then she raised her chin and said belligerently:

"Yeah, well, I wanted somewhere to have a quiet ciggy, okay? That's not like a crime, is it? I tried to have one on the terrace and Azalea saw me and was, like, reading me the Riot Act—so I thought if I went into the back alley, she'd be less likely to find me there. But I was just smoking! I didn't go in the kitchen at all."

"So why did you run away? I saw you," I said accusingly. "You weren't standing there smoking—you were being really furtive, like someone running from the scene of a crime."

"I wasn't 'being furtive'! I just... I was having a quiet smoke, but then I heard voices in the kitchen. One of them sounded like Azalea and I was like: Oh God, she's gonna open the back door and see me and start giving me hell again... so I stubbed my cigarette out and scarpered. I went round the building and went back in through the front entrance."

"Do you think the police are going to believe that?" I asked scornfully.

"The police don't have to know about it," said Gillian Bennett quickly. She looked anxiously at me. "I mean, you obviously haven't told them, otherwise they would have been investigating Freesia much more heavily. So if you just keep this to yourself, they'll never—"

"You can't expect me to just keep

quiet," I said indignantly. "I haven't told them so far because... well, I... I wasn't sure who it was. But if it *is* Freesia, I'm not going to help cover it up—and you shouldn't either," I added, giving her a hard look.

"I didn't commit the murder!" snapped Freesia. "I told you—I didn't even know Azalea's body had been found until I saw all the commotion in the tea bar."

"If that's true, then why did you ask Professor Bennett for an alibi?" I asked. "Why did you need her to pretend that you were with her the entire time?"

Freesia scowled at me. "I didn't ask her to do that. *She* suggested it. She said we needed to tell the police that we were together the entire time—"

"I didn't want the police to jump to conclusions," Gillian Bennett cut in. "They might have seen Freesia's journal entry and then thought—"

"But I deleted that entry—I told you," said Freesia impatiently. "It was just to vent a bit, but I deleted it as soon as I finished writing it. The police would never have seen it, so they'd have nothing to make them suspicious."

"You're forgetting the fact that you were seen running away outside the kitchen..." I trailed off suddenly as I realised that the only person who had seen that was *me*.

I was the only person who had seen Freesia, but I hadn't told the police about it. So they had no idea that she was anywhere in the vicinity of the kitchen that night. Similarly, they didn't know about the fight I'd witnessed between Freesia and Azalea because, once again, I had kept mum about that. And, with the Chinese penchant for "saving face", I doubted that Mrs Chu or even Magnolia would have revealed the tensions between Freesia and her older sister, which meant that the police wouldn't have known about the conflict in their relationship. In fact, if they *were* going to suspect any member of the family, it would have been Magnolia because she actually *had* a motive: she could have wanted revenge for her sister's affair with her husband.

My thoughts started spinning. If the police hadn't known about the figure in the back alley and they hadn't known about Freesia's animosity towards her sister—*and* the journal entry had been immediately deleted as well, then what reason would the police have had for suspecting Freesia?

None, I realised. They wouldn't have suspected her beyond any of the other people at the tea bar that night. And yet Gillian Bennett had known this and still insisted on concocting a false alibi to protect her...

I froze. *No, I've got it completely back to front.* Slowly, I raised my head and met Gillian Bennett's eyes.

"It wasn't Freesia who needed that alibi—it was *you*," I said. "By saying that Freesia was with you all the time, you were effectively providing yourself with someone who could vouch for you at the time of the murder. *You* killed Azalea."

Chapter Thirty-Three

"Wh-what?" Freesia took a step back, her face turning pale.

"That's nonsense! Freesia, don't listen to her," said Gillian Bennett urgently. "She doesn't know what she's talking about—"

"But... but it's true that you kept insisting we lie to the police, even though I told you I didn't understand why I needed an alibi in the first place," said Freesia, an expression of dawning horror on her face. Her eyes widened suddenly. "That... that cast-iron teapot I found in the bottom drawer of your desk yesterday—you said it was just something you'd bought ages ago and forgotten about. But then why did it have some tea leaves in it that were still damp?"

She drew a sharp breath, backing away from the older woman. "You lied to me, didn't you? The police said that Azalea was killed by a blow to her head and they thought the murderer used one of the cast-iron teapots in the tea bar... *That* was the teapot I found, wasn't it? *Wasn't it?*"

Her voice was rising and becoming shriller and shriller, tinged now with hysteria.

"That was the teapot used to kill Azalea and you've been hiding it! That was why you looked so weird when I found it and tried to change the subject so quickly." Freesia threw a glance at me, then turned back to her tutor. "She's right—you murdered my sister!"

"No… I…" The Oxford don took a step towards the distraught girl. "Freesia, it's not like that… I mean…" She hesitated, then took a deep breath and said: "Yes, all right, I admit it. I killed Azalea, but you must understand, I did it for you!"

The girl gasped. "For me?"

"Yes, for you! Azalea was suffocating you! She was bullying you and controlling your life and denying you the chance of realising your true potential. You told me that night, after your fight with her, that she had threatened to stop paying your college fees. She was going to force you to drop out of Oxford and squander your talents and… and… take you away from me!" cried Gillian Bennett. "I couldn't let her do that! I had to stop her. After you went out to have a second cigarette, I saw Azalea go into the kitchen, so I followed her in there and tried to reason with her—but she just wouldn't listen. She was so arrogant and sneering, and she started making horrible insinuations about us. I couldn't bear to hear her talking about you and me like that! I had to shut her up. I had to teach her a lesson. And it was so easy—she turned her back on me and I just grabbed one of the teapots nearby and whacked her on the head. She went down without a sound..."

Freesia stared at her, the whites of her eyes showing starkly. "No... no... no!" she cried, taking a faltering step backwards. "I can't believe you killed her!"

Professor Bennett reached out towards the girl. "Freesia, listen to me, you might not see it now, but in time you'll understand that it was for the best—"

"No! Don't touch me! Don't come near me!" cried the girl, backing away. She stumbled and tripped over a loose piece of gravestone, nearly falling over backwards. Then she regained her balance and, with a muffled sob, turned and bolted.

"Freesia!" shouted Professor Bennett, as she rushed after her, and I followed suit.

The girl paid no heed. She pushed her way frantically through the bushes until she reached the side of the churchyard at the edge of the road. Without pausing to look, she stumbled blindly out into the middle of the thoroughfare.

Horns blared suddenly and the dazzling glare of car headlights bore down on Freesia standing silhouetted in the middle of the road.

I gasped in fear and horror, just as Gillian Bennett screamed and hurled herself toward the girl.

"FREESIA! Look out! Nooooooo!"

The air was rent by the squeal of brakes amidst shouting and screaming. I realised that one of the voices screaming was my own.

Everything was a blur. I saw Freesia thrown sideways.

Then the awful, muffled *thud* of an impact.

I blinked. The car had come to a stop at an angle in the middle of the road, its engine still throbbing, steam rising from its metal bonnet. The driver had the door open and was staggering out, his face ashen. I ran out into the road and my stomach lurched as I saw the huddled figure on the ground beneath the car's front bumper. I wanted to rush over, to cry out, to do something, but I couldn't seem to move.

"Professor! Professor!" cried Freesia, hobbling over and crouching down next to the prone figure.

"She j-just c-came out of n-nowhere," stammered the driver of the car.

"The prof was... trying to save me," said Freesia, her voice breaking on a sob. "She pushed me out of the way and she got hit herself."

"I did try to b-brake—I did!" said the driver, his face distressed. "But everything just happened so fast—"

"An ambulance! Has anyone called an ambulance?" came a new voice.

I realised a crowd was gathering. Passers-by were stepping off the pavement and coming towards us. People were pouring out of the church door and hurrying over.

"Oh God... yes... an ambulance!" I cried, coming suddenly out of my daze.

I scrabbled for my phone and dialled the number for the emergency services. But when I tried to speak, I found that my voice was shaking so much, I struggled to make sense. I felt a hand on my shoulder, and I looked up to see a kindly parishioner standing next to me. Gladly, I relinquished my phone and stood dumbly next to him as he relayed the necessary details of the incident and our location. A few other churchgoers began directing others to manage the gathering crowd, check on the driver, bring some blankets and hot drinks...

Through it all, I stood numbly, staring at where Freesia was huddled by the car. The wail of sirens, when the ambulance came, brought an audible sigh of relief from the crowd, but I couldn't help wondering, looking at Gillian Bennett's still and silent body, whether it was all too late...

Chapter Thirty-Four

There is always something unpleasant about hospital emergency waiting rooms—you can almost taste the worry and anxiety in the air, and everywhere you look is the sight of distressed patients awaiting their turn or the strained faces of friends and relatives, slumped in rows of plastic chairs. I was one of their number now, sitting with Freesia as we waited for news of Gillian Bennett's fate. To be honest, I didn't have to come to the hospital, but when Freesia had been told that she needed to be checked for injuries too, I'd decided impulsively to accompany her. I knew the police would want to interview me about the accident, but until Mrs Chu could be notified and brought to the hospital, I didn't like to leave the girl alone.

I glanced at her now, where she sat huddled in her chair, her face ghostly pale and her eyes blank. She had been cleared of any physical injuries, bar minor bruises from her fall when she was pushed to the side of the road, but I had a feeling that the real wounds were in her mind. I hoped it was true that her writing would provide the means to work through emotional trauma.

My thoughts were interrupted by a suavely handsome man dressed in scrubs, with a stethoscope around his neck, striding out into the A&E waiting room. He paused a moment to scan the room, then he spotted us and hurried over.

"Freesia," he said, touching the girl's arm. "I didn't realise you were involved in this accident. Have you been checked over?"

The girl nodded distractedly. "Have you been looking after the prof, Dax? Is she going to be okay?"

"Yes. She was extremely lucky. She has concussion and a couple of broken ribs, but with rest and care, she should make a full recovery." He turned to me and added with a perfunctory smile, "I'm Dr Hutton. Are you Professor Bennett's family?"

I looked at him with new interest. So this was Dax Hutton, Magnolia's wayward husband! Was it a dreadful irony that he should be the doctor looking after the woman who had murdered his mistress?

"Prof Bennett doesn't have family, Dax," Freesia said before I could answer. "She isn't married and she hasn't got any children. Her parents are dead; she had a brother, but he died of cancer a few years ago, so she's pretty much alone." Freesia paused, then added in a small voice, "Prof used to say that we—the students at Pendlebury—we are like the daughters she never had."

"Oh." Hutton looked slightly unsure how to respond to this. Clearing his throat, he turned to me and said, "I'm sorry, so you are...?"

Freesia glanced carelessly at me. "That's Gemma. She came with me. Her mum is friends with Ma."

"Ahh... is your mother coming to pick you up?" Hutton asked the girl.

"Yeah, they said Ma's on the way," Freesia muttered, her mind obviously elsewhere. She looked over his shoulder to the corridor beyond, which led to the emergency ward cubicles. "Is she awake? Can I go and see her?"

"Yes. In fact, Professor Bennett has been asking for you. They're transferring her to the Short Stay admissions ward where she'll be kept under observation for twenty-four hours, and then discharged home if she doesn't relapse."

It won't be home that Professor Bennett will be going to—it'll be straight into police custody, I thought grimly.

"Come on, I'll take you through to see her," said Dax Hutton, putting a hand under Freesia's elbow.

I watched them go with troubled eyes. As a murder suspect, Gillian Bennett should really have been under guard until she could be taken into custody—and I ought to have been hurrying to notify the police, so that they could come and arrest her. In fact, maybe I shouldn't have even let Freesia see her tutor. But I remembered the way the Oxford don had flung herself into the path of the oncoming car and pushed Freesia to safety. She had certainly saved the girl's life and there was no denying her maternal love for Freesia—however misdirected it might be.

In a way, you could say that even the murder had been motivated by misplaced love and devotion, rather than greed or malice. If she hadn't been a single, lonely, childless woman, would Gillian Bennett have taken her "pastoral care" duties to the extreme? With the absence of anything else in her life to love, had she directed all her hopes and dreams, all her nurturing and protective instincts onto the young women in her charge—and especially onto Freesia? Perhaps it was wrong of me to feel sympathy for her, but I was reluctant to deny the Oxford don one last chance to speak with Freesia before the police descended on her.

Police officers had accompanied us to the hospital and now they took me aside, keen to get a statement about what had happened. But I only repeated the basic details of the accident and carefully omitted the reason for Freesia's headlong rush into the road. These weren't CID detectives, and it would have been too complicated trying to summarise the whole background to the murder investigation. No, much as I hated it, I really needed to speak to Inspector Roberts and tell him that this time, I really *did* know the identity of the murderer.

Deciding that it would be easier to speak to Roberts in person than try to explain over the phone, I took a taxi from the hospital to the police station in Oxford. When I alighted, I was surprised to see the front car park awash with lights, and as I walked towards the entrance, I realised that there was an impromptu press conference being held in front of the station. A dozen or so reporters and camera crew were huddled around the base of the front steps. Standing in the middle of the crowd, flanked by the DCC on one side, was Inspector Roberts. He had a smug expression on his face and was obviously enjoying all the attention as he faced the cameras.

"...constantly evolving situation. But Oxfordshire CID have spared no resources in this investigation, and I am honoured to say that they have assigned their *best* officer to the case." Roberts gave a fake modest laugh and paused to preen himself. "Furthermore, we have used highly advanced forensic techniques to inspect the crime scene and—"

"But after nearly a week, you haven't made any real progress in the investigation, have you, Inspector?" one of the journalists interrupted him. I craned my neck and was surprised to see that it was Mark Scott. He stepped forwards and added in a provocative voice:

"And if you really want the best people on the case, shouldn't you be enlisting the help of Gemma Rose?" Scott gave a taunting smile. "She's been responsible for helping to crack some of the biggest murders in the past year—often solving the case faster than the CID."

The DCC frowned and looked at Roberts, who scowled ferociously.

"I don't need the so-called 'help' of silly amateurs!" he snapped. "Detective work is a serious job for professionals, not nosy tea shop owners with over-active imaginations. And... and I'll have you know that we *are* making progress with the case," he added hurriedly. "In fact, I have... I have made great leaps forward in deduction and I already know the identity of Azalea Chu's murderer!"

"You do?" said Scott sceptically. "So why haven't you made an announcement?"

"I... well, that's... that's why I called this press conference!" said Roberts, ignoring the look of bemused surprise on the face of the DCC behind him. "I can now exclusively reveal that Azalea Chu was not killed by anyone in her immediate social circle. Ohhh no! It's convention to focus on the victim's friends, family, and business contacts, but I've always had the gift of being able to think outside the box. Yes, that's right... and so I've been able to see what everyone else has missed: that Azalea Chu was murdered by the Yakuza!"

"*What?*" I burst out with an incredulous laugh.

Somehow, my voice came out louder than I'd expected, and suddenly I found myself the focus of attention as everyone in the crowd swung around to look at me.

"It's Gemma Rose!" cried Scott excitedly, looking like someone who'd just seen their favourite wrestler enter the ring.

I ignored the crowd and pushed my way up the front steps to stand next to Roberts. "That's a load of rubbish!" I said. "Why on earth would you think that Azalea was murdered by what is effectively the Japanese mafia? I mean, what possible connection could she have with them?"

"Well, she… she was a businesswoman, wasn't she?" blustered Roberts. "So it's well known that businesses often run into trouble with organised crime. It wouldn't be surprising if she was having to pay 'protection money' to gangs from her own country."

"Yes, except that Azalea wasn't Japanese," I said coldly. "She was Chinese, from Taiwan."

Roberts waved a hand. "Chinese, Taiwanese, Japanese… there's not much difference really—"

There was a gasp of outrage from the crowd and an East-Asian female reporter thrust herself forwards, her eyes narrowed on Roberts. "What did you just say?" she demanded. "Are you suggesting that the Chinese and Japanese are all the same?"

Roberts attempted an urbane laugh. "Well… I mean, come on… you have to admit, it's easy to mix them up."

"How dare you!" cried the female reporter, her face flushing bright red. "These are two separate countries with two distinct cultures and histories. I can't believe you think you can just swap one for the other—oh, I suppose you think just because we all have black hair and slitty eyes, we're all the same, huh?"

Roberts took a step back, his smile slipping. "Uh… um… well… you do look very similar, you know," he said weakly. "And you all drink tea and eat noodles and… uh… like soya sauce… don't you?"

The woman was seething now. "Oh yeah? And I suppose Brits and Americans are all the same, because you all drink beer, eat chips, and like to bake in the sun?"

"That's... that's different," stammered Roberts.

The DCC stepped forwards suddenly and pushed Roberts away from the microphone. Turning to face the irate reporter, he assumed a sombre expression and said smoothly:

"I apologise for any distress caused. I'm sure Inspector Roberts did not intend to give any offence and this is all an unfortunate misunderstanding—"

"Deputy Chief Constable, did you realise racism was so prevalent in your force?" asked one of the other reporters.

"Do you agree, sir, that people of Oriental descent all look alike?" another piped up.

"Shouldn't a detective who has to work in the community be more educated on differences in cultures and nationalities?" demanded another journalist.

"Have you got any Chinese or Japanese officers in the station, sir? Can you tell them apart?" asked Mark Scott cheekily.

The DCC flushed. Clearing his throat, he cut through the barrage of questions and said, "*Ahem*... Oxfordshire Police has great respect for different cultural identities, and we make a great commitment to understanding the nuances and distinctions—"

"Hard to believe that when one of your own inspectors thinks being Japanese or Chinese is the same thing!" said the female reporter scathingly. "If that isn't an example of wilful, ignorant racism, I don't know what is!"

Several other journalists were nodding their heads and making notes, and camera flashbulbs exploded, lighting up the DCC's alarmed expression.

"Look, this is not a forum to discuss those topics," he said desperately. "This press conference was called to provide information on the investigation of Azalea Chu's murder—"

"So *is* there any proof that she was murdered by Yakuza? What about the Triads? Or maybe it's the drug cartels from Latin America?" asked Scott with a smirk, looking like he was enjoying himself immensely.

The DCC cleared his throat again. "I'm sure that my officers are in the process of compiling evidence and, as you can appreciate, the details must remain confidential until we can make an arrest—"

"You don't need to waste time and resources on that," I spoke up. "I can tell you who murdered Azalea Chu."

There was a gasp of delight and everyone turned to me, their faces expectant.

Mark Scott leaned forwards, looking almost like a dog salivating at the prospect of a bone. "Miss Rose, have you cracked the case?" he asked.

"Well, I can tell you who the murderer is," I replied. "It's Gillian Bennett, one of the dons at Pendlebury College in Oxford."

"And where's your proof?" sneered Roberts, thrusting himself forwards again. "You're just making that up so you can brag about solving the case before the police—"

"What? No!" I cried. "I'm not making anything up! If you just listen to me explain, I can tell you where Professor Bennett hid the murder weapon and—"

"I'm not going to waste time sending my men on a wild goose chase!" snarled Roberts. "I've already checked Gillian Bennett and cleared her from the list of suspects. I don't need you second-guessing expert police work. Professor

Bennett is a respected member of the Oxford University faculty and has no motive to murder Azalea, so unless you can produce some proof for your ridiculous accusation, you'd better—"

He broke off as a figure stepped out suddenly from the police station and tapped him on the shoulder. I realised that it was Devlin's sergeant. He caught my eye, giving me a surreptitious wink, before turning to Roberts:

"Sir? There's a phone call for you."

"What? Can't you see that I'm in the middle of a press conference, Sergeant?" asked Roberts irritably. "I can't believe you're interrupting me for a phone call."

"Well, I'm thinking you'll want to take this one, sir," said the sergeant, deliberately raising his voice so that it could be heard across the crowd. "It's one of our boys at the hospital. He says Professor Bennett has just confessed to murdering Azalea Chu and he wants to know what to do next."

There was a delighted silence. Roberts went white, then purple, his mouth working uselessly as he tried to think of how to reply.

Mark Scott sniggered and called out: "Hey, you reckon Miss Rose can brag a bit now, Inspector?"

The DCC shouldered Roberts aside again and took over the microphone. "This press conference is over. Thank you for your attendance, ladies and gentlemen. We will inform you as soon as we have any new developments."

Ignoring the sudden clamour of questions from the reporters, he turned his back on the crowd and fixed Roberts with a hard eye.

"In my office, Roberts—now," he said grimly.

The other man cringed and slunk back into the police station with his tail between his legs. The DCC started to follow, then paused and met my eyes. I braced myself, half expecting him to castigate me for interfering with police work again, but to my surprise, I saw him looking at me with new respect. There was a long moment, then he inclined his head slightly, the ghost of a smile touching his lips, before he turned away and disappeared into the station.

Chapter Thirty-Five

After the excitement and high drama of the night before, it was a bit surreal arriving at work the next morning and stepping into the Little Stables to find the tearoom just the same, with its exposed wood beams, mullioned windows, and inglenook fireplace exuding the same comforting period charm as always. Customers began arriving, and as the hum of conversation and laughter, accompanied by the gorgeous smell of fresh baking, filled the air, I revelled in the warm, cosy atmosphere. It was nice to feel that here, at least, things were always safe and familiar.

Well, maybe not quite so familiar—but in a good way, I reminded myself with a smile. There were subtle changes, from the brand-new menus now filled with gorgeous photographs and mouth-watering descriptions of our signature dishes, to the beautiful arrangements of fresh baking, pretty teapots, and matching teacups that now graced the various tables. I stood beside the counter and looked around the room, feeling a rush of pride as I saw the obvious enjoyment on people's faces.

My mother's idea of themed afternoon tea set menus had been a resounding success. The "Classic Afternoon Tea" package was—unsurprisingly—the most requested, with its three tiers of traditional treats, including a selection of finger sandwiches, dainty cakes and tarts, and, of course, our famous scones, all accompanied by a choice of two tea blends. But many of the regular customers—particularly single patrons like Mr Prendergast—really appreciated the new "Cream Tea for One", with its two fluffy, buttery scones accompanied by home-made jam and clotted cream, and a pot of your favourite tea. Meanwhile, the "Chocolate Lovers' Afternoon Tea" had been a big hit with the ladies, the "Champagne Afternoon Tea" was beloved by those wanting to splash out or celebrate a special occasion, and the "Teddy Bears' Afternoon Picnic" was requested by every family with children under ten.

The success of the changes had breathed new life into the Little Stables and I was looking forward to brainstorming other ideas with Cassie and finding new ways to keep things fresh and exciting. *Ironic to think that this is Azalea's legacy*, I thought dryly—although I doubted that the Taiwanese businesswoman would have appreciated knowing that her entrepreneurial spirit was living on in my little tearoom!

My thoughts were interrupted by the tearoom door swinging open and Cassie bursting in. She had popped out to go to the village post office, and I was surprised to see her return with her arms full of different newspapers.

"Look at this, Gemma!" she cried, whooping with delight. She dropped the papers onto the counter in front of me and fanned them out so that I could see their front pages. My eyes widened as I took in the various headlines, accompanied by photographs of Inspector Roberts's smug face at the previous day's press conference:

"OXFORDSHIRE CID – HOME OF IGNORANT RACISTS!"

"Chinese, Japanese... they're all the same! says Oxfordshire senior detective"

"YOU ALL EAT NOODLES AND LIKE

SOYA SAUCE, DON'T YOU?"

"Oxfordshire Police DCC apologises unreservedly for senior officer's remarks"

"Wow…" I said. "He's really kicked up a hornets' nest."

"Yeah, somehow I don't think Roberts is going to be on the DCC's Christmas card list this year," said Cassie, chuckling. "I mean, public image is *everything* these days. Companies and organisations are more terrified of being seen as un-PC and 'un-woke' than of anything else. People have been fired just for saying the wrong thing on social media… *ten* years ago! So this—" She indicated the papers. "—is a complete disaster. Roberts can complain about your involvement in cases but, while it may not have been totally kosher, at least it always brought *positive* publicity for the police force. Whereas what *he* did…!" She smiled with malicious glee. "Ooh, I hope Roberts gets a real kick up the arse. He bloody deserves it." She gathered up the papers and turned towards the kitchen. "I can't wait to show Dora!"

The door had barely swung shut behind her when the tinkling bells attached to the tearoom entrance signalled the arrival of new customers. I looked up in surprise as I recognised the two women who had just stepped into the tearoom. It was Mrs Chu and Magnolia, the former pulling a small travel case on wheels.

"Mrs Chu!" I cried, going forwards to meet them. "How nice to see you here! Let me show you to a table—"

"Oh no, we can't stay long. My mum just wanted to come and say goodbye," Magnolia said. "We're actually heading off to the airport, but she insisted on making a detour."

"Oh, of course, the funeral," I said, recalling the traditional cremation that had been planned for Azalea's body. I turned to Mrs Chu. "I hope you have a good flight and that everything... um... goes smoothly. I'll look forward to seeing you when you return—"

Mrs Chu shook her head. "No. I go back my country," she said.

"You're returning to Taiwan for good?" I said in surprise.

She nodded, then her attention was distracted by the sight of a little tabby cat standing up and stretching on her cushion by the window. "Muss-Lee!" she cried in delight, rushing over.

Magnolia watched her go, then turned to me and said in an undertone: "My mum only moved to the UK because Azalea kept pressuring her to, after my dad died. But she never really wanted to come, and it's all been a bit of a culture shock for her. She misses her friends and her life back in Taiwan, so she's decided that she'd prefer to go back. She says she's too old to be trying to make a new life in a new country."

"But… what about you and Freesia?" I asked.

Magnolia's expression hardened. "Freesia will cope. It'll probably be good for her to learn to stand on her own two feet. She's been babied for too long. As for me, I'm not sure how long I'll be remaining in the UK myself. My husband and I are getting a divorce."

"Oh. I'm sorry to hear that," I said, surprised.

She shrugged. "It was a long time coming, to be honest with you. I'm fed up with putting up with Dax's affairs. That's what I told him when we went out to dinner on the night of the murder. And he couldn't believe it! The arrogant sod thought that all he had to do was wine and dine me, and give me some expensive jewellery as a sop, and I'd go crawling back into his arms again." She gave a bitter laugh. "You should have seen his face when I told him to take a running jump. He was so shaken up he had to pretend that he needed to go back to work, just to save face—"

"Oh, so *that* was why he went back to the hospital that night," I said. "I wondered about that since he wasn't actually meant to be working a shift that night."

"Yeah, well, it's always been about his ego with Dax. It's why he's always chasing after some skirt or other. To prove his virility. But this really was the last straw." Magnolia shook her head, her expression angry and incredulous. "It was bad enough with the nurses at the hospital, but with my own sister? Yes, I blamed Azalea—but I blamed Dax more. He was supposed to be the one person in the world who would never hurt me, and he completely betrayed me."

"I'm... I'm really sorry," I said, unsure what to say.

She shrugged again. "You know, I've always been the model Taiwanese daughter: I studied hard, got into one of the world's top universities, married a doctor, produced two kids, was the perfect wife and mother... and where did that get me? Maybe Freesia had it right all along. Maybe you should just follow your own dreams and passions and to hell with duty and cultural expectations." Then she gave a cynical laugh as she saw my expression. "Don't worry—I doubt I have the guts to actually do anything crazy. I'll probably just go back to being the 'goody-goody' I always am." She gave a wistful sigh. "It's nice to vent sometimes, though, and imagine you could be different..."

I stared at her, feeling both a rush of empathy for her and also guilt for having suspected her of Azalea's murder.

Magnolia might not have been the most easy-going, affable personality, but I suddenly wished that I'd had more time to get to know her better. Despite our different cultural backgrounds, we had a lot in common. I knew better than most how difficult it could be to walk the tightrope of societal expectations and personal passions.

We were rejoined by Mrs Chu, carrying Muesli in her arms. She set the tabby down at our feet, then turned to me and said: "Jem-Ma, I have some Taiwanese sausage for Muss-Lee. You give her after I go?"

"Oh… er, sure," I said, watching in bemusement as she eagerly unzipped her travel case and pulled out a small bundle, which she thrust into my hands. A smoky, sweet aroma rose from the package and Muesli looked up, her little pink nose twitching.

"*Meorrw!*" she cried excitedly.

Mrs Chu bent to give the tabby another pat. "I miss you, Muss-Lee," she said with a fond smile. "But I go back Taiwan. My cat waiting for me."

"You know, *my mother* is really going to miss *you*," I told her, thinking of all the forlorn pink slippers in my parents' house.

Mrs Chu smiled. "Yes, I miss Mrs Rose also. I am happy come to England, make good friend." She brightened. "But I tell your mother: must come visit me in Taiwan one day! You also!" She clasped my hands and squeezed them. "Thank you, Jem-Ma. You give big help with police."

"Oh no, I… it's nothing, really," I said awkwardly. "I… I'm really sorry again… about Azalea… and everything…"

She gave a sad smile. "In Taiwan, we believe this is the life which happen to you. I think in English is call 'fate'?

"Yes, fate," I agreed.

She nodded. "There is old Chinese proverb: '*cannot change your fate, only change your attitude*'—so have to accept life and continue in best way."

"That's a very wise saying. I'll remember that," I said, squeezing her hands in return.

"I say bye-bye," said Mrs Chu. Then she surprised me by suddenly leaning forwards and giving me a light peck on each cheek. Then she said, with a twinkle in her eye: "Mrs Rose teach me English way: do kiss-kiss... like this?"

I laughed. "Yes, that's right. My mother would be proud of you."

Mrs Chu turned to go, reaching for her travel case handle. But it stuck and rolled sideways as she attempted to pull it.

"Wait..." I said, spying a suspicious-looking bulge beneath the cover of the case. I bent down and realised that Mrs Chu hadn't quite zipped up the case properly when she'd been retrieving her bundle of sausages. Now, as I pulled the zip back and lifted the corner of the flap, a little furry head popped out.

"Muesli!" I said in exasperation. "What are you doing in Mrs Chu's case?"

"*Meeeeorrw!*" said the tabby cheekily.

"I think she want to go Taiwan with me," said Mrs Chu, laughing.

"Hmm… I have half a mind to let you have the little minx," I muttered darkly, reaching down to scoop my cat out of the case.

We zipped everything up properly again, and then, with final goodbyes and wishes for a safe journey, I stood outside the tearoom and watched mother and daughter walk away up the village high street.

"*Meorrw?*" said Muesli, from where she was clutched in my arms. She reached up and nuzzled my chin.

"Oh no, you don't," I said. "Don't try to butter me up. I saw what you did—mercenary little beast. It's true what they say about cats: any lap in a storm!"

Chapter Thirty-Six

I was tired when I got home that evening, but it was a happy kind of tiredness, with the feeling of fulfilment from a day of work well done. Business was booming again at the Little Stables and we seemed to be attracting many new customers. I was relieved and delighted and filled with a sense of hope and excitement about the future. The only cloud on my horizon was Devlin and the chasm that seemed to have opened up between us since our last argument. But he was coming around to my place after work that night and I was sure that once we'd talked through a few things, everything would be fine in my world again.

I rushed to change out of my grimy work clothes and into a pretty cotton blouse and jeans. Then I ran a quick brush through my hair and applied a bit of gloss to my lips. Even if this wasn't going to be a romantic dinner, it never hurt to look your best—or at least as good as you could, in the circumstances. I was just wondering whether to rustle up some snacks when my doorbell rang.

"Hi!" I smiled at Devlin, waiting for him to sweep me into his arms.

Instead, he hesitated, then leaned forwards and gave me a quick peck on one cheek. "Hi, Gemma," he said, his voice tired.

I frowned but tried not to read anything into it. "Long day?" I asked sympathetically.

He nodded as he followed me into the cottage. "This case in Blackbird Leys is a real bastard... but at least the end is in sight now. We just need to get hold of one more piece of evidence to seal the conviction."

He was stopped in his tracks by a little furry figure rushing up and rubbing herself ecstatically against his legs. From the moment she first met him, Muesli had decided that Devlin was her most favourite person in the world, and she practically did feline cartwheels every time she saw him. Now her purring sounded like the engine of a Formula One race car revving up for a circuit lap as Devlin bent to pick her up.

He busied himself stroking her for a few moments, then he glanced up at me. "I heard about your part in helping to solve the Azalea Chu case," he said in a carefully non-committal voice. "Congratulations."

I looked at him uncertainly. His polite, distant manner was beginning to make me nervous. "Thanks. I'm just glad that nobody was hurt in the end. I mean, Gillian Bennett will be facing charges now, but I wonder if they might be lenient on her, given her motivations and the fact that she did save Freesia's life."

There was an awkward pause, then Devlin said: "And you're sure you've had no ill effects from the accident?"

"I'm fine. I told you—I wasn't anywhere near the road," I assured him. "If anyone is feeling the fallout from the events of last night, it's Inspector Roberts. Have you seen the papers today?"

"Yes," said Devlin wryly, putting Muesli back down and leaning against the kitchen door jamb as he crossed his arms. "The whole station is talking about nothing else. Roberts was noticeably absent in the CID offices this morning and his desk has been cleared. The DCC informed me that he's gone on 'temporary leave' while he attends a

Cultural Re-Education programme."

"Really?" I laughed. Then I digested what he said. "Wait—you had your meeting with the DCC? What happened?" I asked, looking at him worriedly. "Did he… you haven't been suspended, have you?"

"No. The DCC told me that in light of recent events, he's inclined to disregard Roberts's report against me. However…" Devlin paused, giving me a reproving look. "He did warn me about maintaining 'the correct boundaries with civilian contacts, especially with regards to sharing confidential police information'."

"Oh." I tried for a determinedly cheerful tone: "But at least you're not suspended! And with Roberts gone, hopefully everything will blow over and things will get back on track for your promotion."

Devlin sighed. "It's not that simple, Gemma. There might not be an official inquiry anymore, but that doesn't mean everything is forgotten. The DCC made it very clear that there were serious doubts raised about my eligibility for a promotion."

I swallowed. "I'm sure, when they consider everything you've done, they'll realise how much you deserve it."

Devlin didn't answer. Instead, he glanced at his watch. "I'm going to have to go. I'm meeting an informant who might be able to help us access crucial evidence for this Blackbird Leys homicide."

I tried to hide my disappointment. "Do you think the case will be wrapped up by next week?"

"I bloody hope so," said Devlin, running a hand over his face and through his dark hair. I noticed that he needed a shave and that his eyes looked slightly bloodshot.

"You look exhausted," I said. "Why

don't you ask for some time off next week? Surely they can't expect you to keep working like this; everybody needs a break. You'll burn out and then you won't be able to help anyone."

Devlin massaged his neck tiredly. "Actually, the DCC did order me to take some time off after this case is wrapped, and the Super reiterated that when he saw me afterwards."

"Oh, that's great!" I said. "I'll take a few days off too, and then maybe we can go away for a mini-holiday? How about a weekend trip to Rome? I saw some great deals online the other day. Or, if you don't want to go far, we can just rent a little cottage in the Cotswolds and—"

"Gemma..." Devlin stopped me. "Actually, I've been doing a lot of thinking during the recent stake-outs..." He hesitated, his blue eyes not meeting mine. "I... well, I thought it might be good if we have some time away from each other."

I froze. "What do you mean?"

Devlin took a deep breath. "I think... we should take a break."

I stared at him. "Are you saying we should split up?"

"No—I mean, in a way, but not... Look, I just think we need some space and time apart... It'll give us a chance to think about what we really want and what's important to us—"

"You're still angry, aren't you, about the whole Roberts thing?" I said in an accusing voice. "You're punishing me for getting involved in the investigation—"

"No, it's not—" Devlin broke off and took a steadying breath. "Okay, I admit, I *was* angry that you ignored me and kept meddling in the Azalea Chu case. I know you didn't do it on purpose," he said, holding up a hand as I started to protest. "But all the same, your actions nearly cost me my job, Gemma! And they could still very well cost me my promotion." He sighed and shook his head. "You're just incapable of turning a blind eye to anyone in trouble. You can't help yourself—you always seem to get involved. That's just 'you', and I realise now that you're never going to change... but I don't know if that's something I can live with.

"It's not just about me," he continued gently. "It's about *you* too. *You* have to decide if you can be with someone whose work will usually have to come first, who will often have to put the needs of total strangers before yours, and who won't be by your side most of the time, doing all the usual things that boyfriends are expected to."

I stared at Devlin, feeling like I was suddenly looking at a stranger. How could he be saying all this? How could he be doing this to us? The hurt and betrayal crashed over me, like the tidal wave that every surfer secretly dreaded, the one that could only end in a total wipeout. I wanted to scream, to shout, to beat my fists against his chest, but something—maybe it was pride—wouldn't let me react, wouldn't let me show him just how devastated I was.

I wasn't the product of a repressed, upper-middle-class upbringing for nothing. Raising my chin, I kept my face carefully blank of expression and said in a voice that only wobbled slightly: "Fine. We'll take a break."

Devlin blinked. He looked as if he expected me to say more, but when I remained silent, he bent to give Muesli a half-hearted pat, then turned to go. At the door, he paused and looked back at me. The expression in his eyes almost made me run to him, but I bit my lip and held myself back.

"If there's anything... if you need help with anything... you know you can always call me. Any time," he said awkwardly.

I nodded, not trusting myself to speak.

He hesitated. "Take care, Gemma."

Then he was gone. I stood staring at the closed door, my emotions swirling through me in dizzying waves. I felt sick and angry and crushed and confused— and a dozen other things I couldn't put a name to.

"*Meorrw?*" said Muesli, standing by the front door, looking forlornly up at it.

Then she turned and padded over to me. I half expected her to start demanding food or attention, but to my surprise, she simply sat down by my feet, curling her tail neatly around her paws. She didn't look at me or try to nuzzle me or anything, and yet there was a simple solidarity in her actions which I found very touching.

I was just bending to pat her when the front doorbell rang. My heart leapt, wondering if it might be Devlin coming back to say that he had made a terrible mistake, and I had to pause a moment to compose my face as I went to open the door.

"Darling! I'm so glad I caught you at home. I wondered if you might be out at a pub with Cassie and Seth…"

I fell back as my mother wafted in on a cloud of Givenchy perfume, carrying several packages in her arms. She placed these on my dining table with the flourish of a game show host displaying the top prizes.

"The things I'd ordered for you arrived, so I thought I'd bring them straight over," she said, beaming.

"Oh… um… thanks, Mother," I said, struggling to control my emotions as the wild hope I'd had that Devlin might be returning was replaced by bemused horror at the sight of multiple fuchsia-pink Flexible Knee Pads swamping my table. "I… I thought you were just ordering one pair of knee pads?"

"Oh, they were such good value, darling, and they had a special offer where you could get eight pairs for the price of five!" said my mother enthusiastically. "So I thought—why not get a couple of pairs each for Cassie and Dora as well? Then you can all benefit from superior knee protection while you're at work."

"It's a tearoom, Mother, not an ice hockey rink," I said irritably. "It's not like we're going to get into a scrum with the customers."

My mother ignored me. Instead, she said: "I saw a black Jaguar leaving the cul-de-sac just as I was arriving. It looked like Devlin's car—did I just miss him?"

"Yes," I muttered.

"Oh, what a shame! I was hoping to ask him whether he'd like a pair of knee pads too. When will you next be seeing him?"

I took a deep breath, preparing to put on a brave face and mumble some lie, but I surprised myself by bursting out: "Mother... Devlin says he wants a break!"

"A break? A break from what, darling?" asked my mother in puzzlement.

"From us. From the relationship," I said miserably. "He wants us to spend some time apart."

I began to tell her everything that had happened, feeling a strange sort of comfort and relief as I did so. I knew I wasn't a little girl anymore and that I was long past the time when I could run to my mother and she would fix everything that was wrong in my life, but still, there was something nice about having a maternal shoulder to cry on. Figuratively, anyway. My mother would have been horrified if I'd actually shown any strong outward emotion or—heaven forbid—produced any actual tears.

"Well, really, darling, if the silly boy doesn't appreciate you, then it's his loss," she said at last when I'd finished.

"How can you just say that?" I gasped. "It's… I always saw my future with Devlin. I don't know what I'll do if he isn't in my life—"

"Nonsense," said my mother briskly. "You'll manage just fine. Remember, a woman needs a man like an octopus needs a hairdryer."

"Er… I think you mean fish needs a bicycle."

"Don't be silly, darling, fishes don't need bicycles."

"That's the whole point, Mother. The original saying—oh, never mind." I rolled my eyes.

"In fact, if we're talking about fishes, then there are plenty more in the sea, you know," my mother continued blithely. "Helen Green is having your father and me over to Sunday lunch this weekend, with a few other friends and family. Why don't you come with us? It'll help to take your mind off things."

I gave her a suspicious look. "Mother..." I said in a warning tone. "You're not going to start trying to set me up with Lincoln Green again, are you?"

"Of course not, darling. I've accepted that you've chosen Devlin and, having got to know him better now, I think he's a very nice boy. But he's not the only nice boy in the world, you know," she added.

"He is for me."

She made a tutting noise, then said brightly, "You know what you need, darling? A nice cup of tea. Now you sit down while I fetch you something..." Her voice faded away as she bustled into the kitchen.

I sighed and flopped onto the sofa, deciding that submitting to my mother's exasperating ministrations was better than being left alone with my brooding thoughts. Then I noticed a new sound above the noise of clinking crockery and boiling kettle. I glanced up in surprise to see Muesli trotting towards me. She was meowing softly, although the cries were muffled by the item she was carrying in her mouth.

As she jumped up onto the sofa beside me, I realised that it was a chunk of sausage meat. The little minx had obviously decided to break into the bundle that Mrs Chu had given me and help herself to a piece of the exotic treat! But to my surprise, instead of eating the juicy morsel, she had brought it over to me and was now carefully depositing it in my lap. Then she looked up at me, her green eyes enormous, and rubbed her chin against my hand.

Suddenly, I understood. I had read

that when cats bring you a mouse or other prey they've captured, it was really a gift of love. This was Muesli's way of offering sympathy and comfort.

"Thanks, Muesli," I said, breaking into a smile in spite of myself.

It wasn't quite a dead rodent, but considering how highly valued Mrs Chu's treats were, the fact that Muesli was offering to share them with me was the ultimate feline gesture of caring and affection!

Eiplogue

"You know, I think your mother's right," said Cassie. "If Devlin can't appreciate you as you are, then sod him! You don't need the stupid plonker. I mean, you managed fine without him for eight years when you were overseas, didn't you? And if you hadn't come back to Oxford and that American had never got murdered in your tearoom, then you might never have met him again anyway—and you would have been perfectly happy! But okay, you're back now and Devlin's here, but that doesn't mean that you need him in your life. With the tearoom and Muesli and your mother and the Old Biddies... you've got more than enough on your plate to keep you busy—"

"Cass…" I said, putting a hand on her arm and trying to calm her down.

"No, no—in fact, Devlin should be bloody *grateful* that you're back in his life," continued Cassie, working herself up into a fine rage. "And he should be bloody grateful that you helped on all those cases! The whole of Oxfordshire Police should be thanking you on their knees! You've given them more good publicity and high case clearance rates than they could dream of, and they should really be making you an honorary member of the CID—"

"Oh, Cass!" I laughed in spite of myself. "You know that's a silly thing to even suggest. Besides, I don't want any honours from the police. I don't care if they appreciate my efforts or not. It's not really about them; it's about Devlin—"

"Yes, well, Devlin is acting like a

moronic git partly because of them, isn't he?" retorted Cassie. "Honestly, I can't believe he wants to 'take a break'! Where did he get such a stupid idea from? I have half a mind to go and speak to him and tell him what—"

"No!" I cried. "No, don't—please, Cassie. I know you mean well but... this is between Devlin and me. It's something we need to work out. Ourselves."

Cassie regarded me silently for a moment, then she sighed and pulled me into a fierce hug. "All right. But you know I'm here. Any time you need me. For anything."

"I know." I hugged her close, touched by her protectiveness and loyalty. "Thanks, Cassie."

We broke apart at the sound of a sudden commotion outside. Hurrying to the tearoom window, we peered out. It was still early in the morning, with most tourists and visitors not having arrived in Meadowford-on-Smythe yet, and the village high street would normally have been fairly empty at this time of day. But to our surprise, we saw a small crowd of people gathered a few hundred yards down from the Little Stables.

"What on earth is going on?" murmured Cassie.

"Come on, let's go and find out," I said, hurrying towards the tearoom door.

It had been raining in the night and the skies were still overcast, with the promise of more rain to come. Water gleamed in several puddles along the pavement and Cassie and I had to dodge these as we hurried down the street to join the crowd. We arrived to see a dishevelled woman being assisted to her feet by several villagers, and hovering beside her were four familiar figures in raincoats, with clear-plastic rain bonnets tied over their woolly hair. The Old

Biddies.

"...absolutely disgraceful that such a thing should happen in the middle of the village high street," Mabel was saying indignantly. "But don't worry, I have already called Oxfordshire CID and demanded that they send their best man immediately."

"In the meantime, what you need, dear, is a nice cup of tea to recover your equilibrium," Florence said kindly. "And we know just the place! The Little Stables Tearoom. You'll feel much better after you've had some tea and one of their marvellous scones."

"Ah, Gemma, dear—what perfect timing," cried Glenda, looking up and spying me. "We were just going to bring poor Mrs Murchison to you. She arrived in Meadowford this morning to visit her sister and now she's had her bag snatched from her by a teenage ruffian!"

"It must have been the most

frightening experience," said Ethel, looking at the woman sympathetically. "We all think you were very brave to try and resist. It's a shame you still lost your handbag."

"Never fear," said Mabel briskly. "Once the police get here, I will inform them how to go about nabbing the young hooligan and you'll get your handbag back in no time."

"Th-thank you," said the woman, looking slightly bewildered as she allowed the Old Biddies to usher her down the street towards my tearoom.

A few minutes later, she was sitting at the heavy oak table by the window, fussed over by Ethel, Florence, and Glenda, while Mabel issued instructions on how to make the perfect cup of tea:

"...and be sure you steep the leaves for exactly five minutes, no more, no less," she said. "But no stirring or squishing the tea leaves! Just leave them to brew in peace. Then pour into a cup, add milk—a good glug—and sugar. Six teaspoons."

"*Six*?" spluttered Cassie incredulously. "Are you sure?"

"Six teaspoons," repeated Mabel. "Traumatic experiences require a strong, sweet tea, and this is my mother's tried-and-trusted recipe. Never failed to restore your composure."

"Never failed to give you diabetes either," muttered Cassie under her breath.

"Eh? What was that?" asked Mabel. "Do you need me to come and show you?"

"Uh—no, no! We'll be fine; we'll do it exactly as you say!" I cried, grabbing Cassie's arm and dragging her across the dining room.

The last thing we needed was for Mabel to follow us into the kitchen to personally supervise the process. The tearoom kitchen was strictly Dora's domain, and meetings between the two equally bossy women usually had the rest of us ducking for cover. However, just as I was pouring the boiling water from the kettle into the teapot, I heard raised voices in the tearoom outside.

"Oh God… what now?" I sighed, putting the kettle down and hurrying back out to the dining room.

I found the Old Biddies standing at the window, with their noses pressed against the glass as they watched a car sliding to a stop on the street in front of the Little Stables.

"The police have arrived!" said Glenda excitedly. "Ooh, I hope they've sent a dishy young sergeant…"

The tearoom door swung open with a cheerful tinkling of the attached bells, and a young man poked his head nervously in. He scanned the empty room, then his eyes bulged as he spotted the Old Biddies by the window.

"Aha!" boomed Mabel. "If it isn't our favourite young detective constable!"

"Oh, is that the young chap with the healthy willy?" asked Ethel, taking out her spectacles and peering at him.

"I thought he was the one with the sensitive hands?" asked Florence, frowning.

"No, no, dear, your memory is dreadful," chided Glenda. "He was the one who was Dutch. Or was it Danish?"

"Whatever he is, he'd better be a good detective," declared Mabel, marching towards him.

The young constable gulped, the Adam's apple bobbing wildly in his throat as he watched the Old Biddies approach him with something akin to pure terror on his face. He turned blindly, stumbling for the exit, but tripped over Muesli, who had arbitrarily decided to sit down and wash her face in the front doorway. She sprang up with a hiss as he narrowly missed stepping on her tail and turned on him with reproachful wails.

"*Meorrw!*" she yowled. "*MEEEEORRW!*"

"You'd better go and rescue the poor bugger before he develops a permanent phobia of cats and old ladies," said Cassie, chuckling next to me.

I was surprised to find myself laughingly agreeing, and as I began making my way across the tearoom, I realised that, for a few moments, I had completely forgotten about Devlin and our "break" and my confusion and misery.

Maybe Cassie was right; maybe the answer was simply to distract myself with other things… and, with Muesli and the Old Biddies around, it certainly looked like there was going to be more than enough to keep me busy!

THE END

Glossary of British Terms

A&E – Accident & Emergency department at the hospital (*American: ER*)

Arse - buttocks, the behind (American: ass. NB. "ass" in British English only refers to a donkey)

Blast! – an exclamation of annoyance

Blimey – an expression of astonishment

Bloody – very common adjective used as an intensifier for both positive and negative qualities (e.g. "bloody awful" and "bloody wonderful"), often used to express shock or disbelief ("Bloody Hell!")

Bloke – informal term for a man, similar to American "guy"

Blusher – a cosmetic cream or powder which is applied to the cheeks to give it a rosy colour (American: blush)

Bollocks! – rubbish, nonsense, an exclamation expressing contempt

Bonkers - crazy

Bop – (v) to dance or (n) a dance; a term often used by university students

Bugger(!) – (1) an exclamation of annoyance or dismay; a variation is used in frustration and an admission of defeat when it's decided that something isn't worth doing. eg. "oh, bugger this!" when repeatedly failing to fix a broken item and giving up. (2) can also be used to refer to a person, usually male and usually in a contemptuous way (although it can also be used as an affectionate term, eg . "the cheeky little bugger" when talking about a naughty child—depending on context).

Bum – buttocks, the behind (American: butt)

Cow – mildly offensive term to refer to a woman, usually an annoying, unlikable one, although it *can* also be used affectionately between friends eg. "you silly cow!"

Cuppa – slang term for "cup of tea"

Dishy – handsome, attractive (used for men)

Dodgy – shifty, dishonest

Git - someone despicable who has taken advantage of you

Hammered – very drunk

Knackered - very tired, exhausted (can also mean "broken" when applied to a machine or object); comes from the phrase "ready for the knacker's yard"—where old horses were slaughtered and the by-products sent for rendering, different from a slaughterhouse where animals are killed for human consumption)

Jumper – a warm, often woolly garment, which is worn by being pulled over the head, similar to a sweater. Contrast this with a cardigan, which has buttons down the front. *(NOTE: this word has a different meaning in the United States, where it refers to a type of girl's dress, a bit similar to a pinafore)*

Lose your rag – to lose your temper, to suddenly become very angry

(to) Muck around / about – (1) to "muck around" is to act silly and behave in a childish way, play around and waste time; (2) to "muck about" with *something* is to tinker or play around with it; (3) to "muck *someone* around" is to deliberately inconvenience them and treat them badly, eg. "he kept mucking her around and changing the time of their date"

Nark - annoyed, exasperated

Natter - to gossip, have a friendly chat

Off your own bat – spontaneously, at your own instigation, without being prompted by someone else. Originated from a cricketing term.

Pissed – drunk (*not to be confused with the American meaning of this word, which means "angry" – in the UK, that meaning would be conveyed by "pissed off"*)

Plonker – an idiot

Poncy – pretentious, affected and ostentatious (NB. *original meaning was to describe an effeminate man, so may be considered mildly offensive in modern culture*)

Porter – usually a person hired to help carry luggage, however at Oxford, they have a special meaning (see *Special terms used in Oxford University* below)

Posh – high class, fancy

Queue – an orderly line of people waiting for something (*American: line*)

Quid - slang term for one pound

(to) Ring – to call (someone on the phone)

Row – an argument (pronounced to rhyme with "cow")

Shag – (v) to have sexual intercourse with or (n) the act.

Shaft / Shafted - treat (someone) harshly or unfairly ; to be treated badly or unfairly eg. "the lawyer shafted me with his fees"

Snog/Snogging – kiss/kissing

Sod – a term used to describe someone foolish, idiotic or unfortunate. Can be used in both a contemptuous manner ("He's a lazy old sod!") or in an affectionate or pitying way ("Poor sod— he never saw it coming.")

Sod off – "get lost", go away, stop bothering me; milder version of the phrase using the F-word.

Telly - television

Tosser – a despicable person

Up to snuff - up to the required standard. The phrase originated in the early 19th century and is derived from the practice of inhaling a powdered form of tobacco called 'snuff', which was considered important for the fashionable gentlemen of society. (Similar to "up to scratch")

Wanker - a despicable person

Willy – penis

(to) Wind someone up / to be wound up by – this has two similar but subtly different meanings: **(**1) to tease someone or play a joke on them, get them agitated on purpose but usually in a non-malicious way; (2) to deliberately annoy or provoke someone.

The meaning will depend on context. eg. one friend laughing at another friend's incredible story: "You're winding me up!" (first meaning: you're teasing me!) – VS one friend complaining about the second friend's music (second meaning eg. "You're really winding me up! Stop playing your music so loud!")

SPECIAL TERMS USED IN OXFORD UNIVERSITY:

College - one of thirty or so institutions that make up the University; all students and academic staff have to be affiliated with a college and most of your life revolves around your own college: studying, dining, socialising. You are, in effect, a member of a College much more than a member of the University. College loyalties can be fierce and there is often friendly rivalry between nearby colleges. The colleges also compete with each other in various University sporting events.

Don / Fellow – a member of the academic staff / governing body of a college *(equivalent to "faculty member" in the U.S.)* – basically refers to a college's tutors. "Don" comes from the Latin, *dominus*—meaning lord, master.

Gown – formal black academic robe worn by students and staff, particularly during Formal Hall, Examinations and during Matriculation and Graduation. There are various types of gowns: the simplest is the short, sleeveless Commoner gown which all Freshers start with; if you have shown outstanding achievement in your first year, you then receive a University scholarship and can change to the longer, bat-winged Scholar's gown.

Formal Hall – three-course formal evening meal in the college dining hall, with a dress code: gowns must be worn, together with jacket and tie for men, smart outfit for women. The meal is preceded by the banging of the gravel and the reading of college grace in Latin. Some colleges have Formal Hall every evening whereas others only have it on certain nights of the week.

Fresher – a new student who has just started his first term of study; usually referring to First Year undergraduates but can also be used for graduate students.

High Table – refers to both the table and the actual dinner for the dons of a college and their guests. Often situated at one end of the dining hall.

Porter(s) – a team of college staff who provide a variety of services, including controlling entry to the college, providing security to students and other members of college, sorting mail, and maintenance and repairs to college property.

Porter's Lodge – a room next to the college gates which holds the porters' offices and also the "pigeon holes"—

cubby holes where the daily mail for students is placed.

Quad – short for quadrangle: a square or rectangular courtyard inside a college; walking on the grass is usually not allowed.

Tea Eggs Recipe

Tea eggs originated in China and have become a popular snack food in Chinese communities across Asia, often sold by street vendors and in night markets. They are especially popular in Taiwan, where they have become ubiquitous in local convenience stores (it's estimated that over 40 million tea eggs are sold per year!).

They are a delicious, cheap, and healthy snack, and although it takes a bit of time, the recipe is actually very easy to make at home. It is basically hard-boiled eggs, steeped—in their shells—in a marinade of fragrant tea, soy sauce, and a variety of spices. The key step is that the egg shells are gently cracked before soaking in the marinade, so that the "tea-and-spice broth" can seep through. Thus, when the eggs are peeled, they are revealed to be covered in a beautiful marbling pattern and the eggs themselves are infused with the subtle flavour of the tea and spices.

INSTRUCTIONS:

1. Place the eggs in a pot with enough water to cover them completely and bring to the boil. Lower the heat to medium so that the water is not bubbling too vigorously (this prevents the egg whites becoming hard and rubbery). Traditionally, tea eggs are hard-boiled (10 mins) but if you prefer your eggs with softer/runnier yolks, you can boil them for a shorter period (eg. 7 mins for medium, 5min for soft-boiled eggs)

2. Take the eggs out and let them cool (you can use an ice bath)

3. Pick up each egg and gently tap with the back of a spoon to crack the shell all over. Ideally, you want cracks evenly distributed over the surface. Don't worry if bits of shell come off, leaving small gaps, but be careful not to crack so hard as to remove large sections.

4. Put the cracked eggs in a small pot together with the tea leaves, soya sauce and spices. Add water until the eggs are completely covered.

5. Bring the mixture to a boil, then reduce the heat and simmer for about 20 mins.

6. Turn off the heat and leave the eggs soaking in the "tea broth" marinade for another couple of hours at least before eating. Ideally, they should be soaked overnight as the longer they have in the marinade, the more flavour is imparted to the eggs. You can transfer the eggs

& marinade to the fridge after cooling and let them soak overnight, then heat them up again to a gentle boil before serving the next day.

7. Take the eggs out of the broth and peel to reveal the delicate, marble-like pattern on the surface. They can be served in a small bowl with a bit of the marinade, to further flavour the egg after peeling.

NOTES:

- Black tea leaves (ie. roasted/fermented) must be used. Green or white teas do not have enough fragrance or flavour. Oolong tea is a good choice, although any black tea should work. You can also use a mixture of Chinese tea leaves and "regular" black tea bags, for a more intense tea flavour.

- The eggs can be stored in the marinade, in the fridge, for 4 – 5 days.

They will continue to soak up the broth and become saltier and more flavoursome over time.

- If you would like a saltier flavour, simply increase the amount of soya sauce used. However, remember that the eggs will become saltier the longer they soak in the marinade.

- Dark soya sauce has a deep caramel colour and richer, more subtle flavour than regular soya sauce. "Dark" does not mean it's saltier—it refers to the colour, which is used to impart a rich, reddish-brown colour to many Chinese dishes.

- If you decide to add ginger to the marinade, make sure you use fresh ginger. Do not substitute dried ginger, stem ginger, or candied ginger.

Enjoy!

About The Author

USA Today bestselling author H.Y. Hanna writes fun cozy mysteries filled with clever puzzles, lots of humor, quirky characters - and cats with big personalities! She is known for bringing wonderful settings to life, whether it's the historic city of Oxford, the beautiful English Cotswolds or the sunny beaches of coastal Florida.

After graduating from Oxford University, Hsin-Yi tried her hand at a variety of jobs, including advertising, modelling, teaching English, dog training and marketing... before returning to her first love: writing. She worked as a freelance writer for several years and has won awards for her novels, poetry, short stories and journalism.

A globe-trotter all her life, Hsin-Yi has

lived in a variety of cultures, from Dubai to Auckland, London to New Jersey, but is now happily settled in Perth, Western Australia, with her husband and a rescue kitty named Muesli. You can learn more about her and her books at: www.hyhanna.com.

Join her Readers' Club Newsletter to get updates on new releases, exclusive giveaways and other book news!

https://www.hyhanna.com/newsletter